LION
The Elmnas Chronicles Book 3

Kaylena Radcliff

Science Fiction and Fantasy Publications

LION

KAYLENA RADCLIFF

Science Fiction and Fantasy Publications
HTTPS://SCIFIFANTASYPUBLICATIONS.CA
A division of DAOwen Publications

Copyright © 2023 by Kaylena Radcliff

All rights reserved

DAOwen Publications supports copyright. Copyright fuels creativity, encourages diverse voices, promotes free speech, and creates a vibrant culture. Thank you for buying an authorized edition of this book and for complying with copyright laws by not reproducing, scanning, or distributing any part of it in any form without permission. You are supporting writers and allowing DAOwen Publications to continue to publish books for every reader.

Lion / Kaylena Radcliff

Edited by Douglas Owen

ISBN 978-1-998029-02-0
EISBN 978-1-998029-03-7

This is a work of fiction. Names, characters, places, and incidents either are the product of the author's imagination or are used fictitiously, and any resemblance to actual persons, living or dead, businesses, companies, events, or locales is entirely coincidental.

Jacket Art by MMT Productions
Https://mmtproductions.ca

10 9 8 7 6 5 4 3 2 1

*For Becca and Lisa, my faithful editors
and loving nags*

1

Year 113 of the Glorious New Era
    45th of Sun's Wane
    Pardaetha, Gormlaen

Arcturo Vipsanius rested his elbows on the edge of his open window and stared down at the titian gray of the Mican Sea. It stretched to the horizon, meeting the low mist that settled upon it. From where he looked, there was no distinction between sea and sky. They roiled together, a cauldron of cloud darkening and disappearing into the void as nightfall drew near. He brought his clenched fists to his lips and peered closer. With some effort, Arcturo could still make out the edges of the frothing waves tinged with the reddish haze. He had always been ambivalent toward the sea, but in these latter days he had grown to despise it.

What monsters might surface from that hellish abyss? he wondered.

Arcturo grimaced as the next thought mocked him.

Would it matter? The monsters have already come. And they've devoured the world.

He looked down, watching figures move slowly along the gray shore. Some of the poorer citizens of Pardaetha stooped along it and picked through the refuse that had collected on the beaches. Certainly, there was enough of it. Father's many factories made sure of that. Farther down and out of sight of Arcturo's window, they never slept, and cast-offs from their production processes ended up in the sea and found their way to the beach below. Here in Kyma and in most of the city, Arcturo could almost forget that pitiful sight, as long as he chose not to look. Though time had swallowed the sun-soaked Pardaetha he knew as a boy, it was still no less the Jewel of the Coalition Empire. In progress, wonderful progress, the city marched on. Pardaetha had long outgrown the old city and now sprawled well into the northern countryside. Order and efficiency reigned in its many districts and hovercraft-filled streets. Great, paved roads brought profitable traffic in and out of its limits. The people, many of them, anyway, had their fill of prosperity, accustomed to every modern convenience that gold could buy. To be certain, no other city in all the Four Dominions held a candle to Pardaetha's progress.

Still, Arcturo looked to the shore. In the last century he watched as it aged, its pristine, sparkling white sand fading to the gray, stinking garbage heap it was now. And despite all the augmentation had done for his body, his spirit felt much like the Pardaethan beach below.

It is nothing but a phantom, he thought. *Sagging and withered with years of regret.*

The sky darkened, and a desolate, obscuring shadow spread along the beach until it was formless. Gingerly, Arcturo tore his gaze away.

He closed the frosted glass shutters, clasped them tight, and rubbed his hands together as he surveyed his private quarters. Those who ignored the details could easily miss its opulence, but Arcturo saw it in every item. Though sparse, his decor included the expected: a Coalition standard, showcasing the two red lions on a field of black rearing up with their forepaws touching, artisan bedroom furniture, including his magnificently attired four-poster bed, an elegant writing desk, a holograstone, and a full-length mirror. An exquisite rapier gleamed on its wall mount above his bed; the one which had won him some distinction in the fencing competitions among the most elite members of the Coalition Assembly. Arcturo stared at the polished rapier. He would be lying if he said he did not think fondly of it, but nevertheless every award and honor won with its skill lay collecting dust beneath his bed. A little delight mired in a slough of self-loathing. Arcturo had that particular relationship with most things in his life.

With a sigh, he glanced toward the small wooden door between the desk and dresser. Through that door, his room adjoined to Tyranna's own lavish quarters. When they were first married, Arcturo felt obligated to leave it open, allowing her to spend the night in his bed as she pleased. He had only spent one night in hers. Their wedding night. Decades faded away, and with them, so did the commerce between rooms. In only one month in Arcturo's recent memory did that change, seventeen years ago, for one singular purpose. Since then, the door had remained closed.

Arcturo walked softly toward it, rested his ear upon the cool wood, and listened. Quiet, as expected. Tyranna usually left her quarters by this time to brief with Father before supper, and never once had she shirked her duties as the Coalition's Prime Ambassador. If she was not with Father, she was likely out of Kyma altogether, carrying out the Supreme Chancellor's wishes in whatever ruthless way she saw fit. Arcturo continued to listen, holding his breath to distinguish any sound. He could never be sure, of course. Tyranna could prowl like a cat when she wanted to, and these days, more than ever, she might find reasons to sneak about. Nothing stirred. Arcturo exhaled slowly.

With a decisive twist, he engaged the lock.

Arcturo swept toward the holograstone, stopping short as he reached it. With tentative fingers outstretched, he stared hard at the dormant surface between the spindles. Once more he glanced at his bedroom doors. With a sharp breath, he kneeled down and activated the stone.

"Senator Vipsanius."

The murky shadow of a hooded man's face swam into the orb as it sparked to life.

"Constan," Arcturo breathed in relief.

The man bowed in deference. "I was beginning to worry."

"I apologize for keeping you waiting," Arcturo whispered. "I had to be certain I was alone. What news?"

Constan leaned in, his face growing larger in the holograstone. He pushed back the hood of his coalition cloak, revealing grim, dark eyes and a stubbled, strong jaw.

"Your suspicions were correct, Sir," he answered in a low voice. "Miss Vipsanius is in great danger. The marriage to the Grand *Imyr's* eldest is indeed a trap... for the *Imyr himself*. My sources have uncovered a scheme that even I could not believe had you not shared your own concerns. She is to be assassinated by a Heibeiathan in the royal court who believes he is acting on the Grand *Imyr's* own orders. It will end the treaty and be an occasion for conquest against all of Heibeiath."

Constan's eyes flicked away from the stone. He held his fingers to his lips for a moment as he watched somewhere Arcturo could not see. Arcturo held his breath and stared into the orb nervously. Finally, Constan's gaze returned to his, and Constan leaned forward again.

"The Ambassador arranged for it all," he whispered.

Arcturo shut his eyes, fighting the tears that threatened to fill them. "You swear this is true?"

Constan nodded. "On my life, Sir."

"Then you are the only friend I now have."

"These many years, I have served House Vipsanius," Constan said gravely. "But my loyalty lies with you. Ask of me anything, and I will see it done."

Arcturo rubbed his face. The weight of his years, of everything he had ever done and seen done, crushed his soul like a mountain. An all too familiar fear accompanied it; paralyzing him, shrinking him, outing him as the coward he always was. With a tremble, Arcturo glanced at his paling reflection in the mirror beside him.

A man, tall and lean like Father and handsome like Mother, gazed back. The face in the reflection had none of Father's resolve, strength, or inscrutability. Instead, it wore every emotion as plain as day - doubt, weakness, and terror showed the true colors of the man behind it. And none of Mother's haughtiness (may her spirit find rest) shaped his features, either, but Arcturo's own vanity exposed itself in other ways. No, he could not hide any of that. Nothing could hide the tragic combination of genetic traits that made him abhorrent to Father, even as he obeyed his terrible bidding.

There you go, he thought ruefully. *Shifting the blame, just as you always have. How can you live with yourself?*

If he did nothing now, for *her,* the only treasure he had left, he couldn't.

Arcturo cleared his throat. "If I could get you a craft, would you be able to take her to safety?"

"I would certainly try," Constan nodded. "But where in Reidara is safe?"

"Nowhere." Arcturo swallowed. "The Supreme Chancellor is making certain of that."

"To Heibeiath, perhaps? The Grand *Imyr* could protect her, and would have ample notice to fend off the planned Coalition coup."

"No... she never wanted... I never agreed to give her to the next Grand *Imyr*. It wouldn't do, anyway. She would be just as close to danger and to fulfilling the Supreme Chancellor's design." Arcturo let out a heavy sigh. "No, Constan, you must take her far from here. You must escape into Elmnas."

Constan's expression darkened. "Sir, the stories..."

"Are stories." Arcturo waved his hand. "I do not say only stories, but the Mistwolf threat is greatly exaggerated to keep border traffic under control. And the Coalition has a far less stable grasp of the territory than it lets on. Far north, there is a place the Elmlings still control. They call it free."

"A... free Elmnas exists?" Constan's face creased in disbelief.

An edge of bitterness crept into Arcturo's voice as he replied.

"Indeed, Constan, it does. I would not have believed it either, had I not discovered the truth myself just this past week. It should not surprise you. Kyma is built on lies." Arcturo composed himself with a steadying breath. "I will transmit coordinates to where you might cross, perhaps gain asylum. I daresay the Elmlings might welcome even their prisoners of war more humanely than the Coalition does its allies."

Constan looked doubtful, but nodded. "It is done, then. Orders, Sir?"

"Gather an escort of your most trusted people. A half-dozen would do and fit comfortably in my personal craft. I'll have it readied and make arrangements for Miss Vipsanius to be in the bay during the third watch tonight." Arcturo glanced at the doors again. "Get a message to the Grand *Imyr*, if you can. Now that I know the Supreme Chancellor wants to end the treaty, he will accomplish that with or without my daughter as the tool. Perhaps the *Imyr* can do something. We'll drown in both Gormlaean and Heibeiathan blood alike otherwise. I'll contact you in the usual way within a fortnight. If I don't..."

Arcturo clasped his shaking hands together, wringing them to get the frozen blood flowing once more. *I'll die for this.*

But the thought did not make him any more afraid than he already was. How could he be? He had been afraid his entire life. And in one hundred years, not one of his spineless compromises allayed his terror. Indeed, what was he so afraid of now? Pain? Death? Father? Fear was only a useful tool if the hell it kept Arcturo from was worse than the hell he occupied now.

Isn't it better to die for this than for nothing at all?

"Expect the worst. I cannot bind you to protect her forever, but... please, if you cannot escape north, then take her east, to the islands of the Agwanii. It is said they are a noble people. Perhaps they will offer some hospitality. You fulfill this, my last wish, and you are free."

Constan shook his head. "Upon my life, I and my company will remain with her until the very end."

"You are a good man, Constan."

The man in the holograstone said nothing, but crossed his arms in the Coalition way. Arcturo de-activated the orb, staring between the prongs long after the image fizzled and faded. With a long sigh, he glanced once more out the window. The darkness had deepened, and a light drizzle tapped against the pane. Father would expect him at supper soon. It would not do to be late.

Every limb felt heavy as lead as he pulled himself upright. Arcturo stumbled toward his bed, aching to fall into it, to sleep and forget the world. He stared at it numbly, trying and failing to empty his mind of every black fear that conquered him.

Arcturo closed his eyes and inhaled. He opened them, finding his gaze resting on the chest he kept at his bed's end. He reached out, hands hovering just above its lid. Gingerly, he lifted it. For the first time that day, his terrible, frightened grief softened. Arcturo reached inside, pulling out memories of his daughter's early years: her Presentation Day clothes, a stuffed toy lion, a crinkled parchment with a child's drawing of the two of them together. These he held close to his chest, breathing in the scent of innocence and joy. Arcturo looked further down, more of his daughter's things crowding the bottom.

So many beautiful memories.

He let them fill his mind, pushing away all the empty years before. And as Arcturo focused on those happiest thoughts, he almost forgot the darkness that always crouched behind them. Almost.

Beneath the collection of his child's things, another object caught his attention. Laying the other items on his bed, he tugged the object free: a tired oud, battered with age and a violence that had cracked its short, straight neck and curved body. Arcturo ran his fingers along the instrument's contours and cracks, eventually brushing against the still-intact strings. They hummed in dissonance, long out of tune after years of disuse. He gripped the neck and strings to deaden the sound.

Kaylena Radcliff

His thoughts grew troubled, returning to the night when he plucked the oud from the gutter by the Fish Gate; when he removed the final piece of evidence exonerating the Samrasine musicians of his sister's horrific attack. Father did not care how he disposed of it. He cared only that it was gone. Arcturo kept it, a solemn reminder of the moment he forfeited his soul.

The sound of the strings echoed in his brain. Arcturo stared at the oud, shaking.

Did you make that sound when the Drake flung your owner to the pavement? Did the sound of your destruction drown out his?

Tears filled Arcturo's eyes as he beheld it, but he refused to look away.

Not this time, not ever again.

2

55th of Sun's Wane, Year 113
   The Priory of the Ameliorites
   The Wolf Barrens, Elmnas Territory

Sister Alba stood in front of the narrow passageway, peering into its dark recesses with a mixture of terror, relief, and excitement. Even with the torch extended before her, she could not decipher just how deep the passage went. But she could see the artistry of ancient Guardian runes carved along the passage's walls and into its carefully crafted steps, all faintly alive with the dim sheen of glowing fungi anchored in the etched crevices. She had read the stories of such things in the sacred writings; of runic pathways that came to life beneath the feet and hands of true Eneshkin, of power and holiness beyond the reach of most mortals. Yes, she had read about all that, and more: Sister Alba, the Prioress of this convent of Ameliorites, had committed most of the existing Guardian writings to memory. Still, it was altogether a much different thing to behold that of which she had only read. Even dormant, the First Words rendered her speechless.

Air as warm as breath seeped out of the passage, washing over the

Prioress in a continuous exhale that made her winter habit feel even stuffier than usual. Her torch guttered. By now, she had grown accustomed to the brisk, autumnal air that frosted the last flowers in the Priory's courtyard and chilled its heartless corridors. If winter did not arrive within the week, it would surely come soon after, bringing with it the bitter cold and violent snowfalls that always seemed to hover over the valley of the Wolf Barrens until spring. Even the deepest parts of the Priory, like the Guardian-crafted rooms and halls where the sisters slept, still suffered during the harsh winter months against the Jagged Jaw Mountains. But the passage here felt different. It burrowed into the mountain range itself, and heedless of whatever storms raged outside, tapped into the heat rising from the roots of the earth.

No traveler need fear the elements, Sister Alba thought, *although the darkness and whatever may wait within it might be a problem.*

Oddly enough, that did not frighten her. She gazed into the passage, her free hand deep in her pocket as she rolled her Cardanthium prayer gem between her fingers and garnered comfort and strength from its own innate spark of warmth. The gem that she possessed now, like all the treasured Cardanthium prayer gems in the Priory, did not carry the power and life found in the ore of the forged Guardian sword. This was different, although her gem did carry *something*. She did not know exactly what made it different or why, even with her many years of study on the subject. Guardian sword lore had long fascinated her. Still, the deepest secrets of the ancient Way remained veiled despite all its textual references. Perhaps there were some things outsiders like her were not meant to know. At least not yet.

The gem felt alive just the same. Its constant, humming presence served as a reminder that things both much smaller and much greater than herself existed, and that dwarfed any disappointment in Alba's inability to understand. She felt awed to be part of it at all, to walk between the planes of comprehensibility and get a glimpse of glory.

Like this moment, she thought, closing her eyes in a prayer of thanksgiving.

"Well, Sister Ilidette," she said after a moment, placing the torch in its sconce on the opposite wall. "What do you think?"

The other Sister stood beside her, hands tucked into her habit, face drawn tight in anxious consideration. Sister Alba saw the struggle there on the younger Ameliorite's features. Ilidette had always disliked sharing an opinion that conflicted with her superiors. *Which is often enough.* The Prioress almost chuckled. *No wonder she started her time here with a vow of silence.*

"Please." Sister Alba smiled encouragingly at Sister Ilidette.

"I'm not so sure what to think," Sister Ilidette finally replied. "But I can't see what good it will do. We can't know where it goes– if it goes anywhere, that is– and even if it does go somewhere, who is to say what's waiting on the other side or anywhere along the way? Or suppose the passage splits off, or there's a cave-in, or any number of things that would mean dying of thirst and hunger or worse? Maybe this is a mistake."

"Thank you, dear Sister. It is quite alright to voice your concerns, especially in times such as these." The Prioress nodded with solemn sagacity. "But consider another idea. What if this is a gift? What if it is the providential hand of the Unseen? How else could our discovery be explained? Would we have ever found it had not Sister Daiuma stumbled on that exact stone in this exact place, steadying herself on this one narrow ledge that opened this singular secret door into the very mountain itself? A mountain range we know harbors the cloister of our brothers only a few days' walk from here. It is simply extraordinary."

Sister Ilidette peered into the passage skeptically, but shrugged in resignation. "Whatever it is, I suppose it is the only way now. Unseen preserve us. We must trust that Sister Raelin will manage."

"Not just Raelin," Sister Alba said. "You must go, too."

"Me?" Ilidette stepped back and shook her head. "No, I-I can't. I was to stay with you. I can't leave you all behind. You will need protection, Sister. I still have my bow! I... I can fight."

The Prioress held up a hand. "It is not the time for that. Not now, and not for you. But it is time to put your skills to other use. For all of Raelin's medicinal knowledge and ability, she is no pathfinder, like you. She did not have to survive the Dell woodlands on her own with four other mouths to feed besides. But you did, dear one. The elder Sisters and I are all in agreement. We are not the ones in need of protection and guidance. We commit that responsibility elsewhere. But the novitiates and orphans in our care do. Both you and Raelin must provide that. There is no other way."

Ilidette bit her lip, eyes glistening. "What will become of you?"

A small, sad smile quirked the corner of Sister Alba's mouth. "The Unseen knows."

Ilidette buried her face in her hands and let out a muffled sob. The Prioress took hold of Ilidette's shaking shoulders and pulled her upright. Ilidette looked up. Alba searched her tear-filled eyes. "You mustn't think on that, little sister. You must have courage. Is it not written? 'Where mortal sight cannot suffice–'"

"Trust that which Sees and Knows." Ilidette sniffed and rubbed her sleeve across her eyes. "I will try."

Alba smiled and patted Ilidette's arm. "You do well. Quickly now, return to your cell and take only that which you will need for the journey. I have seen to all the other details already. All is prepared. Raelin and the novitiates should be on their way here as we speak."

Ilidette nodded and drew an unsteady breath. "How much time do we have?"

"Not much now," Alba replied, her countenance darkening. "If we are to believe the news Dane received while he was in our care, the inquiry craft could arrive at any moment. Let us pray they are delayed. You will need all the time we can spare."

"Then I shall be quick, Sister." Ilidette wrung her hands. "Is this goodbye, then?"

Alba answered with an embrace. Ilidette grasped her fiercely in return.

"Warn the Brothers of what is to come," Alba whispered. "And protect these small ones. The Unseen guide you and light your way."

Ilidette nodded into her shoulder before pulling free. With one last tearful look, Ilidette took off down the dark corridor at a run.

The Prioress wiped her own eyes as she turned on her heel and strode briskly the opposite way. The sloping passage turned, winding away from the interior of the mountain and toward the man-made walls of the Priory. Slabs of granite changed to mortared stone, and Alba could once again feel the cold air whistling through the arrow slits built into the fortress passage. To her left, a winding staircase peeled off from the main passage and climbed up to the outer battlements. She shuffled up the stone stairs, only letting go of the curving wall when she reached the exposed top. The wind whipped at her as she exited the safety of the Priory. Overhead, the sky churned. Alba lowered her head and hid her hands in her habit as she hurried toward the main gate.

As she went, the Priory's bell sounded. Alba listened as she walked, counting each knell and the seconds between. Two quick rings echoed around the courtyard. *One, two, three,* the Prioress counted. A final, heavy clang rolled out of the bell tower, and Sister Alba's stomach dropped. She lifted her robes above her ankles and ran to the gate.

"What news, Krelah?" Alba said, huffing as she caught her breath.

The old woman peered down at the Prioress from her perch upon an overturned crate. Even with the box beneath her feet, Sister Krelah could barely see over the battlement. With a scowl, she steadied herself on Alba and gingerly stepped off the box.

"See for yourself." The elder sister gestured. "Won't be long, now."

Alba did not need the crate, but she climbed up on it anyway and gazed over the side. The stiff wind rippled across the wide vale leading to the Priory and over the grassy slopes in angry gusts. It reminded Alba of the cold swell of a winter sea just before a storm. She pushed away the dark image, unwilling to dwell on what it might portend.

Atop the final hill crest, just above the rutted path to the Priory, a transport craft idled five feet above the ground. The sleek, black exterior glinted like a sharpened knife. Shiny, red designs, indistinguishable from this distance, nonetheless marked it as a Coalition military vehicle. The guns mounted on the sides made that clear as well. Alba furrowed her brow.

The craft dropped, maintaining its hover inches from the hill, its spinning discs splaying the grass below it. Its door hissed open, and several hulking figures hopped down from the transport. Hands passed weapons out of the open transport door as black cloaks with the twin lion emblem caught in the wind.

"Why do this?" Alba whispered. "Why not bring their craft right to the Priory's gates? They could have done that quite easily."

Krelah scratched her chin. "Oh, to make a show of it, I expect. Our Coalition always had a flair for theatrics, don't you think, Prioress?"

Alba murmured in assent as she watched the last figure emerge from the craft. A young woman in charcoal body armor stepped in front of the others, shrewd eyes scanning the fortress. Even at a distance, Alba could see both how lovely and how terrifying the woman was. Hair as black as a raven and as straight as the edge of a sword flew out in all directions. She threw back her illustrious cloak, its outer side black like the others but lined with blood-red satin. The woman placed a hand on the sheathed weapon by her side, her haughty eyes finding Alba on the battlement. She flashed a wicked grin and started down the hill, her entourage close behind.

"Snow," Krelah muttered.

Alba turned and looked down curiously. "Pardon, sister?"

"It feels like snow today, eh?" Krelah rubbed her knee. "I feel something coming, I tell you."

"Indeed, something comes to us this day," Alba mused. She stepped down from the crate and clasped hands gently with the elder Ameliorite.

"Do what you must to hold them outside our walls as long as you can. I fear it won't be enough, but we must give Raelin and Ilidette a fighting chance."

Krelah's ancient face wrinkled further in a mischievous smirk, and her dull eyes twinkled. "Oh, they'll have to excuse us old women for our doddering. Can't expect to have the gate up too fast. Teach these young Coats some patience, eh?"

Alba squeezed Krelah's hand. "That shall do."

3

The gate inched upward as Sister Alba waited in the courtyard, shivering beneath her habit. Several of the middle-aged Sisters slowly cranked it open, which Alba could see had begun to rankle the waiting Coalition Inquiry. Heavy boots stamped or tapped the ground with growing impatience. The feet of their leader, however, remained stationary. The gate rose further, revealing the hard faces and cold stares of ten Coalition men and women. And these were no standard Coalition forces, either. Extraordinarily crafted dark armor gilded with red glinted beneath their cloaks. They carried the most superior energy weapons Alba had ever seen. An unfamiliar insignia on the right breast of each warrior also caught her attention: a red marking detailing the profile of a single lion's head, mane flying and mouth open in a fierce roar.

Not even Gormlaean city Sentinels are as outfitted as these, Alba thought darkly.

Her gaze came to rest on the woman before them all. She stood jauntily with arms crossed over her chest. Confidence and pride exuded from every inch of her, including her beautiful but cruel face. Alba thought she had seen that face before – long ago smiling on the holograstones or plastered upon the propaganda posters on city walls – but it had been so many years since she had been in Gormlaen proper, that she could not say for sure. The woman sized up Alba, and with a dismissive sneer, she walked under the still opening gate and into the courtyard. Her elite force followed, eyeing up the Sisters who stiffly went about their chores within the Priory's walls. The soldiers fanned out and stationed themselves around the four corners of the courtyard.

The Prioress smiled, as she did for every visitor who entered her walls, and lifted her voice for all to hear.

"Welcome to the Priory of the Ameliorites, our humble home and a rest for weary travelers on the forsaken Wolf Barrens," Alba said pleasantly. "We poor Sisters are honored to invite in such a large and illustrious party. To whom do we owe the pleasure of offering our hospitality today?"

"You must be Alba Avetti, the overseer of this sorry place," the woman scoffed. "Some welcome. Many thousands would have groveled at my feet to beg my mercy before asking that question. Or do expatriates and traitors not recognize their own rulers?"

Alba continued to smile, but her tone grew terse. "We have no holograstones here. We mean no offense."

"Then mark it well, Sister." The woman glared before addressing all in the Priory. "Attention!"

The Ameliorites present ceased work immediately, straightening and turning to face the speaker. Alba forced a mask of serenity as she surveyed them, praying that her sisters would find the courage to do the same. They tried, but they could not hide all the anxious energy building in the courtyard. Alba looked back at the woman, and a hot anger rose in her cheeks. *The fiend's enjoying every moment of this,* she thought. She slipped her hand into her deep pocket, caught up the Cardanthium jewel in her fingers, and squeezed.

"I am Prime Ambassador Tyranna Vipsanius, second only to the Supreme Chancellor himself. Some of you may be wondering why the honor of my presence has been bestowed upon you this day, but I regret to inform you this is no happy occasion. This is an Official Inquiry into actions conducted in direct violation of Coalition law."

For the Sisters' part, no one looked aside or gave any reason to find guilt. They watched the Ambassador with the same slightly troubled faces. But Alba's eyes narrowed.

"And what law is that, if I may, Ambassador?" she asked pointedly.

Ambassador Vipsanius strode toward Alba, stopping only inches from her. Alba stood nose-to-nose with her, unflinching even as the Ambassador's sneer turned to open disgust. She spoke in a low voice only Alba could hear.

"I know all about you, Alba Avetti. You, who disgraced your eminent House and shamed your family name by throwing your lot in with these..." The Ambassador gestured vaguely to the women around. "These castoffs, illegals, mongrels. How can you stomach it? You're even worse than the Elmlings."

"I dwell with my Sisters in the house of the Unseen. It is enough for me."

"Ah yes, a strange, foreign god to go with your love of strange, foreign things. It is fitting."

The Ambassador stepped back and raised her voice. "Your Prioress is under arrest for the harboring of enemies of the state. We know that a fugitive, alias Mouse, and her companion, Berr-Toma Breythorn, passed through your gates within the past two cycles. Hold your protests and claims of innocence. They were pursued in Ervandas, and there is nowhere else they could have made the journey and survived except from here. Under the law, I could hold you all guilty, but I am a just ruler. If any of you come forward now and tell me what you know of these events, you will be pardoned for your superior's crimes."

"Shall we speak of Coalition law again? You level serious charges with no evidence," Alba replied coldly. "I am a natural born Gormlaean and a Coalition citizen. You have said so yourself. Not

LION

only do I have the right to a fair trial, but you have no grounds to intimidate and harass my people under that law."

"Coalition law does not apply to treasonous old fools," she said, smirking. The Ambassador turned to her people. "You four. Search the grounds."

"You cannot..." Alba fumed, charging forward, but relented as a soldier yanked her backward with a heavy hand and pressed an energy pistol against her back. None too gently, he wrenched her arms behind her and clapped cuffs tightly on her wrists.

She watched helplessly as the four other soldiers saluted Ambassador Vipsanius in the Coalition manner and broke off from the courtyard. They entered the Priory. Alba cringed as the sounds of frightened screams, shattered pottery, and splintered doors followed. Ambassador Vipsanius stared down at the terrified Sisters.

"The offer still stands," she said in a melodic, inviting voice. "But not for long. I do not wish for harm upon any of you, but what I must do will be done. For the good of the Coalition. For the good of all."

Alba gazed upward, watching the swirling clouds as she tried to pray. Despite all her recitations of the sacred writings, her wise counsel for any who would ask, and the ancient songs daily filling her hours and leaving her own lips, Alba could find nothing now. *Please*, was all she could think. *Please.*

The soldiers had moved closer to the clusters of Sisters standing in the courtyard, and Tyranna Vipsanius looked expectantly to each one of them. No one spoke. With as much emotion as she dared to convey, Alba also looked to her Ameliorite Sisters and offered each a slight, grateful nod. *You are so brave,* she wanted to say. *It will not be forgotten.*

The Ambassador allowed a few more breaths of fraught silence before clucking her tongue in mock regret.

"Pity," she said with a smirk.

The soldiers chuckled ominously. More crashing, shouting, cries from inside. Alba inhaled sharply. More than anything, she wanted to be there for her Sisters. The wait might be unbearable out here, but what was happening where she could not see? She tried not to think about that. Alba's gaze wandered back to Tyranna, who was already staring back. Questions swirled through Alba's mind. *Why isn't the Ambassador questioning me? What does she think she'll find inside? Why make us wait like this?*

Ambassador Vipsanius cocked her head and approached Alba once again. Alba's shoulders were beginning to ache. She struggled to straighten out as the Ambassador came closer, hoping both for a more comfortable and more dignified position without agitating the soldier behind her. Tyranna looked down at Alba's feet. Alba did the same and gasped.

Something glowed faintly in the grass. *My prayer gem. It must have fallen out of my pocket.* Alba's heart pounded as the Ambassador stooped to pick it up. She straightened and held the gem up to the sky. The prayer cord dangled as she turned the gem slowly, examining it. A cruel smile split her lips.

"What do we have here? A contraband Cardanthium crystal?"

Alba's lip quivered. "It is rightful property of the Ameliorite community."

"How very selfish of you, Alba," Tyranna murmured. "For the good of all, both Cardanthium ore and crystals are highly regulated by the Coalition. What are you even doing with it, anyway? This ought to have been converted. My, you could have even brought this fortress of yours out of the dark ages. Surely your odd little commune would find *that* far more useful. Why hold on to such power like a trinket?"

"Respectfully, Ambassador," Alba said curtly. "We have different ideas about what such power is for."

The Ambassador rolled her eyes. "Not only is your possession illegal, but it's rather unfair for you to hoard Cardanthium when so many must do without."

"If your Coalition hadn't devoured it all in the first place, such regulations would be unnecessary."

"Quite an opinionated blood traitor, hmm?" Tyranna said. "You sound as if you have a bone to pick, Sister. Tread lightly now. That is not the way to make your case."

Alba said nothing, but held Tyranna's proud, testing gaze. The Ambassador smiled as she addressed her soldiers again.

"Search all the women here for contraband Cardanthium. You're certain to find it."

Only a few cries of protest rang out as the soldiers took hold of them. Brutal shoves forced the shouts into whimpers. Alba struggled, but a sharp blow to her temple sent her reeling. She would have fallen had the soldier who dealt it not wrenched her upright. Blood trickled from her head and stained her veil.

Tyranna laughed. Stars burst in Alba's periphery, but still she staggered forward, trying to do something, *anything*, to provide comfort to her crying Sisters. Her weak attempt barely registered with the soldier holding her back. When her vision cleared, she saw some Sisters upon the ground, others bleeding, still others standing with arms raised. The gleam of Cardanthium winked like green stars in the hands of the Coalition force. They gathered the gems greedily and stuffed them in a communal loot sack. In moments, the starry glow was gone. The wave of grief that hit the Prioress then surprised even her. Tears flowed down Alba's cheeks.

Suddenly, one of the Priory's doors slammed open. Terrible, ear-splitting screams came from within. Alba recognized those screams. *Sister Brenna.*

Two soldiers emerged, prodding out ahead of them many of the Sisters who had been indoors. They lined the solemn group up around the courtyard, cursing and pushing the elder women who could not move faster even as they tried. The screams grew louder, and Sister Brenna stumbled out the door. Another soldier followed quickly behind. He planted a swift kick in her ribs. Only groans escaped her then, and the courtyard echoed with the sound of suffering.

"Mercy," Alba whispered. "Have mercy."

Tyranna either ignored her plea or had not heard it all. Her gaze turned to the last miserable woman, Sister Eliese, prodded forward by a cruelly grinning soldier. The Ameliorite slumped to the ground after exiting, her head hanging as her shoulders shook with sobs.

"What did you find?" Tyranna asked.

"This Elmling scum," the soldier scoffed, gesturing to Sister Brenna. "Interfered with our investigation. Tried to keep this one from talking."

He pointed to Sister Eliese as she sniffled and wiped her eyes.

"Is that so?" Tyranna asked. "What are they hiding?"

The soldier behind Sister Eliese yanked her upright. "Talk."

Sister Eliese raised her head slowly. Her eyes were puffy and red with tears. She looked around, her gaze resting on the Prioress. Terror and pain etched her anguished features, and her eyes pleaded with Alba to help. *You should not have stayed, little sister*, Alba thought with sorrow. *You are just barely out of the novitiate. You are not ready for this.*

Alba did not dare to move, but she tried to convey comfort, strength, and peace to the frightened young woman.

"Do not do it, Sister!" Brenna screeched desperately. "Do not sell us to the Coats!"

Alba flinched as her outburst was met with another blow. *My brave Brenna.*

Tyranna crossed her arms over her chest and flashed an impatient smile. "Well?"

Eliese's breath shuddered. "They were here."

Alba would not give Tyranna the satisfaction of her disappointment. She stared straight through Eliese; ever composed, equally stern and equally loving, as any good Prioress ought to be. Alba tried not to notice the new tears on Eliese's cheeks, the burning anger in Brenna's eyes. *Forgive*, she willed. *Forgive, she doesn't know any better.*

"Where are they going?" Tyranna demanded. "What are they trying to do?"

Tyranna nodded to the soldier as Eliese stared at the ground. He jabbed something into her back. Her shriek of pain sent shivers down Alba's spine.

"East, I think!" Eliese cried. "They thought the girl might be a seer. I don't know why. I don't know anything else, I swear!"

"Mouse *is* a seer!" Brenna shouted. "She is the Harbinger, and the Phoenix comes! Elmnas will rise from the ashes! She will reach the gathered tribes! We will not be silenced!"

The soldier did not raise his foot this time, but his pistol.

"No!" Alba shouted as the other Sisters too began to wail.

"Halt." Tyranna held up a hand, and the confused soldier paused. "I have something I would like to say."

He stepped back from Brenna. Silence, except for Sister Eliese's sniffles, filled the courtyard once again. Tyranna walked to its center, pausing to sweep her audience with inscrutable, terrible eyes.

"From my reading about your little cult and from my experience with you today, it has become clear that the Supreme Chancellor has dealt far too graciously with you. Here I believed the Ameliorites were submissive, impartial, given to acts of charity and humble living. Good citizens of the Coalition, even, despite your insistence on backwardness. And what have I found instead? Fanaticism, criminal insubordination, treachery, rebellion, hatred, thievery! Why, your lot is no better than common Mautardu pirates or the Jackal Syndicate! The ties we've discovered among your communities begin to make sense. You are cut from the same cloth."

The Ambassador leveled a glare at Alba before turning it to Brenna. "The saddest part about it is you believe you are right. You inclined your ears to these cunning Elmlings. What did they tell you? That they have a hero hidden somewhere in those northern wastes who could liberate you from the miserable existence you've brought upon yourselves? Did they tell you all the incredible advances of the Coalition which have improved life in the whole of the Four Dominions are somehow evil? Do you truly believe these Elmlings, these that refuse to see reason and light even when it smacks them in the dimwitted heads, do well to sow discontent and bitterness instead of working toward peace? Ah, but I see they have bewitched you. You will not see that they speak nothing but lies. Their promises, their invisible god, their seers are the wild creations of a people too fragile to accept reality. And still, you throw your lot in with deranged fugitives and infectious malcontents. So weak, so foolish, so... pathetic."

Alba raised her chin and smiled serenely. "We would be weak fools with clean hands than the noble strong who stink of innocent blood. But you are wrong, Ambassador. We do have a hope. I suspect that is why you hold the weak and foolish at gunpoint."

Tyranna laughed. "Hope? We shall see about your hope."

She raised her wrist and spoke into the black device wrapped around it.

"Bring him in, but control him. He need not be wasted here."

Alba heard the rumble of the hovercraft as it drew closer to the Priory. It rushed over the vale and to the gate in only moments. The door of the craft fell open. Something came out.

The Sisters gasped when a giant of a man jumped down and lumbered through the gate. His red hair whirled in the wind as his piercing, green eyes surveyed the courtyard. He grasped the haft of his colossal battle axe and growled with rage. Alba's eyes grew wide, for she had seen his likeness before.

"Behold, your champion," Tyranna said. "Grigus Gildar no longer serves Elmnas. He has seen the error of his ways, and as you can see, has been rewarded with eternal youth for it. Today, he serves me."

Alba heard moans of horror and whispers of "It cannot be!"

Not just it cannot be, she thought. *It should not be.* The young warrior looked exactly like the leader of the Elmling Rebellions of forty years before, strikingly similar to the old portrait hidden in the Priory's storage cellar. Too similar, she decided, to be a son or grandson of the legendary man. But not for one moment did she believe the proud Grigus Gildar would abandon Elmnas and fight for the Coalition. Alba's head spun. Despite the paradox before her, he seemed no counterfeit. Was that so impossible? Not long ago everyone had believed him executed when the rebellions were quelled. But Mouse had shown that to be a lie, and Alba believed her. He had lived, even grown old in Misty Summit's prison before his supposedly final demise.

But what about his youth? How could he be young again if not through the ancient Guardian Way?

Alba dismissed Guardian blessing or involvement. Though she knew there had been Guardians who had misused the Way – the writings recorded those evil deeds and the consequences they had on latter generations – this was not a manner in which the Way could be twisted. The Way only granted the Guardians slowed aging; they could not reverse life's natural course. Even the most perverse of the ancient Elmlings could never accomplish that, though given the sordid histories, they may have tried. But this, whatever had happened to Grigus, was not a natural youth. And it was all wrong. Alba peered closer, now aware of the emptiness in his eyes and the hungry, animal expression etched on his hard features. She could not decide if he was truly a man, or if he had become something else altogether.

"What have they done to you?" Alba whispered.

"You see it plainly now," the Ambassador continued, sweeping her gaze over the terror-struck Ameliorites. "There is no hope in your backward beliefs, no triumph in your treachery. There is nothing left but to beg for my mercy."

The Ambassador turned, locking eyes with Alba yet again. She reached into the sheath on her hip. Alba inhaled sharply as a dull, green glow emanated from the scabbard. Tyranna raised the etched, sharpened sword into the air, allowing the women to behold it and murmur their confusion. Slowly, she lowered it, pointing the razor tip toward Alba. The Prioress cocked her head.

"It looks sick," Alba said. "No wonder. It is ill gotten."

Tyranna bared her teeth in a grin. "To the victor goes the spoils, Sister. And when your precious Guardians fell one by one to the

Coalition, such spoils there were. Cardanthium enough to power the Glorious New Era for another millennium."

Alba smiled. "I admit I am no expert on the Way of the Twin Blades, but I do not believe you could get even one minute of power from a Guardian-forged sword."

The Ambassador shrugged. "Does it matter? The Guardians are gone. Their silly blades are destroyed or adorn the mantlepieces of Gormlaen's greatest houses. The Coalition won this war a hundred years ago. Why are you still fighting?"

She drew closer to Alba and waved the guard behind her away. He stepped back, and Tyranna brought the sword point only inches from Alba's chest.

"You haven't started begging," she said. "Denounce all your disloyalty, confess your sins, and perhaps you may spare some of these here the fate you brought upon them."

The Prioress gazed slowly around at the Sisters in her charge. She saw them for what they were; poor, scared women, the sturdiest and youngest among them, startlingly frail beside the armored soldiers. Perhaps there was nothing she could do. Nothing but beg that the Coalition not silence all of them. Alba looked into each of their eyes as she could. Women she had loved and cherished more than natural daughters and mothers. Fond memories of each of them sprang to mind, piercing her heart with both joy and sadness. Her gaze rested at last on Sister Krelah. Her old face betrayed only a little fear. Shining through even brighter was a peace and comfort that passed understanding, softening Krelah's wrinkles with arresting, otherworldly beauty. How had Alba never seen it before? She reveled in it, drawing upon it even as she stood bound and at the edge of the sword.

She turned her attention back to Tyranna, who wore a gloating smirk. Alba shook her head with a knowing smile.

"Fate is not mine or yours to bring. The Unseen sees—"

The sword flashed forward, driving beneath Alba's breastbone. Agony exploded in Alba's chest. It stole even her ability to scream as

Tyranna buried the blade to the hilt. Alba sunk to her knees, choking as breath and blood flowed out of her together. With a disgusted twist of her lip, Tyranna raised her foot. She kicked Alba away as she yanked back the slick blade. The Prioress tottered and fell with her face to the ground. Tyranna's voice rose over the wails of her Sisters.

"Kill them all. Take what you please and burn this cursed place to the ground."

Screams and hissing blasts reverberated in the courtyard, but they echoed on and on as if down a corridor miles long. Alba turned her battered face out of the dirt, gasping in pain and in desperate need of air. Thudding, crashing, crackling, screaming. In Alba's narrowing vision, a purple habit smoked in the grass. She could smell it; fabric and flesh burning. *No, not that. Let me not see that.*

The last prioress of the Wolf Barrens strained to lift her gaze out of the confines of her graveyard. Above the Priory wall, she could just make out the rolling, reddened sky. Further up still, and it rolled faster. Magnificent blue pierced through the clouds. Sky, unadulterated sky. Everything else faded away. Yellow light poured through the hole, bathing everything in spectacular warmth. Alba smiled, unable to see or feel anything but light, a light now taking shape and form. Her vision narrowed, and her lips worked, but the words she wanted to sing would not come. She did her best.

"H-he is... here."

4

Smoke rose in puffs from the battlements and slowly circled up into the sky. From his hidden perch overlooking the vale, Dane saw it better than smelled it. The harsh, northern-eastern wind normal for this time of year had died for a while, but when it picked up again, it would scatter the caustic haze across the Priory's valley. For now, the smoke mushroomed and hung over the Priory, rippling with heat and black ash. Dane was not sure how long it would go on like that, but given the size of the fortress, it could burn for days. He watched as tongues of fire licked over the walls, consumed whatever detritus it could find, and then retreat. The puffing smoke and spouting flames produced an image of a dragon in his mind, crouched in the courtyard just beyond sight. Dane couldn't see the courtyard. He didn't need to.

'Tweren't no proper dragon, he thought, crossing his arms and spitting off the tree stand platform.

He followed the arc, watching it plop into the orange needles and dead leaves collecting at the base of his pine tree. The little sound disturbed a red squirrel burying acorns. It chittered angrily as it shot up the tree trunk beside Dane and twitched its whiskers toward him with some annoyance. Dane ignored it, hunkered down, and hoped the sound wouldn't draw undue attention. Not that anyone was still around. He caught sight of the Coalition transport and its heavily armored entourage exiting the Priory's entrance. That was a lucky coincidence. If they had not been in such a hurry to leave, they might have seen Dane hustling out of the tree line. They might have seen him freeze, like a deer in a glade, suddenly sensing the hunter's bowstring already drawn tight. As it was, he only had moments to scramble up into his lookout before the transport crested the hill. Only moments to lie flat on the stand as they roared past. He was lucky. When the approach of winter and its brutal winds shook the other trees naked, the evergreen hid him. His gamble to build in the wobbly pine and not the sturdy oak had paid off.

This time, he thought. *And only 'cuz I was stupid.*

He cursed himself softly under his breath, wishing he had not come back at all. When his Syndicate contact caught wind of the Inquiry and alerted Dane, the smuggler did what he did best in those situations: he got out. That was the Syndicate way. Heads up, and head out. Sure, he had warned Alba. A safe house needed to know when it was no longer safe. But she would not budge. She would stay with her Priory, like a captain going down with its ship. Dane inhaled sharply and raised his eyes to the fortress once more.

You mean, crazy, holy old bat.

Flames shot above the battlements as some new fuel fed the fire. The smoke poured out in thick billows now, obscuring the fortress and turning the scattered smoke scent acrid. Once again, Dane rued his return with a mumbled obscenity. He had his getaway made. A Syndicate contact had already arranged his passage back to the sewers. All he had to do was get to the crossing on time. Instead, like a moron, he missed his rendezvous and came back for the Ameliorites; one more attempt to change their minds. He knew it was pointless. Even if he had gotten here in time, he knew his pleas would fall on deaf ears. Alba and the other Sisters would never leave. They were always going to face the Coalition. They were always going to stand up and die.

Dane's hard, angry eyes rested on the Priory, now engulfed in the blaze. For fear of the Coalition soldiers' return, he had hesitated to go down to the Priory. This sort of prudent action had saved Dane's skin plenty of times in the past, but today it had wasted the opportunity to do anything meaningful. The small hope of giving the Sisters the burial they deserved went up with the flames swallowing the fortress.

Better fire than them Mistwolves.

Dane spit again with the force of a curse. He wondered if those mutant mongrels would venture into the flames, regardless. The thought horrified but did not shock him. Mistwolves might be the only thing on par with the Coats themselves in terms of degeneracy. And as the sky continued to darken, Dane rather hoped not to meet any now. With a wary glance in all directions, he climbed down from the tree stand. Cautiously, he edged away from the tree line, sweeping his sharp gaze up and down the vale for any sign of trouble. As always, it remained a silent wasteland, a place where even the bravest travelers feared to tread. Dane turned away from the burning Priory and looked back through the trees. The young people had gone that way, but he didn't know where they were headed or understood why. That day when Mouse and Toma left with the young Sister flashed into his memory.

He had liked Mouse. Dane always had a soft spot for kids who toughed it out like her. And to be honest, he had a soft spot for that oaf Toma, too. But he sure didn't care for what they were up to. Such ridiculous, un-derailed purpose, even as they ran straight toward danger. Even when Blade guided them, Dane thought it suicidal to head to Elmnas, of all places. What good could anyone do here? But there was something about Mouse; he saw that on Thunder Run, even if he had no categories to understand what had actually happened. He had his ears open at the Priory though, and he had heard the whispers of "Harbinger." Dane did not ask what that meant, or what their journey deeper into the Elmnas' wilderness could accomplish. He knew not to ask such prying questions. That was all part of the job: be discreet and aloof. Still, he wondered what they knew that he didn't. Or maybe they didn't know anything at all. Surely, they could not anticipate the terror that was tracking them down and scorching the earth in its wake.

Dane looked up at the sky and shivered as the wind howled past him. He pulled his bearskin coat tight and pushed the fur-lined cap down tighter over his ears. White flakes spiraled in the air and stuck in the wiry hairs of his beard. Within hours, snow would suffocate the valley, and any chance of anyone knowing what had happened on this black day would remain trapped here with him.

"Ain't nothing fer it," he grumbled.

Dane glared at the Priory one last time. Tearing his gaze away from the flames, he wiped at his eyes. They stung and watered. The bitter cold had a way of doing that.

5

62nd of Sun's Wane, Year 113
   Aruacas Rainforest
   Southwestern Gormlaen

Hot, thick air blanketed the jungle basin of the Aruacas Rainforest. Deep in the jungle's heart, beneath its expansive canopy, and removed from the sickly haze of the red-clouded sky, Blade could almost forget the civilized world. This world remained ever green, untainted by Coalition progress, almost devoid of humanity's mark, except for this deserted guard tower. Still, even this place was melting into the jungle. Vines grew up and over the tower's ancient walls, pushing through its interior and out its decaying roof in search of water and sunlight. Slabs of stone, eroded and strangled with overgrown roots and vines, dotted the immediate area around the tower. Blade supposed some long-forgotten people of Southwestern Gormlaen must have built the fortress here years ago.

A defensible place, Blade thought approvingly.

The basin stretched out below, and from his place in the tower, he had an acceptable view of anything coming through or around it, though traversing the basin itself would be a feat for any would-be attacker: it flooded constantly with the frequent downpours. Even as a shadow of its former self, the tower offered refuge and formidable defense. Of course, the fate of those who built it, like many before and after them, Blade could only guess. Something unexpected and stronger than they took them, he decided. Invaders, sickness, infestation, or famine, perhaps. Whatever it was, the jungle had now taken the stronghold for itself. In the end, it always repossessed what man proclaimed belonged to him.

From his perch on an upper floor window of the old ruin, Blade searched the steaming undergrowth for any sign of trouble. A heavy tropical rain had quieted the basin, but as it began to pass, a bird trilled out a tentative song. Creature cries and calls echoed amidst the slowing rain patter. Another bird cawed in distress, and the trees closest to the fortress shook. Blade's sharp, hawk-like eyes found the source: a troupe of tiny monkeys leaping onto the wet branches and converging on the succulent fruit near the harassed bird's nest. It cried indignantly as it flapped and winged out over the basin and through the dense tangle of limbs on the far side. Blade stroked his beard thoughtfully as he watched it.

Monkeys and birds in abundance. Now where are the leopards and other manner of beasts known to feed on them?

He searched the jungle floor again, knowing well the Aruacas Rainforest was unpopulated here for a reason. Many years had passed since he wandered this part of the country, but his last visit, a hunting engagement, had left him wisely wary of jungle dwellings. When the inhabitants of a river-side village had contracted him to take care of their Yacumama problem, Blade encountered more trouble than just the monstrous snake terrorizing them. Even with a guide, he would not venture far into the jungle on his own. It was a deadly place. Deadlier still for city-dwelling thieves with no working knowledge of a world beyond concrete and smokestacks. But what choice did they have? The Jackal Syndicate had nowhere else to go.

Blade reclined on the broad sill of the window, one foot hanging over the interior wall with the other planted on the crumbly stone as he resumed his self-appointed watch. He crossed his arms gently over his chest, still aware of the tenderness of his ribs. Blade snorted with annoyance. *Sticks and stones might break my bones,* he thought, recalling the childish rhyme. *But a Guardian stops at nothing.*

Indeed, Blade could still fight, still contribute. By the time they had cleared Lilien and fled to the woodlands west of the city, Blade's old strength returned to him. Not even his ordeal in Myergo's arena would stop him. And though Woldyff wanted him to rest, he knew as well as Blade the Syndicate depended on the beast hunter's guidance to survive. Woldyff had no say in that matter. Blade led them into the rainforest and to the Syndicate's emergency hideout there. And yet, once they arrived, Woldyff finally put his foot down. He refused Blade's offer to continue to help with the Jackal Syndicate's relocation. Instead, he gave Blade strict orders to relax.

Relax, Blade scoffed. *After my liberation cost them everything? How could I presume upon such a luxury?*

That was asking a lot. Blade could not allow the deed to go unpaid, even if Woldyff insisted he need not worry about that now. Yes, the Syndicate knew the risk – Woldyff had said as much – but even if they had all agreed to help him and had foreseen what the consequences would be, surely they did not fully grasp the implications. And they lived those implications now. Every Syndicate member in Lilien, whether involved in the battle or not, had to flee for their lives because of him. Could Blade not at least give what he may to alleviate their transition into life as refugees?

To Woldyff's annoyance, Blade planted himself here, on this window, and played sentry for the past week. That was as close to relaxation as he could manage. He refused to be totally useless, not when he knew the Aruacas better than any member of the harried band of thieves. And so, Blade scanned the jungle, both night and day, and the Syndicate cleared out the old tower and set up camp.

The week had passed without excitement. Myergo had not pursued, and no hungry creatures dared draw near their fires or flashing weapons. For now, that was more than the Syndicate could have hoped for. But something told Blade that peace would not last. He surveyed the jungle with suspicion.

With no more rain to tamp it down, the humid jungle air rose to meet him. Blade always forgot how warm it remained in this part of the country, even as winter approached in the north. He shed his outer cloak and laid it beside *Av'tal* and *Ub'rytal*, his twin Guardian-forged swords.

Noises below drew his attention, and Blade looked down to see two Syndicate members trotting up a small path toward the base of the tower. Between them, they carried a fresh kill, a wild boar, as well as a dripping net of fish. Though red-faced with exertion and soaked to the bone, one looked up and smiled. He and his companion waved enthusiastically. Blade nodded.

They entered the tower at the base, to whoops of celebration from the Syndicate members within. Blade hopped down from the sill, meaning to help prep the boar for dinner. The Syndicate members had enthusiasm to spare, but by no means did they understand what wilderness life demanded. Some could hunt and fish, but fewer still knew how to butcher fresh meat without ruining it. Blade stalked quietly down the winding stair, stopping just short of the second floor. He paused as a loud screech and hissing blast of an energy pistol reached him. Out of habit, he pressed himself against the wall.

"What the–" A voice he recognized as belonging to Maren, one of the Syndicate's chief mechanics, yelped in horror. "S-s-snake."

Another voice, Woldyff's, laughed loudly. "Wow, the size of that thing! Nice reflexes, Mar. Think we could eat that?"

Maren groaned. "Augh, why would you even say such a thing? Disgusting!"

"Not a time to be picky, dear." Woldyff clucked his tongue. "People gotta eat."

"You go on if you like," Maren growled, and then groaned again. "Oh, for heaven's sake, it's still lookin' at me!"

Blade inched toward the room, hesitating in the shadows on the stair as Maren stood over the snake's still quivering form. To her credit, the creature stretched several feet across the tower floor. Not so large as a Yacumama, but then again, normal snakes were unpleasant enough without being the size of an elephant. Maren had blown a hole through this snake's upper vertebrae, nearly severing its head. She muttered ominously to herself as she finished the job, straightened, and chucked the head out the second-story window.

"Of all the blasted places in Reidara," she said. "It had to be here. In the stinkin', sweaty jungle. Why, Woldyff? Why'd you have to bring us to be here?"

Woldyff shrugged. "Is it really worse than a sewer?"

Maren dug her fingers into her hair. "Not just any sewer! *Lilien's* sewer, the most perfect sewer for Syndicate operations in the Four Dominions! Where else would you find a tunnel system like Lilien's? With *working* locospheres? We could just pop right up into the ritziest district of the city and be gone in a flash. Ain't no one would see us coming or going! And we knew those tunnels like the back of our hands. We could get anywhere and do anything. All of it under the richest city in Gormlaen aside from Pardaetha. We had it made!"

Blade retreated further into the shadows, sensing his intrusion into this conversation would be worse for Woldyff in the long run. He heard Woldyff sigh as he turned to wait out the discussion in the tower.

"Listen, Mar," Woldyff said, his voice echoing up the staircase as Blade ascended. "I know we had it good, but you know as well as me that we weren't safe there. Myergo was always coming for us. He was just happy to collect rent in the meantime. And if he didn't come, the Coats would. We were stirrin' up too much trouble in the city. You know, a raid was overdue."

Woldyff paused, and Blade could almost hear the grin in his voice. "Besides, it smells better here."

Maren sniffed. "Wasn't that bad."

"We were just used to it," Woldyff chuckled.

"None o' that matters now," Maren said icily. "We're still in trouble. How in the name of all that is unholy are we gonna get back on our feet? All because we had to save your friend up there, the most wanted man in Gormlaen and not even a Syndicate member. Was it really worth it?"

By now, Blade had reached the third floor of the tower, but he could still hear every word. Years of hunting creatures quicker and stronger than him had honed his senses, and his bond with *Av'tal* and *Ub'rytal* sharpened them well beyond natural human ability. He returned to his post by the window, the farthest point from the stairwell, but the small, circular room afforded no privacy for the argument brewing below. Woldyff's voice echoed up the staircase with a threatening rumble.

"Watch it, Maren. Blade's done a lot for us. More than you know. You ain't been 'round long enough to run your mouth like that."

"No. Don't you talk to me that way!" Maren shouted. Mastering herself, she lowered her voice to a harsh whisper. "I've earned my place here, and I'll speak my mind. I won't put my trust in someone who slums it with us when it suits 'em and then leaves us when we still need 'em 'round. King o' the Shadows or not!"

Blade distinguished a thump and a grunt; probably Maren shoving Woldyff aside. A soft, fleshy thud suggested she kicked at the snake's carcass as she stomped toward the stairs. Silence stretched for a long moment before Maren's voice, calmer but still distressed, echoed toward Blade.

"You always said to never kick the hornets' nest," she said. "Even when I lost friends, too many of them, to Myergo, I thought it was right. Our young fools didn't deserve their fates, but they knew the consequences. We couldn't go bustin' down the door for them, not if we wanted to survive in Myergo's world. So, what changed, huh? Why give up everything for this one? Was his life really more important than the score of friends before him?"

Woldyff said nothing.

"That's what I thought."

Blade waited for the echo of her footsteps to fade before he made his way back down the stairs. He entered the room silently, finding Woldyff hunched over the dead snake and rubbing his chin. His friend sighed deeply as Blade emerged from the shadows and stood beside him.

"That is quite the monstrosity," Blade said. "Unfortunately, that is not the largest I have ever seen."

"I'd have a perfectly coarse rejoinder to that, if I were in the mood for it," Woldyff sighed. "And don't insult me. I know you heard us. How much of it, though? That's the real question."

Blade crouched beside him and traced the patterned black strips on the reptile's otherwise muddy blue scales. A river python. Not venomous, but dangerous enough in its own right.

"It does not matter," he replied.

Woldyff stood up and passed his hands over his face. He paced toward the window and leaned against the sill. "She's just upset about losing the Den. It's the first real home Maren and her brother knew. Always tough to let places go when you're young."

"But she is right," Blade said, following him. "You ought not to have gone after me. You could have gotten yourself killed."

Woldyff snorted. "It's bound to happen, eventually. I'd first look death in th' face then be hidin' in a drain waiting for it to come."

"And yet not every one of your members feels that way," Blade countered.

"How many times do I haft'a say it? We wouldn't have come after you if the Syndicate didn't agree to it! And it wasn't even me doin' the convincing!"

"Speaking of the devil," Blade said in a low voice. "Where did that bounty hunter get off to?"

Woldyff shrugged. "Beats me, but I wouldn't worry so much, Falky. Fox is in it, just like us. Did you see Myergo's face when he realized she was helping us? I never thought a man's veins could stick out that much without poppin'!"

"Still, you would do well to keep eyes on her. She is hiding something." Blade closed his eyes and pinched the bridge of his nose. "And do not call me that."

"It's more endearing than Falkir," Woldyff said with a laugh. "Although your dear mom and dad must've known you'd turn out this way by calling you somethin' like that. Oh ho, so serious. He'll be a stout one."

Woldyff puffed out his chest and tried to match Blade's impenetrable expression. Blade glowered, but even in his annoyance, had to admit the imitation was a dead ringer. The illusion broke as Woldyff's lip quivered into a wide-mouthed grin. Blade leveled a glare as Woldyff laughed louder.

"That name is a remnant of someone I no longer am," Blade said curtly. "Someone I no longer deserve to be. Any of your other inane epithets I will suffer, but not this."

Woldyff's grin died away. "Why? Because you stooped to filching from Coats who never deserved what they had, anyway? My... Maren was onto something, wasn't she? Do you have to be a sanctimonious neddy to be a Guardian up there in Elmnas, or do you really think associating with the likes of us makes you a bottom feeder?"

"The reason why has nothing to do with you, Woldyff," Blade replied sharply. He sighed and looked down at his hands. "You do not know the worst of all I have done. You could not understand."

"Must have been pretty bad," Woldyff whistled. "Didn't think your face could get gloomier. You always surprise me."

He slapped the back of his hand against Blade's arm. "But hey, maybe it's not as bad as you think. Maybe you're just so wrapped up in it, you can't see it for what it is."

Blade looked back at Woldyff and said nothing. Woldyff grinned.

"Come on, we're friends, aren't we? Try me. It's not like I have the right to be judgin' a soul."

Despite the disapproving shake of his head, Blade returned Woldyff's grin with a small smile of his own. He turned, grasping Woldyff's forearm firmly in affirmation. "Yes, we are friends. And I am a better man for it."

"That's right, you are!" Woldyff returned the gesture before patting Blade heartily on the back.

"I mean it," Blade said. "I still stand by my word. You risked too much for me in Lilien. But I am forever grateful. You and every one of the Syndicate members have my sincerest thanks."

"No need to thank us," Woldyff chuckled. "But you do owe us. Get the Syndicate outta this place and consider your debt paid."

"I'll do what I can," Blade nodded.

"First thing's first," Woldyff said, pointing to the snake. "We can eat that, right?"

6

The smell of simmering meat lingered in the twilight air. Blade scooped the last piece of boar from the bottom of his bowl. He would have preferred it on the spit, slowly roasted over the coals, but they lacked the luxury of patience for something like that. Their flight into the Aruacas had preserved the Jackal Syndicate, but it had also left them lean with hunger and ragged with exhaustion. The band of thieves, many of them barely adults, were accustomed to a different sort of jungle. That one did not generally require long hours of trekking through dangerous wilds to hunt for meals to survive. And with dinner duties falling to a handful of junior Syndicate members whose only experience with raw meat was the cuts they had stolen from the butcher shop's window, Blade took it upon himself to oversee the work. Not a single one of them could afford a botched meal. Into the pot went the boar, snake, and fish alike. And after Blade's careful attention and instruction on which plants could improve the meal instead of poisoning them, the young cooks-in-training finally crafted something edible.

He set the bowl down beside him and gazed out from his roost, overlooking the fortress ruins. Blade gave up his tower haunt for the communal meal, instead resting on a portion of the toppled but solid walls that outlined the perimeter of the fortress complex. From there, his tower loomed behind him, and another tower rose in front of him about a half mile to the north. That one was uninhabitable, and to Blade, not worth the trouble of exploring. Behind the camp and the adjoining remnants of fortress wall, great heaps of stone dotted the landscape for about another mile, monuments to the impressive structures the grounds had once harbored. Despite the erosive damage of time and rainwater, the ground within the lost complex remained reasonably level. Here, most of the Syndicate had erected tents, tarps, and whatever else the fleeing members thought to grab on their way out of the sewers, and spread them out among the ruins. Now, as supper time wound down, people moved among the tents to resecure canvas flaps and protect supplies from the next downpour. Lanterns and campfires gave off a cheerful, welcoming glow. Those finished with their daily tasks sat on rocks, rubble, and fallen trees dragged to the fire. They talked in subdued tones, a low murmur among the ever-present life of the rainforest. Occasionally, though, a laugh or two echoed throughout the camp above all else. A flute warbled somewhere. Daylight faded fast beyond the forest canopy.

With a nervous clearing of his throat, someone called up to Blade. "Take your bowl, sir?"

Blade gazed down at a Syndicate recruit, a young man of Maiendell barely out of his teens. He smiled tentatively as Blade watched him for an unblinking, silent moment. Blade caught himself, forcing his expression to soften. He found it easier now, after his journeys with Mouse and Toma, but still he had to remember his habit of detached observation unnerved even the boldest among the group. People knew what to do with smiles, frowns, and tears. They could respond to that. Neutrality, however, terrified them. Blade imagined the youth was Toma, and his humanity came a little easier.

"There is no need for that," Blade answered gently. "I am more than happy to do my part."

The young man relaxed and reached up. "Oh, it's no trouble at all. Consider it my thanks for getting supper off without a hitch." He added in a whisper: "My friends are great, but they sure can't cook to save their lives."

Blade allowed a small chuckle and handed down the bowl. "No doubt, but you managed today. There is hope for them yet."

The young man grinned, and with a nod, turned back to collect dishes from the rest of the camp. Blade watched him disappear into the pop-up settlement.

Satisfied, he leaned against the inclined slab at his back and rested with his knees up and swords at his sides. Out of habit, he searched the surrounding jungle. It seemed that the fortress had once extended farther, but the trees had crowded in and overtaken whatever was beyond their small clearing. Mounds of moss-covered rock hidden in the canopy shade hinted at a far bigger compound than he initially realized. Blade studied the layout of their clearing. Strips of flat stone stretched at parallel and perpendicular angles from the tower. It looked to Blade like fragments of road, split and separated as the jungle sprang up through it. *Perhaps not just a military installation*, he thought. *Perhaps a great city of ancient times.*

He tried to imagine what the streets must have looked like before, lined with massive buildings and alive with city life, full of the sounds of carts trundling, merchants shouting, children laughing; heavy with the scent of cooking fires and humid jungle heat. Perhaps they believed they were safe here, tucked deep into the jungle behind impressive walls. Perhaps they were still buying and selling, laughing and walking, eating and drinking on the day of the city's destruction.

Most do not know the end is coming until it is already upon them.

Another image flashed through his mind: a city he knew, its wide, cobbled streets lined with timbered homes, their roofs dusted with a late spring snow. The familiar scents of roasting mutton and juniper berry wine filled his memory, followed by the sensation of a touch; the soft touch of a familiar hand. His eyes lighted upon the hand and traveled up toward a familiar face. *Her* face. She smiled. Blade remembered the snow drop he was holding, and the feel of silky, golden hair as he tucked it behind her ear.

What do you think, Falkir? Will you still be putting flowers in my hair in a hundred years?

Blade could still see the playful smile, the joy and mischief twinkling in her eyes.

As long as you do not come to your senses and leave me for one who deserves your love.

He felt the soft touch of lips against his as she leaned in and kissed him, giggling.

Only you could sound so noble while being so self-deprecating. If you can put up with me for that long, I'd say you earned it.

Theana.

The memory of his speeding heart thumped again in his own chest. He saw the impish grin turn serious at the sound of her name. She looked up, sky blue eyes softening as they met his.

What, my love?

Let me be yours.

Even for a hundred years?

If the Unseen grants it, for always.

Blade sighed and looked down at the piled rubble on his left. A few inches from his fingers, a pink flower poked up through the mossy crevices of broken stone. He did not know the name of this one. Rainforests had too many to name, and in his trade, only the ones with medicinal or edible uses mattered. The unknown and probably useless pink flower looked back at him. *Useless*, he thought. *But beautiful.*

He plucked it, twirled the stem between his fingers, and wondered if Theana would have liked it. *What was her favorite color again? Was it purple or pink?* He stared at the petals, studying the indigo spots that darkened near the flower's pistil. Why was it so hard to remember? The long years of his life had dulled those memories, those little details once clutched tight. He had held them looser in these latter days, allowing the joy so mingled with pain to slip out of focus. Memory was a burden, a burden he had been too weak to carry. Blade had laid it down long ago.

But something had changed. *Mouse*, he thought. *Another young woman with her life ahead of her.* Mouse had stirred up the past, and her amnesia brought only natural curiosity about that same past, the one that, in many ways, they shared. It had forced him to recall, to conjure up the sorrow and agony, to tell the story that needed to be told. And burden though it might be, how could he will himself to forget the past when others had so cruelly ripped it away from Mouse? Blade could pick up the burden again. He could be strong for someone else.

Magenta, he remembered. *Theana's favorite color was magenta. She was always so particular.*

Blade wasn't sure if the pink flower between his fingers was magenta, but it seemed close enough. Theana would have liked it all the same. He looped it through a buttonhole in the top of his shirt.

A soft rustle outside the crumbled fortress wall caught his attention. Blade jumped up, swords poised defensively in the direction of the sound. He turned his head to the side, listening carefully to the faint crunch of undergrowth as light feet trod softly upon it. *Human feet.*

He bounded over the wall and sped to a sprint as soon as his boots touched the ground. Weaving through the vines and trees that rimmed the gurgling basin, Blade careened along the ruins toward the alien sound. Twilight darkened the jungle. Blade peered through its twisting shadows. A shape resolved. He extended *Ub'rytal* toward the intruder's throat. A flash of green met his sword with a resonating clang.

"A little jumpy today, are we?" Fox smirked in the light of the blade's glow. "I shall remember to be a little louder next time I come back. Or perhaps softer. It might be fun to see if you would discover me at all when I am actually trying."

She pushed the tip of *Ub'rytal* down with her own sword. Blade sheathed it and sighed.

"What do you mean by disappearing all day?"

Fox crossed her arms with a pouty smile. "Were you worried about me? How sweet."

Blade raised his eyebrow. "Some might find such behavior suspicious."

"Be still, oh vigilant one," Fox said, her voice dripping with sarcasm. "I was scouting the jungle. I would have invited you, but I'm still not certain that would be prudent."

"Though I do not trust you, it would be ignoble to take your life now. Certainly not alone in the dark. Still, I have not decided whether I ought to challenge you to open combat for past offenses," Blade replied.

"I was talking about this," Fox said, poking a finger into his ribs. "But thank you."

He winced.

"Anyway," she smirked. "I've had enough of traipsing about the wilderness for the day. Shall we?"

The two walked together toward the Syndicate camp, and Blade considered the woman again. Fox moved with graceful ease through the tangled brush, as silent and as at home in it as the creatures it harbored. She had pulled up her thick, crimson-touched hair, which had seemed to grow even thicker in the wet air. Her skin glistened with sweat, and her muddied and blood-stained clothing was damp with it. Even so, Fox retained her uncommonly arresting beauty, deep scars and all. A shallow person might call the marring a pity, but Blade could not imagine who she could have been without it. The Arctura Fox, who never received such wounds, would be someone else entirely. Indeed, most likely a person Blade could never abide or respect. And for all their differences and his own misgivings about her, she at least had earned that from him.

Still, she seemed every bit the ruthless bounty hunter who, only weeks before, had trapped Blade and his fellow travelers on the Coalition's orders. Fox remained indifferent about having sold him to Myergo. It was only business, she had said. When Woldyff asked about the fates of Dane, Mouse, and Toma, she had simply shrugged. So, what was she doing here, now? What did she hope to accomplish? Whose side was she really on?

Blade had not discussed much else with her since their wild journey out of Lilien to the Aruacas, and certainly not in private. There had not been time, for one thing. For the other, Blade had little desire to engage her in conversation without knowing what she truly wanted. And that not knowing unsettled him. Blade could read anyone. As her captive in the wilderness, he thought he had read her perfectly. The sharp edge of a cruel world had honed her own cruelty even sharper. With that sharpness, she made the world pay. That was simple. Blade had dealt with her type before, and it always ended the same. But then she had bewildered him. Of all possible outcomes in Myergo's arena, the bounty hunter responsible for his predicament now leading the charge for his rescue had not been one of them. Why would she do that? What had changed?

Her mention of Hiraeth continued to roll around in his head. It made him wonder. And worry.

"Find anything of interest in your scouting?" Blade asked instead.

Fox scoffed. "Other than a hungry leopard and four million mosquitos? Not much. I see no evidence of Coalition presence here in the rainforest, so we are safe from them for a time. As for Myergo and his lot... They know we are in here. I saw a few idiots wandering about, but they don't seem keen to venture too far into the jungle. Just enough to keep us from turning back east toward Gormlaen."

With deadly wastes west of the Aruacas, only open ocean south, and the myriad dangers in the heart of the jungle north, Blade understood Myergo's strategy immediately.

"Then it is a squeeze. They expect to wait us out on the eastern border."

"Precisely," Fox said. "And if anyone can afford to do so, it would be Myergo."

"I should not want to fall into his hands again," Blade said knowingly.

Fox smirked. "Neither should I. It will be most unpleasant for the both of us."

They came to the remains of the crumbled tower. Blade paused at its base, resting his hand against the slick, broken stone. Fox stopped as well, her fierce eyes meeting his in the gathering dark.

"Why did you help me?" Blade asked. "You had nothing to gain from it and everything to lose. You have signed your own death warrant from the Coalition and our unpleasant mutual friend alike. They will never stop hunting you. I should know. It has been my life for a century."

Fox scowled as she looked up at the forest canopy. Blade followed her gaze, watching in silence with her as the refracted red of the clouds streamed between the gray-green fronds.

"I was born on this day," she said softly. "One hundred and sixteen years ago. I have been told it was a beautiful, clear night, and the light of *Arcturan*, the Archer's Constellation, shone down on the place of my birth. It is said that when I first breathed, a meteor shot through *Arcturan*'s bow like a flaming arrow. In those days, our people still believed in signs and wonders, so from *Arcturan* I received my name. A good omen for Gormlaen."

Fox scoffed and shook her head. "My father hated the old superstitions of our people, the worship of stars and trees. Such things were already passing when I was a child, and he refused to entertain them. No one but my nurse would tell me why I was named for the Archer. 'You are his fiery dart,' she would say. 'Who can say how far he means you to fly? Will you pierce the dark? Or shall it swallow you whole?'"

Blade said nothing as Fox stared off into the shadows, absent-mindedly stroking the scars on her cheek. She stopped abruptly, her keen eyes turning on him with ferocious intensity.

"I hated her for that."

At this, Blade smiled. Fox sighed and leaned against the deteriorating wall adjacent to the tower. "A strange thing to remember, after all these years. And yet there are stranger things still. Would you not agree, Falkir?"

Blade remained silent as he judged Fox's intent. Arms crossed, she peered back at him. Blade moved closer.

"Before you turned me over to Myergo, you spoke of someone. An ancient Guardian, a legend, of my people," he said. "You spoke as if you met him. Were you lying, or was he the one who showed you the Way?"

Fox smirked. "Is it so hard to believe?"

"That Melek Tzedek, the only Elmling known to command all three Guardian gifts, stepped out of the pages of the Sacred Writings and took you under his wing?" Blade snorted. "He was the greatest among us. Never before or since has any Guardian like him existed. Indeed, there were many Masters of my time who did not believe he ever did."

Her eyes narrowed. "What do you mean?"

"If it was truly Melek Tzedek, the same Hiraeth whom you say you knew, he would have been thousands of years old. No other Guardian, not even those most attuned to the Way, had ever lived that long."

Fox jumped up, rubbing her chin in thought as she paced in front of him.

"Is it possible?" she murmured, more to herself than to Blade.

He tilted his head. "So, it is true."

"You want to know why I came for you," she said. "It is because Hiraeth came for me."

Blade raised an eyebrow. For the first time, a humble uncertainty crossed Fox's features.

"I cannot explain it. What I saw in the wilds of Gormlaen went against all sense and reason. He appeared out of nowhere. I thought it just a fever dream, and even now I wonder if I imagined his transformation into that fiery bird of prey. But he *touched* me. I know Hiraeth lives." Fox looked into Blade's watching eyes. "He prepares for something. Something that holds the fate of us all. I was given a choice."

Blade stroked his beard distractedly, his expression darkening. Turmoil churned inside him. Could it be? Was this Hiraeth of Guardian lore, whom Blade had long believed only myth, not only real but also Elmnas' prophesied redemption? Was the Phoenix indeed returning to Elmnas in its time of need? Fear, doubt, and pain swelled in Blade's chest, but something else rose, something he was not sure could ever rise again. Hope.

He breathed in deeply before speaking. "This is why you gave up your pursuit of Mouse and returned to help me?"

Fox nodded.

"And who do you believe this Hiraeth is?" Blade asked. "Is he worth the path you have abandoned?"

"I do not know," she admitted. "But I believe it is as he said. The time comes when all will be revealed. What I have done, I have done. The burden of this decision is not the heaviest I have had to bear."

"Then I, too, have made a decision." Blade drew closer to Fox and thrust out his arm. "We shall not do battle this day."

Fox looked down at the proffered forearm with a smile before grasping it. "Strange times, indeed."

Blade held hers in return, a small smile forming on his own lips. But as he opened his mouth to speak, a sound reached his ears. Something rustled in the jungle just behind them.

Fox's eyes narrowed, indicating that she had heard it, too. Without a word, Fox and Blade reached into their sheaths. Together, they moved toward the sound, crouching stealthily as they weaved along in the undergrowth. By the glow of their swords, Blade searched the jungle. Ahead, a slow shape maneuvered through the thick tangle of trees. Blade could hear the man's labored breathing, as well as his muttered curses. The Guardian held up his hand. Fox nodded and edged around the approaching stranger. Blade split off in the other direction, closing in on the other side.

The man drew nearer. As he crossed within sight of the fortress ruins, Blade and Fox surged out of the jungle. Before the man could shout, four swords pointed at his throat and chest. He cursed instead.

"Just what I needed," the man grumbled. "A ghost back from the dead and the one who killed him."

7

"Dane." Blade quickly sheathed his swords, a rush of astonishment and excitement coursing through him. He observed the Syndicate smuggler with calm silence, even as a dozen questions raced through his mind. *Dane is alive,* he marveled. *But where is Mouse and Toma?*

The Syndicate smuggler glowered at Blade and Fox in turns. He looked better than Blade remembered at their last parting. Of course, he was unconscious then and had a gaping hole in his shoulder. Raw, raised skin with still-dissolving stitches sutured the wound together. Blade saw its distinct outline through Dane's thin undershirt stained with sweat at the collar and armpits. More sweat poured off his balding head as Dane passed an arm across his forehead. His other layers he had peeled away and shoved into the bundle slung over his back. The corner of his fur cap and the sleeve of his winter coat hung out of the top, and Blade wondered at how long he must have traveled through the Aruacas to find them. A pistol remained strapped to his side. Dane had no time to even reach for it when Blade and Fox ambushed him. Otherwise, he carried nothing else. His long, wiry beard and hollowed, weary face hinted at the incredible journey. And despite enemies and natural dangers, he had made it here. Blade nodded with appreciation.

"There are many foes skulking around the rainforest," he said. "I am pleased to see you are not one of them."

"I'm not so sure I'm not," Dane grumbled, eyeing Fox with wary disdain.

Blade barely registered the comment, his thoughts fixed with urgency on his young charges. Distractedly, he held out his arm in welcome. "What news of Mouse and Toma?"

Scowling and still glaring at Fox, Dane reached for Blade's outstretched arm.

"Alive and well, since last I saw them, despite the best efforts of some folk."

Blade's eyes misted as relief flooded through him. For the first time in many years, a once reflexive litany of thanks leaped from his heart into his mind. *Praise the Unseen, the One who sees and moves.* He grasped Dane's arm a little tighter. "You bring welcome news."

"Yeah, well, the rest ain't too pretty," Dane replied, his scowl deepening. "And beggin' your pardon," he growled, jabbing a finger toward Fox. "But *what* is she doin' here?"

Fox had already lowered her swords and respectfully backed away from the smuggler, but she did not bother hiding the presumptuous smirk as she watched the pair's greeting.

"That is an extraordinary tale," Blade answered. "I cannot do justice to it here, but know that our former adversary has made herself an enemy of both the Coalition and Myergo for my sake."

Dane's wiry eyebrows shot up in surprise before settling back down in his familiar scowl. He harrumphed as he crossed his arms gingerly.

"If I may, smuggler, I am impressed to see you alive," Fox said. "It appears anything's possible with a gifted healer and a mulish will to live. I surmise you had both. Nevertheless, it was nothing personal."

With a pained expression, Dane pointed fiercely at the wound.

"You almost shot my arm off!" he growled. "Turns out I was still usin' it!"

Fox sighed. "Yes, and if I hadn't missed, we wouldn't be having this conversation at all, would we?"

Something between anger and horror paled Dane's face. Blade sighed as he clapped a hand on his good shoulder.

"There is much to speak about," he said. "You shall want to hear more of our tale, and I am eager to hear yours. But come, let us not waste breath and time out here where enemies may fall on us. The Syndicate camp is not far."

"Alright," Dane relented, but not before shooting a dark look at Fox. "You stay where I can see you. And there better be something to eat when we get there."

The three continued on toward the fortress as Blade recounted the details of their last few weeks. Dane listened without speaking, his brow furrowing deeper with every word. As they arrived at the tower entrance, he grunted with annoyed comprehension.

"So, you're the reason all my Syndicate contacts disappeared. Could hardly find a soul willing to take me south, let alone one to tell me what happened to the Den or where to find Woldyff. Just that it ain't in Lilien, and I better keep my mouth shut. You're lucky I got here at all."

"Indeed," Blade said. "It is remarkable that you even survived Thunder Run. What happened?"

Dane snorted. "Mouse happened."

Blade remained silent, gathering himself as even more questions than before began to roil within him. He knew something had drawn him to Mouse, something more than mere coincidence, though he had tried hard to ignore it. Dane's comment hinted at what Blade found impossible to ignore: Mouse *was* the Harbinger.

"Tell me," Blade finally said. "Spare no detail."

"Yes," Fox added, tapping a finger against her lips. "I am most interested, as well. What did the girl do?"

Dane narrowed his eyes at Fox before turning back to Blade. "Not so sure now's a good time for me."

"Believe me when I say she has proven her mettle," Blade said, almost impatiently. "And if she seeks to betray us now, she will not live to regret it."

Fox sniggered. "Do you not think I've done enough betraying for one cycle? I know I hide it well, but it is exhausting."

Dane harrumphed, but began speaking anyway.

"Here's how it happened. We got on the river. A bad idea, obviously, but we had no choice. I couldn't do nothing, 'cept lay there in the bottom of the boat and yell things. The kids tried to steer, but... no use. We were goners. And things were getting hazy for me. But right as we just about went under, Mouse went rigid. Not scared stiff, but trance-like, as if something had come over her. She wrenched the oar from Toma's hand like she was five times his size and rowed like I never seen no one row before, all the while staring straight ahead. We were in the worst of it then, water flooding the boat, me sputterin', that boy lookin' like a great big goon with his mouth hanging open and barely keepin' hold of the skiff. Coulda been the shock, but I swear... she was glowin'. Anyway, I passed out for about half a minute and when I came to, we were safe to shore."

Fox and Blade looked at each other and at Dane without a word. Dane chuckled.

"They thought I'd lost my wits, which is half true. But I did catch her talking to the boy about it, though. She saw something. Some sort of uh... vision, I guess."

"You bring strange tales," Blade said with a smile. "And still not the strangest. But there is more to the story. How were you parted?"

"We ended up at that fortress on the Wolf Barrens, the Ameliorite Priory."

Blade nodded. "The convent of those foreign adherents to the old religion. Yes, I know it. What fortune."

"Not for them," Dane mumbled. "And that's why I'm here."

Blade's stomach tightened, a nervous nausea rising as he gazed into the pain and rage darkening Dane's countenance. He was all too familiar with what news that look meant. His own deep rage quickened, and his swords grew hot in their sheaths.

"Get me in front of the Jackal Syndicate," Dane said. "I got something to say."

"Would it not be wise to be speak to me and Woldyff alone first?" Blade asked.

Dane's jaw grew rigid as his steely glare pierced the dark. "What I have to say, I'm sayin' to everyone."

Again, Blade nodded in assent, knowing it was pointless to argue. He pointed to the tower entrance.

"You'll find the company through there."

Dane shouldered past Blade and Fox. They followed as he entered the tower. Woldyff was just inside the door, speaking quietly with Maren and a handful of other Syndicate members as they hovered over plans laid open beneath the lantern light. His eyebrows shot up at the entrance of the trio, lighting upon Dane with pleased recognition.

"Ho there! You're alive after all!" Woldyff laughed. "What a reunion! And how in Reidara did you find us? I'll tell you, it's been something of a wild ride for us, but you sure are lookin' ready to share a tale of your own."

"Shut yer yap, Woldyff," Dane barked. "No time for that. Where's the rest of this sorry lot?"

Woldyff raised an eyebrow with bemusement, but heeded Dane anyway. He gestured behind him to the doorway that opened into the ancient fortress courtyard. Darkness blanketed the ruin now, but fires brightened the camp. Dane growled and charged through it.

"Listen up!" he shouted. "All of you, get over here!"

Woldyff rounded on Blade.

"What's this all about?" he muttered. "He's sourer than a Coat sucking a lemon. That's sayin' something, given his usual temper."

Blade stared back, expressing his sense of the weight of the situation with even more sobriety than normal. Woldyff sighed.

"Don't like the looks of that," he said. "Alright, let's go hear 'im out."

Woldyff turned, followed by the Syndicate members with him. Maren was the last. She met Blade's gaze, her lip curled and arms crossed. With a withering look, she exited the tower. Blade heard Fox snort behind him as they streamed into the courtyard.

Outside, a crowd had already begun to gather around the smuggler. He stood atop one of the piles of ruins, his stern, fierce features sharpened in the shadow and glow of flickering firelight. As the final members stepped into the circle, the low murmur quieted, and Dane spoke.

"Listen here," he said. "Ain't no doubt about it, the Syndicate's seen better days. I've heard – bits and pieces, mind you – but I've heard. I was never much for livin' underground, but all the same, I'm sorry we've lost the Den. After all the Syndicate's been through, I reckon you're pretty tired of bad news."

Murmurs of agreement rippled through the crowd. Dane grimaced.

"It's about to get much worse."

He raised his hands to silence the growing volume of anxious whispers and grumbled protests.

"Listen, it wasn't any picnic gettin' through this blasted rainforest to find you. Myergo's people are everywhere. You know what that means. But if he ain't the end of us, the Coalition is."

"What do you mean by that?" Woldyff said quietly.

"While you've been busy robbin' rich chumps in Lilien, outside, things have been changing," Dane said. "Coats are clamping down the borders. All over the Four Dominions, they're gunnin' for outfits like ours. People are disappearin' left and right. The ones who are left have told me what they've seen. Weapons, transports, people. All movin' north. War is headed that way. To Elmnas."

Blade looked around the whispering crowd. They shifted uncomfortably, whispering among each other about the implications of war. In the confines of Gormlaen, and even in Maiendell and

Heibeiath, war remained a foreign concept; a fleeting thought, an incomprehensible matter. Blade tried to imagine what it must have been like for many of them, growing up as Coalition citizens, knowing peace, even if it was kept through the iron grip of fear. Still, none of them could begin to comprehend the terror and suffering of life as an Elmling, a life as truly hated enemies of a grossly powerful state. These young, prideful thieves had only ever rebelled in small ways, chafing under Coalition rule like children weary of living in their parents' household. But for all their feigned bravado and radical ideas, they were still only petty criminals. They weren't traitors. Not really, not yet. But where would their loyalties lie in an open war?

Some have already made that choice, Blade thought, his gaze turning from the restless crowd to Fox.

He had half-expected her to be looking right back at him, an ominous yet playful smirk on her lips as usual. Instead, she stood staring at Dane with a stern, concentrated frown.

"But how's that affectin' us?" Maren challenged. "We're Gormlaean citizens. And we don't do much business in Elmnas, anyway. If we could just get out of this stupid jungle, we'd be fine."

Shouts of agreement rang out in the night.

"Don't you get it?" Dane shot back. "The Coalition is stampin' out its enemies. All of 'em. Ask yourselves, where does the Syndicate fit into that picture?"

The crowd fell silent.

"Let me paint it for you in some more detail," he said angrily. "I watched a Coalition Inquiry burn an abbey filled with unarmed women to the ground. Most of them, Gormlaean citizens, *in good standing*. They were slaughtered. Every last one of them. Still think you'll be fine?"

Maren's resolved gaze fell to the ground as the stunned hush continued.

"They knew Mouse had been through the Ameliorites' Priory," Blade said, interrupting the silence. The crowd's attention swung to him as he continued. "Some of you may yet remember what happened in Lilien the night we first came to you. Make no mistake, there was no city-wide drill on that day. The Coats wanted Mouse, desperately enough to turn the city upside-down just to find her. They will spare no one who has harbored her."

"Them coming after *you*, I get. But Mouse? She's just a kid," Woldyff said in disbelief. "What do they want from her?"

"She has something, doesn't she?" Fox asked.

Blade did not answer as Fox watched him, her brows drawn in thought.

"Perhaps something that could potentially disable the Coalition itself?" she posited. "Yes, that must be it. I was offered pure Cardanthium and my weight in gold to hunt her down. Now, I am good at what I do, but no one, not even the Coalition in previous engagements, has sought to entice my services with that much wealth. Truly, Blade, does Mouse indeed represent the biggest threat the Coats have seen since the Elmling rebellions, or am I underestimating the amount thrown in to get you out of their way?"

"That remains to be seen," Blade said.

A cryptic half-smile formed on his lips as Fox's gaze bored into him. He sensed the piqued interest of the Jackal Syndicate as well; Blade felt their stares, their minds probing and mulling over what a young fugitive from one of the Coalition's most notorious prisons could know or have that would bring the full weight of the state's power down upon her. Not that Blade could give them an answer, even if he felt it appropriate and necessary. What would he say when Woldyff pressed him on it later? What did he understand of experimental Coalition technology and the evil uses they intended for it?

And yet she *might understand,* he thought, still holding Fox's gaze. *What an irony. Not long ago even torture would not have drawn anything of value from me. But if there is an answer...*

With a knowing smirk, Fox turned back to Dane. "Tell me, smuggler, the raiding party that burned the Priory. What did it look like? Who led it?"

"Didn't get the best look at 'em," Dane grumbled. "Too busy tryin' to stay out of sight and alive. About a dozen people, though. I thought I saw a lion on their armor? Just one, not like the usual Coalition getup. Not your run-of-the-mill Coats, either. That's for sure. It was a woman who ran the outfit."

"This woman," Fox said. "What did she look like?"

Dane shrugged. "Youngish, I suppose. As pretty as you and I'm bettin' just as mean. She had long, black hair. Now that I think about it, I feel as if I've seen her somewhere before."

"No doubt you have," Fox replied with a grim smile. "Though perhaps it has been a while. The face of Prime Ambassador Tyranna Vipsanius has not graced the holograstones, the propaganda posters, or indeed any of the public arena in nearly forty years. Mainly, I suspect, because it has not aged a bit in all that time."

Whispers among the Jackal Syndicate began anew as Fox tapped on her wristband. Blade watched with interest as a miniature image popped up and orbed above her wrist like a bubble on the surface of a still lake. A face swam to the surface of the orb, but disappeared and reformed in the cloudy swirl as a new face, and then another, as she continued tapping the band. Fox flipped through her catalog of faces, and Blade grimaced as a likeness of Toma and then of Mouse floated by.

"There you are," Fox murmured as the image she was looking for swirled and settled on the bubbled surface. She moved closer to Dane and raised her wrist to eye level. "Is this the woman you saw in the Wolf Barrens?"

Blade peered down at the face alongside a squinting Dane. The Gormlaean woman pictured was haunting in her loveliness. In her eyes she carried the look of all high-born. Noble, powerful, proud. Her perfect, red lips curled up in a seductive and cruel sneer, giving Blade the impression she knew too well the extent of both her power and beauty. A strange familiarity came over him, and Blade searched his long memory for a time he might have seen her before. Was it in the holograstones? In his many years, Blade never looked at them long. He never knew who could be looking back. But then a faint memory came to him; an unannounced Coalition procession through an insignificant Heibeiathan city, about ten years after the Silver Sea Sanctum fell. Blade had ducked into the shadows of an alley, but not before the procession came into view. He remembered one face all too clearly – the first Supreme Chancellor of the Coalition – and in his cowardice and shame, Blade retreated further into the dark instead of avenging Elmnas. That was what he had always remembered of that moment. His shame, his fear. He had tried to remember it no more. So why did it return to him now?

She was there, Blade thought, as he studied the woman. *Beside him.*

His jaw tightened.

All this time Dane was considering the image, brow furrowed in concentration. Woldyff and the other close-by Syndicate members had been leaning in as well, and the entire camp seemed to be holding its breath. Dane released a slow, shaking sigh.

"That's her, alright," he said darkly. His gaze shifted back to Fox. "How did you know?"

Fox spoke quietly and with deliberate calm, but Blade could see the fire rising in her eyes. "How could I not know my own sister-in-law?"

8

A stunned silence fell over the Syndicate. All eyes fell upon Fox, and she stared back brazenly, her face an iron mask of inscrutability. Blade looked upon that face, recognition of her shared features with that Supreme Chancellor he saw so many years ago now hitting him like a stone wall. How had he not seen it before? Unanswered questions sprang to his mind, but these drowned in the flushing heat of rage fomenting in his chest. He unsheathed his swords, now blazing with their signature green intensity. *Ub'rytal* flew forward and its point rested against Fox's collarbone.

"You," Blade growled. "Even knowing you were the cruelest hunter that roamed Reidara and a Coalition pawn, I had believed better of you than you deserved. Had I understood what you truly were, I'd have destroyed myself with gladness as long as you could no longer draw breath."

Fox blinked at the sword, her expression unchanged. "I know."

"Whoa now, steady, okay?" Woldyff moved toward Blade with a nervous chuckle and place a hand on his rigid shoulder. "Let's all just take a step back, and maybe do some explainin' before killin', alright?"

"What is there to explain?" Blade said through gritted teeth.

LION

"She comes from the house of Lucan Vipsanius, Supreme Chancellor of the Coalition, the man who spilled the blood of millions of my kin. The worst of the Coalition stands before you. She ought to die."

Murmurs rippled through the crowd. Woldyff's eyes widened as even he took a step back. Fury blazed through Blade's swords as he held *Ub'rytal* firm against Fox. She winced, but did not move. Her eyes rose to meet his. Blade steeled himself against what he saw there – sorrow and shame, but also courage, determination, and understanding.

"I am guilty of many things," Fox said quietly. "Terrible things that cannot be forgotten. For those, I admit you would bear no fault in striking me down. And as the daughter of Lucan Vipsanius, I carry the shame that is upon that house. But I do not carry the guilt of what he has done to Elmnas."

"How can you expect me to believe such lies?" Blade spat threateningly. "What proof have you?"

"Proof?" Fox wore her same scoffing, arrogant smirk, but her eyes told a different story. They melted into an unbearable sadness. Blade frowned as tears glistened in her eyes. She traced the scars on her jaw, her gaze settling on Blade's pink flower.

"Perhaps this will satisfy you."

With Blade's swords still upon her, Fox reached into her pocket, pulling a thin, watertight box from within. She opened it gently, revealing a yellowing parchment inside. With shaking fingers, she unrolled the parchment.

Blade scanned the document by sword light, his gaze finding the Supreme Chancellor's signature across the bottom. A tuft of black hair fixed to the parchment's corner caught his eye, and his breath caught in chest.

Fox said nothing, but Blade looked into her eyes, recognizing her distant, yearning stare with startling clarity. All at once, his anger subsided. He could not mistake that deepest wound, that inexorable pain, even if buried under years of rage and ruthlessness. The

63

righteous glow of *Av'tal* and *Ub'rytal* softened. Blade lowered his swords.

"Right," Woldyff said, relaxing his grip on Blade's shoulder. "Let's hear 'er out then."

Fox offered Woldyff a curt nod. With an agile leap, she landed softly beside Dane on the ruins. Dane crossed his arms and hid his startlement with an annoyed frown. Her signature smirk returned before addressing the assembly.

"What your friend has surmised and what I have told you is true," she began. "In another lifetime, I was Arctura Vipsanius, daughter of the Coalition Supreme Chancellor and groomed to rule after him. You might also comprehend that this is no longer the case. Like many of you, I am an outcast, and given my actions as of late, a fugitive of the highest order. I shall skip the sordid details, however, and get to the point. Dane judges the coming doom of Elmnas and your own rightly. Prime Ambassador Tyranna Vipsanius will burn and murder her way through a thousand priories to acquire Mouse. She has done such things before. And yet that is only the beginning. I have lived long enough to read the signs. War is coming. The Supreme Chancellor will accept nothing less than your total devotion. Every Coalition citizen will be called to account. I know my father well enough. His forces shall root out and crush all subversion. Neutrality will not be tolerated."

At this, Fox offered a grim smile. "In my brief time among you, I have learned you are anything but compliant. You have been frustrating the Coalition from the outset. But you must also know that you are no longer annoying, trivial criminals. You are enemies of the state. Whether you like it or not, the fate of the Syndicate is now tied to Elmnas. If Tyranna is successful – if the war is successful – it shall be your end."

Uncertain and anxious murmurs rippled through the assembly. Blade looked at the faces of his Syndicate comrades, finding shades of doubt, fear, worry, and disbelief etched upon them. For his own part, Blade could muster little surprise. Like Fox, he had read the signs of trouble stirring the waters, even before he stumbled upon Mouse at Pilgrim's Pass. The urgency of those signs only accelerated in the time he guided Mouse and Toma through the Gormlaean wilderness. He long knew the Coalition's first brutal entry into Elmnas would not satisfy the Supreme Chancellor. No, Lucan Vipsanius required complete submission to his rule. For the last century, his agents worked in secret, searching for something that would stamp out the call for rebellion forever. And once they found it, it was only a matter of time before the total destruction of Elmnas began.

Still, he thought wryly, *this is no easy tale for natural-born Gormlaeans to swallow.*

Woldyff's perplexed expression confirmed Blade's assessment. He rubbed his chin and stared past Fox into the jungle. Blade turned his attention back to Fox, where Dane stood by, his scowl somehow deeper than usual.

"Now, hang on a minute. *Your* father – the Supreme Chancellor who started the Last War – is still alive? You're sayin' that the Coalition is run by a one hundred-and-sixty-year-old man?" Dane huffed. "That ain't possible."

"There are two centenarians standing before you." Fox nodded toward Blade with a sardonic smile. "Surely that cannot be the strangest thing you have heard in these strange days."

Woldyff waved his hand as he interjected. "No, no, he's got a point. You two do the – ya know – glowing swords thing."

He mimicked their signature dual wielding stances and made whooshing noises, drawing some snickers from the crowd. "That's different, it is. You're Ageless because of 'em, because of 'The Way'. I made Blade tell me all about that. Well, as much as I could get outta 'im, anyway. I can't see that the Supreme Chancellor and his kin would be too keen on ancient Elmling Guardian stuff. How can they be Ageless?"

Blade looked back at Fox. Her eyes met his, and her expression darkened. "There are other ways. There have always been other ways, other methods and rituals of which our very own ancestors feared to speak. And if there was another way, the House of Vipsanius would have done everything in its power to discover it."

"And so it would seem that they have," Blade said somberly. He turned to Woldyff. "I now believe Fox speaks the truth. But whether or not the Supreme Chancellor and his kin are Ageless has little bearing upon what the Jackal Syndicate now faces. I have lived this evil before. You are in more danger than you can imagine."

Blade scoured the group, their grim faces no doubt mirroring his own. "You are marked. The Coalition would sooner raze the Aruacas to the ground than allow any of you to escape retribution. And they will not be satisfied with your destruction alone. They will come for everything and everyone you love."

At this, the Syndicate gathering exploded in confusion. Woldyff tried to calm the crowd, but to no avail. In the din, Blade could hear the shouted, desperate questions of the frightened members.

"What about our safe houses?"

"How are we gettin' out of here?"

"What are we gonna do?"

Fox raised her voice over the commotion. "That is for you and your comrades to decide. As for me, my path is determined. Whatever I might be, I shall not be a coward, and I will not wait for war to come. I go to Elmnas to meet it."

She unsheathed her swords. Bright flashes of green danced and weaved in the air as she swung them. The crowd's shouts faded, and Fox grinned wickedly down at them. "I never did get around to getting Tyranna anything special to welcome her to the family. Perhaps the time has come for her to receive what she's owed."

"Ain't no way you're gettin' in there alive," Dane mumbled. "And even if you did, you ain't leavin' in one piece, neither. I seen what that woman and her dirty dozen are capable of."

"You have only received a taste of what they are capable of," Fox replied. "It is far worse than you could imagine. But then again, so am I."

She smirked again, sheathed her swords, and looked at Blade. "And what about you, Guardian? Where does your path lie?"

A rare, slow smile formed on Blade's lips. "Could I suffer the impeachment to my honor if I remained elsewhere, allowing a foreigner to fight my kin's battles and keep the glory for herself?"

Fox chuckled; a genuine, heart-felt laugh with no sarcasm or ill intent. "I should think not."

Blade nodded and then turned to Woldyff. "We can go west and north through the Aruacas, taking a similar route Dane did to meet us. If the Syndicate consents, you can travel with us and out of Myergo's grasp. As long as Fox can bear with a slower journey."

Fox shrugged. "There is something to safety in numbers, I suppose, at least in the jungle. The open plains will be a different story."

"Yes, indeed. We must expect a rough road after that," Blade said. "Perhaps bypassing the grasslands on the Gormlaean side and moving through the Heibeiathan desert will give the Syndicate its best chance of escape. The wastes are unforgiving, but they may offer protection from even deadlier perils."

"We have some contacts out that way," Dane piped up, scratching his head. "Past the wastelands, what's called 'the Desolation', we have a sister guild in operation in some of the cities out there. Could be that they're smart enough to be lyin' low. Give this lot some chance of a place to hide."

Blade nodded. "That sounds promising. We can part with the Syndicate there, and continue on. But to get into Elmnas... I do not know a way. Not through Heibeiath."

"Oh, you needn't worry about a small thing like that," Fox said grimly. "I do. I can get us through at the Kamarians."

"The Kamarians?" Blade raised an eyebrow. "Those mountains still burn in places."

"Then we ought to tread lightly," she replied.

"She's right. It's the best way to cross," Dane said begrudgingly.

"No Coats hangin' about on an active volcano. Not so many eyes up there, either."

"It is decided then," Blade said quietly, surveying the crowd surrounding them. "But will the Syndicate go? Woldyff, what will you do afterward?"

Woldyff rubbed his chin and looked at the gathered assembly. The grumbling had died down by now, but the Syndicate members whispered among themselves. Woldyff beckoned to Maren.

"What do you need?" she asked, stepping forward.

Woldyff leaned in close to her, but Blade could still hear their confident conversation. "I want to do right by you and the Syndicate. What do you think?"

Maren looked over at Blade and Fox, back to the crowd, and then Woldyff. She sighed.

"No one wants to die out here," she said. "By the size of it, these two offer us our best choice. Even I can see the sense in that. But the young ones, they're afraid. Do we really mean to be a part of this fight?"

"That's what we'll need to decide," Woldyff answered quietly. "Maybe not just yet, but it's coming to us, isn't it? Put Blade's suggestion to a vote."

Maren nodded and turned back to the assembly. "Alright, everyone, gather round here. Let's talk plans."

As the Syndicate crowded around Maren, Woldyff waved Blade, Fox, and Dane to him. Blade followed as he stepped farther away from the main group. Fox hopped off the ruins to join them, and Dane scrambled down after her. Woldyff lowered his voice as they came near.

"Well, we'll settle some of it tonight. I don't know where we'll end up. As for me, I'd like to help, but I don't see how we'll do any good. How will you even find the Prime Ambassador? And how in the world do you expect to get through Coats and Mistwolves and whatever else wants to kill you there to find her?"

"We can deal with Coats and avoid Mistwolves," Fox said

confidently. "As for the Prime Ambassador, she will no doubt make herself easy to find. All we need to do is follow the flames."

"Indeed. It sounds as if she almost expects you to do so. Still, it would be ideal to head her off instead of following in her wake," Blade added thoughtfully. "If only I knew where Mouse and Toma were going. We could find them before the Prime Ambassador and her force do, and some lives may yet be saved."

Dane cleared his throat. "Does Titans' Rest mean anything to you?"

"It does." Blade gave him a shrewd look. "Why?"

"They didn't discuss their plans with me, but I'm sure I heard the boy mention it," Dane said. "The Prioress sent one of the younger Sisters with them, I guess as a guide. She's an Elmling, too."

"Titans' Rest, eh? What's that, Blade?" Woldyff asked.

"It is an ancient place," Blade said. "A place I thought long abandoned. Many years ago, it served as a seat of council among the clans. It lies in the northern wilds, a place rumored to still be inhabited by free Elmlings, but I have been gone from Elmnas for too long to know for sure. Either way, it would be no simple matter to get there."

"And what in blazes do they think they'll do there?" Dane muttered.

Blade looked at each of them, his piercing eyes sober. "If any shell of Elmnas' former might exists, they must hope to muster all of her for war."

9

15 days earlier
47th of Sun's Wane
Elmnas

Mouse opened her eyes with a start. Above the droning hum of the small hovercraft, a loud thump and shriek startled her out of the slow drift into sleep. She sat up, her head aching, and her punctured leg throbbing with pain. A panicked "what now?" formed on her lips, but the sound died as she found the source of the commotion. Mouse gasped instead. Toma had emerged from the back room of the craft. He wasn't alone.

"Um, didn't find the med-kit," he said slowly. "But... I found something else."

Her mouth hanging open, Mouse stared at the young woman standing in front of Toma. By the fine black and red gown she wore and the elegant manner with which the young woman, or girl, rather, carried herself, Mouse could see she was not just Gormlaean, but raised in the ranks of the Coalition party itself. Images of Coalition

Party Representatives reflecting out of the holograstones swam into Mouse's memory, and even now, Mouse could detail their similarities with that of the girl before her. However, her disheveled appearance and scrupulous but anxious eyes told the rest of the story; one which, even in Mouse's fear and distaste, she could feel sorry about. No doubt the lone survivor of the horror that had befallen the rest of her misfortunate crew. The girl must have been hiding as Mouse, Rhavin, Fraeda, and Toma had been troubleshooting the malfunctioning hovercraft. Mouse could imagine vividly the terror she must have lived all over again during the Mistwolves' renewed onslaught.

The hovercraft changed speed. Mouse braced herself as it slowed to an idle and guttered as it set down on the ground. The whirring died. Rhavin and Fraeda rushed out of the cockpit, stopping short as they faced the unexpected passenger. Gingerly, Toma guided the girl toward them with the barrel of an energy pistol. She winced in discomfort, but nothing erased the defiance written in her eyes. She swept the trio indignantly as she slowly raised her arms, pausing only to push the long, black hair out of her face. A face, Mouse realized, that was vaguely familiar. Mouse squinted in confusion for only a moment. It hit her like a thunderclap exactly why she felt she had seen it before.

"Even without the scars, you look just like her," Mouse breathed, barely loud enough for even herself to hear. Toma's gaze shifted to her, his eyebrow lifting quizzically.

"Who are you?" Rhavin said icily, breaking the momentary standoff. Mouse turned to see his serious eyes cold and narrowed. He placed his hand in his jacket. A flash of steel glinted as Rhavin held it there.

The girl crossed her arms and turned up her nose. She stared down the end of it with an insolent sniff.

"I am not obligated to tell you anything," she said. "I demand you release me and my craft at once."

Toma snickered. "Sure thing, we'll get right on that. Would you like us to set down at the closest Coalition outpost or should we get out and walk from here?"

The girl huffed, but said nothing.

"She doesn't need to tell us who she is," Mouse said. "I already know."

Mouse glared at the girl, her eyes hardening into stone. Yes, she could see it now. Those familiar, haughty eyes gazed back at Mouse, full of the swagger, ferocity, and arrogance she could never forget. *Just like her*, Mouse thought, anger rising. *Just like Blade's murderer.*

She gritted her teeth as she got to her feet. Pain shot through Mouse's leg, but she could almost ignore it as she focused on her coursing rage. Mouse grasped Fraeda's arm for support, and looking up at the taller girl, she could not imagine she struck anyone as imposing. Still, the haughtiness in the girl's eyes faded as the color drained from her face. She stared down at Mouse, not with the mockery Mouse expected, but with uncertainty... even a hint of fear. Her gaze flitted to Rhavin and Fraeda, and she flinched as Toma pressed the energy pistol into her back.

"You couldn't possibly know that," she tried bravely, but her voice quavered.

"She might," Fraeda said, giving Mouse a knowing look.

Mouse shook her head. "Not a seer thing. Toma, who does she remind you of?"

Toma rubbed his chin, stepping to the girl's side as he examined her with a concentrated frown. His hand froze in the middle of one ponderous chin rub and his eyes grew round.

"I can't believe I didn't see it before!" he said.

The girl's cheeks flushed. "What are you talking about?"

"Yes," Rhavin chimed in, cocking his head. "This I would like to know as well."

"The bounty hunter who attacked us at Thunder Run," Mouse answered, scowling at their prisoner. "This girl looks exactly like her."

The girl's brow wrinkled. "Bounty hunter?"

"Scary lady with two glowing swords and a scarred face?" Toma pointed at his own face and made a circular motion around his eye. "Ringing a bell?"

Her eyes widened briefly, and then her gaze fell to the floor of the craft.

"I knew it," Mouse said coldly.

"It's not what you think," the girl whispered. She looked Mouse in the eyes. "You are wrong about me."

Those eyes. Mouse seethed. She surged forward, arm swinging, her fingers curved like claws and aimed at the Coalition girl's face. Pain screamed through her leg, but Mouse roared louder. Her hand made contact. The girl shrieked as she toppled backward into Toma. Shouts came from everywhere as both Mouse and the girl tumbled to the floor. Vaguely, Mouse registered shouts directed at her. She didn't care. Every injustice, every terror, every hideous thing that had befallen Mouse paraded around her mind, fueling an anger desperate for vengeance. The fury exploded, blinding her, filling every crevice of her being with a hunger to hurt as she had been hurt. Mouse pounced, pinning the girl to the unforgiving floor, drawing her arm back for another blow.

A strong hand caught Mouse's wrist. Mouse pulled hard against it, but the grip did not relent. She looked back, furious, her mouth open to scream her rage.

"Enough," Fraeda said sternly.

Mouse looked back, shocked to see the hand around her wrist belonged to Fraeda. She slackened under the sober, matronly gaze, no longer pulling against her friend's surprisingly firm hold. Fraeda held her frowning stare. Mouse collapsed to the floor under it, all the fight fleeing from her. Defeated, she looked around. A bewildered Toma was pulling the girl from the floor and helping her to the couch. She glared at Mouse as she held a delicate hand to her cheek. Rhavin smirked, his arms crossed as he looked on with naked amusement.

Mouse's gaze returned to Fraeda. With a sigh, Fraeda helped her up and turned Mouse toward her.

"For heaven's sake, what are you doing?" she exclaimed.

Mouse sighed, grimacing as she rubbed her painfully pounding leg. "You weren't there. You didn't see what that woman did to us. What she did to Blade."

"Mouse, I understand what you went through, but we don't know anything about *her*. Just because she resembles the bounty hunter doesn't mean they're related." Fraeda replied, exasperated. "And even if they are, can you look me in the face and tell me you're willing to blame her for what someone else did?"

"I don't know, maybe," Mouse grumbled, her ire rising. "Look at her. Look at her clothes, her tech, her pretty little smug face. She's Coalition, and she's no different from the rest of them. She's hunting us, just like every other Coat in Elmnas."

Fraeda furrowed her brow, her gaze flicking toward the girl. Mouse's eyes followed. The girl stared daggers back at her. Mouse crossed her arms over her chest.

"Come on," Mouse said. "Why else would she be here? I bet she was planning to meet mommy and give her a hand."

"You presume much for knowing so little," the girl said sourly. "You're wrong about everything, or nearly everything. And now that I am certain I know who *you* are, I can tell you I am not your enemy."

Mouse dared a quick glance at Toma, whose troubled eyes were already on her. The girl continued.

"You are the escapee from Misty Summit and you, the Dell boy, helping her," she said, lifting her hand from her cheek and examining it for blood. Instinctively, Fraeda strode over, finding another frozen ration from the box beside the couch and offering it to the girl with a gentle, encouraging smile. Suspiciously, she reached forward, but within moments of examining Fraeda, the suspicion melted into timid acceptance. Fraeda patted her arm lightly as the girl lifted the frozen pack to her face.

Why do you have to be so kind, Fraeda? Mouse scowled, but her own face flushed in shame at the sight of the swelling and four reddened blotches where Mouse's fingernails broke skin. She shook away the guilt, meeting the girl's gaze with renewed steely resolve.

"Fine, you know who we are," Mouse said. "A lot of people have figured that out. Doesn't make you a friend."

"I never said friend," the girl shot back. "But I'm not out to get you. Maybe if you *listened*, I could tell you why."

Mouse clenched her teeth and her fists, but stayed still as Fraeda returned to her side. She placed a hand on Mouse's shoulder, squeezing it. *Was that for assurance, or was it a warning?* Mouse squinted up at Fraeda, but she couldn't tell. Her face was inscrutable. Finally, Mouse sighed and placed her palms on the floor behind her.

"Alright then, we're all calm, and we're all reasonable," Fraeda said soothingly. "Maybe now we can hear our new acquaintance out? We can't decide if her claims are true until she tells us what they are."

"Yeah, whatever, let's give it a shot," Toma nodded, dropping the energy pistol to his side. He squinted at Rhavin. "But uh... quick question first. Where are we?"

Rhavin glanced to the front of the craft, scanned the world outside the windshield, and shrugged. "At the edge of a wood, somewhere. I see no mist. I make no promises about anything else."

"There won't be Coalition this way," the girl sighed. "It's the direction we were going, precisely for that reason."

"You are avoiding the Coalition?" Fraeda asked, surprised. "Why? Who are you?"

"Yes! I'm running away! That's what I have been trying to tell you!" she replied with an incensed huff. "Because I am... because..."

The girl paused to collect herself, taking a deep, shuddering breath. "My name is Linnea. You are right, I am... was, rather, Coalition. It's part of why I'm out here. And yes, I know of this bounty hunter of yours as well."

Mouse's eyes narrowed. Linnea looked to each of the others

slowly, her gaze turning to Mouse last of all. On the surface, her expression remained stoic, refined, impenetrable. *How Coalition Party perfect you are.* Mouse almost smiled. She waited for another snide remark, but it never came. Linnea lowered the frozen ration pack, now staring through her. She blinked once, then twice, and then blinked once again. Her chin quivered. Mouse frowned.

"But she is not my mother," Linnea said softly. Her eyes grew wet as she gazed out the darkening hovercraft window. No one spoke. Not even the craft creaked. The absolute silence stretched on, broken only as the Coalition girl sniffled. With a scoff, she wiped her eyes.

"Even if I resemble her. I know I do. Father always said so. No, you see, my mother..."

Linnea swallowed hard.

"She is far worse."

"How's that?" Toma cut in. "Who is she?"

Linnea wrung her hands and looked at the floor. "I would rather tell you little of who I am. You'd all find it easier that way, I think. Mercy, that would be easier, too. But I can see it's pointless to hide anything. Pointless and tiring. I am so tired of hiding. So tired of hiding who I am."

Mouse let out a resigned sigh. She wished with all her might that her anger and hatred toward the Coalition and everyone associated with them would overrule the small but persistent tug of empathy on her heart. *Why should I give a rip about you?* Mouse thought crossly, but the tug only grew stronger. Her anger abated, if only for a moment, as she looked at the miserable Linnea. Mouse sighed, closing her eyes, and a strange image entered her thoughts: she saw *it* again. *The Phoenix.* Her eyes snapped open, but like a waking dream, it remained there, nothing else in view. The bird looked at her with burning green eyes, and then it was gone.

Mouse blinked. It was only a moment. No one else had seemed to notice.

"Here it is," Linnea continued, taking a deep breath. "I wasn't just part of any ordinary Coalition House. My mother... my family...

we are the worst of them all. Some, in fact, might say... we *are* the Coalition."

Her voice dropped to a whisper.

"After all, where would the Coalition and the Glorious New Era be without Grandfather? Without... the Honored Reign of Supreme Chancellor Vipsanius and his esteemed House?"

10

"Your grandfather is the Supreme Chancellor?"

All the rosiness fled from Fraeda's cheeks as she dropped away from Linnea, eyes wide and mouth open.

Mouse's wild gaze flicked around the hovercraft, resting on the rest of her friends. Rhavin's eyes narrowed, all amusement gone. A frightening anger clouded Toma's face, and his knuckles turned white as they strangled the grip of the pistol. No one moved. Mouse waited with them, all tightly coiled bundles of terror, ready but unsure of how to act upon Linnea's confession. *It's much worse than I know*, Mouse realized. *How could I know? I don't remember like they do.*

She looked again at Fraeda, who flexed shaking fingers at her sides. For as much as she herself hated and feared the Coalition, Mouse still could not grasp the panic gripping Fraeda now. In all their journeys, their talk of the Coalition and its Coalition Party remained nonspecific, and Mouse only had a general knowledge of the Supreme Chancellor; she knew nothing of those closest to him.

What did they do to you, Fraeda? Mouse thought as her friend folded her still-trembling hands in her lap.

"Yes," Linnea said. It seemed the word came painfully, and her eyes reddened as she looked at Fraeda's horror-stricken face. "And I'm so sorry."

"You don't know how sorry you are," Toma said through clenched teeth.

"The House Vipsanius." Rhavin shook his head and clicked his tongue, like he could hardly believe it himself.

"What?" Mouse looked at each of her friends. "What does this mean?"

Rhavin inclined his head knowingly. "It is a problem."

"Her family is directly responsible for *everything* that's wrong with this world," Toma cut in, pointing viciously. "They were the ones that annexed Maiendell. It was *that* family that who conquered the Four Dominions with the Coalition."

"Their House is spoken of only as a curse among the Elmlings today," Fraeda whispered. "Even if much of who we were was lost, we still remember the names of those who killed us."

Tears rolled freely down Linnea's cheeks, and she shuddered with quiet sobs. "I am so sorry, I didn't know... That is to say, not until Father told me... he told me... oh, everything. The truth, everything..."

Linnea buried her face in her hands, unable to stifle the sound of her breakdown. The others sat or stood in uncomfortable silence as each watched and tried to decide what to do. For her part, Mouse frowned at the crying girl, both loathing and pitying her. Like her, Linnea was young, too young, perhaps, to be directly involved in her family's worst crimes. Still, up to this point, she had lived her life in Coalition luxury, bought and sustained through the misery of Mouse's and her friends' peoples. Linnea was responsible in some ways, despite her ignorance. And for all Mouse had been through, why would she forgive her *that*? How *could* she?

Mouse's gaze wandered to the lever of the hovercraft door. *It wouldn't take long,* she thought. *It would be only a moment, that's all. Just a minute to lift the latch, shove her outside, shut it up again, and leave this place forever.*

She lifted her hand and moved it toward the door.

Without warning, the Phoenix burned again through Mouse's mind, briefly searing away the fear and panic screaming in her chest. She concentrated on the green eyes, and as she did, the bird faded, resolving instead into the likeness of a human face. It was ancient, familiar, and Mouse puzzled over where she had seen it before. Its lips moved. *Listen,* Mouse heard. *Will you follow, even now?*

Shame niggled at her conscience. She dropped her hand.

"Okay," Mouse said, breaking the tense silence. The others turned toward her. A mixture of confusion and surprise crossed their faces as each of them was snapped from their own dark thoughts.

"Fine, okay, I am listening." Mouse took a deep breath. "Even if you are what you are, I'll try to hear you out. As best I can, alright? But I'm not the only one you have to convince."

Linnea looked up from her crying. Her eyebrow shot upward for a moment before she squinted at Mouse suspiciously. With a sniff, she looked with uncertainty at the others as well. Mouse glanced around, too, finding her gaze once again locked with Toma's. He worked his jaw in the way he did when he was thinking, judging; weighing the consequences of what might come next.

"Just a minute ago, you were trying to rip her face off," Toma said stiffly.

"Yes," Mouse said, the creep of shame burning up her cheeks. "But maybe that wasn't the way to handle it."

With no small amount of hubris, Linnea scoffed, but Mouse ignored it. She gave Toma a small, tight smile and nod.

"It can't hurt, right?"

Toma did not answer, but he broke eye contact with a sigh and crossed his arms over his chest. Mouse looked at Rhavin, whose dark, sober expression seemed to neither encourage nor discourage action. She turned to Fraeda last.

"Anyway, it's you I want to hear from most. What do you want to do?" Mouse asked.

Fraeda took a deep breath. "'Open your ears to the accused, and hold your tongue unto judgment, lest you blind your eyes to justice.' That's in the Sacred Writings. We must let her speak."

Fraeda's face was a storm. Mouse clasped her shoulder reassuringly.

"We don't have to—"

"No," Fraeda said, her brows drawn in resolution. "Let her speak."

Mouse dropped her hold and nodded. With a sharp exhale, she crossed her arms and looked at Linnea.

"Well, okay," she said. "You're running from your family. Why?"

Linnea dabbed her reddened eyes, but she replied with cool, matter-of-fact detachment.

"Because you are not the only ones they should like to see dead."

"They are after you, too?" Fraeda asked. "Your family is really trying to kill you?"

"Not Father, never him." Linnea scoffed and shook her head. "But I am certain Mother has wanted me out of the way since I was born. It is only these latter days that she has had the occasion and opportunity. And Grandfather... Reidara is his game board and we are all the pieces. Mother can do as she pleases as long as he still wins."

"What is it with rich people and killing their family?" Toma muttered.

"The poor do it, too." Rhavin flashed a grim smile. "We simply do it with style."

Toma huffed, but the corner of his mouth quirked up. Mouse frowned, angry and horrified at the idea of filicide. *How could someone do that to their daughter?* Linnea's mother stood in stark contrast to the picture Mouse had of her own. Niiri, the woman of Mouse's dreams; her mother, the woman who had sacrificed everything... *for her.* The image of Niiri's face lived in Mouse's mind long after waking now; eyebrows drawn, eyes full of love, lips tight. *That is a mother*, Mouse thought. *That is family.*

"I don't understand," Mouse said. "How could she treat you that way?"

"It is a long story," Linnea said. "One I do not always understand myself. But Father tried to explain it to me, and I shall try to explain it to you. It began over a hundred years ago, when Father and Mother first married."

"Wait a minute." Toma held up a finger, paused, and then scratched his head. "What?"

"Yes," Rhavin added suspiciously. "That is not possible. Women that old do not have children as young as you."

Linnea sighed. "And this is why it is a long story."

"Your parents... they must be like our Guardians... what Gormlaeans call Ageless," Fraeda whispered. "In the Prioress' personal library, I have these read Gormlaean myths before. But how? It cannot be the same. In Elmnas, the gift is only given to those who follow the Way, and that ancient path has been lost with the Guardians. Sister Alba and I have talked often about it. Even the Sacred Writings are difficult to decipher on becoming Ageless."

"I believe it is as you say," Linnea answered softly. "Most Gormlaeans think the Guardians and the Ageless alike are myths from ancient times. So did I for most of my life. But when I came of age, Father let me in on the truth... the great secret of the House of Vipsanius. Perhaps all should know it."

Solemn glances passed among the four listeners as Linnea gulped.

"There is another way to becoming Ageless. And Grandfather found it, a century ago."

"Wait, wait, wait. Are you saying the Supreme Chancellor from the Last War..." Toma scrunched up his face as he worked it out. "He's your *living* Grandfather?"

"Grandfather calls himself 'Lucas Vipsanius III' in the official dictums, but there has never been a successor to the first Supreme Chancellor. There has only ever been one. *Him*."

"But how is that possible?" Fraeda asked, her voice tight and thin.

"I'm not sure, exactly, but I know this. It all has to do with the Cardanthium," Linnea's expression darkened. "Everyone thinks it disappeared so fast because it was powering everything, but really, Grandfather had been hoarding much of it, experimenting on his stockpile. He was... how did Father put it? 'Exposing and exploiting the immortal secrets of the Elmlings.' It consumed him. Father said he had often seen Grandfather in his Great Room, studying a Cardanthium crystal, watching it as if it might speak at any moment. He seemed to see it as a living thing."

Mouse inched her hand to her side, where her dagger now remained in a leather holster. She could feel its strange fire through the covering. Even without looking at it, she could imagine its shifting, runic surface, shimmers moving across it like a breath. Her fingertips hovered above the hilt, and as if in answer to her focused attention, a pulse, a spark, like the thrum of a beating heart, met them. To Linnea's obvious surprise, she nodded solemnly in agreement.

"And you are saying that he discovered some connection with Cardanthium and becoming Ageless?" Fraeda asked, her brow creasing further. "Apart from the Way?"

"It is a dark thing," Linnea continued with a shudder. "The way it is done... they call the process 'the augmentation.' Grandfather's top scientists began experimenting with ways to manipulate the Cardanthium, to recreate the Guardians' longevity, not long after he took power. Father says it failed at first. The test subjects died horribly. But Grandfather ordered the testing to continue. They had Cardanthium and people to spare."

Linnea took a deep breath. "But there was a breakthrough. Some of the subjects survived. And now Grandfather could offer near immortality to his inner circle."

"Are there more Ageless than your family?" Fraeda asked in horror.

"No, not anymore," Linnea whispered. "Father isn't sure what happened to the city Senators, but he believes Grandfather knew the augmentation process was not yet perfected. They enjoyed the benefits for a time before..."

She paused and shook her head. "My own grandmother received the augmentation then, too. Father says it was her vanity that did her in. She was beginning to age. She wanted to be the Lily of Kyma for centuries to come."

"But your father and mother..." Mouse said. "They survived."

Linnea nodded. "They did. And then Grandfather received his augmentation. If it is as Father says, he can yet reign for another 500 years."

"Great, just what we needed. Dictators who never die," Toma muttered. He sighed heavily. "Well, how is it done?"

She shook her head. "Father wouldn't– or couldn't– tell me much about it. But he described it as a torture beyond tortures, like being ripped to pieces and stitched together again with red hot skewers. And not one of Reidara's heaviest sedatives could dull that pain."

"Were they to do that to you?" Rhavin asked curiously. "Were you to receive the augmentation?"

"I am still too young. And Father said he'd never let them do it," Linnea sighed. "But I know he cannot resist Grandfather's will, even if he tried."

"So, you're really – actually – young, like us." Mouse's brow furrowed in thought. "Don't your parents have other children? Far older ones? They've had enough time, anyway."

Linnea shook her head. "It is only me. In the early days, Mother and Father could not produce a child. There was some hope the augmentation could fix that, but it only kept them from aging. Grandfather was desperate for an heir, but he was patient. They waited years for the Coalition's top researchers to develop the technology to cure them. I was the result. The only result."

"But if you're the only heir, why in all of Reidara would they want you dead?" Toma asked.

"Father never wanted to tell me." Linnea wiped at the fresh tears welling in her eyes. "But I found a way to hear, anyway. I had learned

Grandfather's researchers had discovered a way to make an heir without a womb. An heir for whom they could handpick all the traits they desired, even down to his eye color. A perfect Supreme Chancellor. Perfect for Grandfather and Mother. Someone... unlike me."

Linnea paused, her mouth twisting into a grimace as she looked down at the floor. Still her puffy eyes spilled tears. Seeing it was no use, Linnea sighed and gazed at the group.

"I only thought they were to send me away. I was to be married, you see, to the next Grand *Imyr*. It's not what I wanted, of course... away from Kyma, my home, Father... but I'd still have a good life. A dignified life, out of Mother's way and Grandfather's plans for the future. But as it so happened, Grandfather *did* have more use for me, beyond my marriage. He needed a sacrifice."

"How would your untimely death be useful?" Rhavin raised an eyebrow. "The marriage would serve well enough to stabilize the alliance between Heibeiath and Gormlaen, would it not?"

Toma, Mouse, and Fraeda all turned to Rhavin with puzzled looks. He shrugged and waved his hand dismissively. "I was to be an *Imyr* myself, remember? Besides, the politics of the Four Dominions is common talk among noble families. All of us know Heibeiath's relationship with the Coalition is... growing cold. The current Grand *Imyr* is not content to be a vassal of Gormlaen. It has been rumored his son," –Rhavin nodded toward Linnea with a smirk– " your betrothed, that is, will work for nothing less than total equality. Sovereignty even. The Supreme Chancellor deals shrewdly by tying his bloodline to the Grand *Imyr's*. It would pacify our people, at least for a time."

"It would seem a goodwill gesture," Linnea answered bitterly. "But I am afraid the Supreme Chancellor has never been interested in equality. He only ever wants complete surrender. And he *could* get it from Heibeiath, as long as he was justifiably provoked. That is where my use comes in, you see. For if, as it would be believed, that the Grand *Imyr* ordered the assassination of the Supreme

Chancellor's only and beloved granddaughter, what other option would there be but total war?"

A stunned silence fell over the group.

Linnea scoffed. "The older Grandfather gets, the more cunning he seems to grow. Imagine the outrage in Gormlaen. The people would revolt if he *did not* invade Heibeiath. And even then, Grandfather could scorch the entire country to ashes and no one would blink an eye."

It was Fraeda who spoke first.

"Like Sister Ilidette had liked to say." She nodded soberly. "Kill two birds with one stone."

Toma crossed his arms and muttered something derogatory about the Coats as Mouse spoke next.

"How did you find out?"

"Father had his suspicions that this was no ordinary arrangement. He entrusted Constan, the captain of Father's personal detail and a man like an uncle to me, to uncover whatever secrets had been kept from him," Linnea answered. "It was Constan who uncovered it all... only the night before I was to leave for the Grand *Imyr's* palace."

Linnea hugged her arms close to her body, her eyes drifting toward the door. "Father woke me in the middle of the night. He said it was time to go. I didn't understand, and even now, it was all like a dream. But I listened. Before I knew it, I was in here, speeding away from everything I've ever known. I didn't even get to tell him—"

She drew a sharp breath and shook her head. "But never mind that. It's not important. Constan and a cadre of Father's most trusted people came with me. We were to get as far from Pardaetha as we could, crossing dominion borders before anyone could know we had gone. Mother and Grandfather had left Kyma on business, you see, and they were not expected back for some time. Even so, it was a terrifying journey. You must understand, these were the bravest people I knew. They'd kept their heads and fought their way through all kinds of terrors. And I had never seen them so tense. Somehow, we'd gotten through all without even stopping. First through

Maiendell and then on past Slate Snake River. News had not gotten out yet, I suppose, for the outpost did not flag us. We went on, into Elmnas."

Toma snorted indignantly and rolled his eyes toward Mouse. "What did I tell you when we first met? They *never* stop a hovercraft."

"Sh." Mouse swatted at Toma and turned her attention back to Linnea. "But you didn't go due north. You came westward instead. Through the mists."

Linnea nodded. "It was the only way. My escape was sure to have been discovered by then. Even getting across the border seemed an impossible thing, and Constan was not one to take unnecessary risks. He believed every Coalition outpost would be after us. But he also thought that if we could just keep moving across the mistlands, we would be safe. They said Mistwolves had never attacked a craft at full speed. So that is what we did. And it was working..."

Linnea gulped and stared at the sealed door. "It was so sudden. The craft just seemed to... die. Mid-air. We had only enough time to strap in before it hit the ground. I remember Constan pulling me from my seat, the red glow all around when just a minute before it was light. They were going outside to fix the problem, he said. The door opened, and all I could see was a wall of gray. Then he took me to the back room, where you found me. Told me not to move until he or one of the others came back."

Linnea's gaze settled on Mouse's torn trousers and bandaged leg. "No one came back."

Mouse looked down as well, grimacing more from the gruesome sight than the throbbing pain. *That was just one bite*, she thought darkly, and her own first brush with the Mistwolves swam up out of her memory. The nightmarish howls and sounds of their feeding frenzy still churned her insides. What if it had not been Slim with his cruel and wicked intentions and instead trusted and loved friends?

Not like that, Mouse shuddered. *But I know all about friends dying for me.* Mouse glanced at Linnea, who now slumped back against the couch and stared vacantly across the hovercraft cabin. The dark circles ringing her eyes spoke of the fear-fueled exhaustion and unspeakable grief Mouse well knew. All of Linnea's cool confidence and arrogant posturing had fled, devastated just as thoroughly as the trappings of her prominent Coalition life. Only the truth remained. Like Mouse, Linnea was lost and alone.

"That's some story," Toma finally said, shaking his head. There was no malice in his voice, but there was not much warmth in it, either. "I don't believe every word, but only a fantastic liar could come up with all of *that*."

"Well, we know the last part is true." Fraeda exhaled slowly, as if releasing a breath held through the entirety of Linnea's tale. Her large eyes rounded on the others. "And someone *did* sabotage the craft. Mouse figured it out."

Toma and Rhavin exchanged looks of surprise as Linnea turned sharply.

"What do you mean?" she asked.

"Well, it's only my first time tinkering with a hovercraft, so I could be wrong," Mouse answered slowly. "But I *think* someone had messed with a crucial connector attached to the power source. Loosened it, just enough to hang on for a while, but once the part totally separated, everything would shut down. That lines up with what you told us."

Linnea nodded numbly.

"Even a really good mechanic wouldn't have been able to find the problem and fix it in enough time," Mouse continued in a low, grave voice. "I'm sorry."

"And yet, you figured it out," Linnea muttered. She sighed, crossed her arms, and turned away from the prying eyes of the group. "It does not matter. I have said all I could and wish not to speak of this anymore. Go ahead. Decide my fate, if you will."

Mouse studied her with a frown, working out whether Linnea meant to insult or compliment her. Worn and deflated as she was from her ordeal, Linnea had seemed to recover her initial bravado.

She pulled herself up on the couch into a ball and stared pointedly into the corner opposite the four friends.

Is she actually brave? Mouse wondered, her frown deepening. *Or is it as obvious to her as it is to me that no one is all that interested in harming her?*

"Alright," Mouse sighed as the other three drew closer together. "What do we do?"

"Well, I don't know. Tie her up and set a watch on her as we head north?" Toma shrugged uncertainly. "Although that seems kind of pointless. What's she going to do? Run away?"

Mouse almost laughed. For all his righteous anger and blustering about the Coalition, Toma was no blind avenger, even with Linnea's family name. It was just like him to be reasonable, forgiving, willing to offer another chance. He had, after all, changed his tune with Mouse when she gave her own sob story, and that saved her life.

"Do you believe her?" Mouse asked.

Toma sighed. "Maybe?"

"I do," Fraeda said with a decisive nod.

Resolve had replaced the terror in her eyes, and Mouse knew it was settled. Fraeda had determined to see past Linnea's history and show uncommon kindness to yet another lost, frightened soul.

"Down to you, Rhavin," Toma said. "What do you think?"

Rhavin did not answer. He toyed with one of his hidden blades and watched Linnea glowering at the corner. Shrewd suspicion darkened his gaze as he pursed his lips. Finally, his eyes darted to the others and his brow furrowed thoughtfully.

"Whether we trust her words or not, our minds are made up, are they not?" Rhavin said. "We have control of this craft, and we go to our final destination. She may come with us, willingly or unwillingly, or..."

"Or?" Mouse replied, raising an eyebrow.

"Or we can leave her here," Rhavin shrugged. "Her choice."

"I can hear you, you know," Linnea scoffed indignantly. "And not exactly a choice, is it? Of course I'll have to go with you."

"How do we know you have no treachery planned?" Rhavin asked, eyes still narrowed.

"By all means, check my person, go through my things, look in all the hidden panels of this craft. If you find anything treacherous, I am certain it was meant to kill me, anyway." Linnea narrowed her eyes with suspicion of her own. "But where would a group of fugitives want to take me?"

"Oh, it's a surprise," Toma said nonchalantly. "A good one, as long as you aren't lying."

11

66th of Sun's Wane, Year 113
Aruacas Rainforest
Southwestern Gormlaen

Blade drew a deep breath as he stared down at yet another tangled thicket of trunk-like vines and unyielding masses of greenery. Grunting, he swung *Ub'rytal* and *Av'tal* into their midst. They sliced right through, but only revealed yet another wall of vines and a cloud of buzzing, biting insects. They rose to meet him, just as annoyed as Blade at their unhappy circumstances. Blade sighed, swatted exhaustedly for a moment, and then paused to take stock of their situation.

It wasn't going well. Blade had spent many long years weathering the inherent discomforts of his chosen way of life, and by all accounts, had grown quite accustomed to it. He had mastered the most inhospitable wildernesses, had haunted the most barren wastelands and had lived to tell his tale. But this? This was by far the worst experience of rugged travel he could bring to recent memory.

No other place he had traversed was as unforgiving as the Aruacas. Over the last few days, she had thrown every weapon in her arsenal at Blade and those with him: raging, drowning downpours, ravenous mosquitos, rampaging ants, roving jaguars, more snakes than Blade could count. Her hostility lived in every root, vine, and branch, which grew into every narrow forest path and cut off nearly all directions of escape out of her disorienting labyrinth. She also housed, as Dane was certain to warn them, certain deep forest dwellers, all with nothing but malicious intent for would-be trespassers.

But worst of all was the sweat. It was everywhere. Sweat drenched every inch of Blade's clothes. It poured into his mouth and stung his eyes. It dripped from his arms as he wiped at it with spare cloth, which, of course, was also covered in sweat. Sweat had become his constant companion, stinking in his nostrils when he slept and returning in full fury after each frequent but brief spell of drenching rain. A scourge for the ages, Blade was beginning to forget what life was like before Sweat and its merciless assault upon him.

Blade wearily raised *Ub'rytal* to strike down the next wall of vines. But before he could begin, a familiar hiss like released steam made him pause. Jets of white light flashed into the thicket, combusting the vines upon violent impact. He lowered the sword slowly, turning to scowl at Fox.

"If we should ever manage to escape this hell, you will rue wasting those shots on mere vegetation."

Fox smirked, blew on the end of her pistol, and replaced it in her holster. She looked as wild as Blade felt, particularly her hair, which by now had expanded to incredible proportions in the humid jungle air. She had pulled it up, winding it tightly on the top of her head, but the valiant attempt to tame it had failed. Rogue hairs shot in every direction. She ran her hands over it, sighed, and crossed her arms over her chest.

"We need to make camp," she said, nodding over her shoulder. "These wretches will not last much longer."

Blade looked to where she indicated, eyes narrowed as he

observed the straggling column of thieves following them. If Blade and Fox were not faring their best, the Jackal Syndicate fared far worse. The jungle was getting to them. No one had died, at least not yet, but Blade feared the inevitable. Hot, damp places like the Aruacas always meant sickness of one kind or another, and over the last two days, the first victims had begun to fall ill. It would spread, and it would kill, if Blade could no longer find enough natural remedies among the flora. It was why he had been pushing them to move, move as quickly as they could through the jungle. The sooner out of it, the better. They tried their best, of course, to keep up and put on brave faces, but most of the thieves were ill-suited and under-equipped for such a journey. Few in the best of circumstances could keep up with Blade's preferred pace; he had expected a slower going. But this? They went now at a crawl. It was excruciating. To stop again meant another night in the jungle; another night full of opportunities for the Aruacas to unleash its evils.

"Here?" Blade tried to say evenly, but the irritation was evident in his voice. "If the beasts do not prevail over us, the mosquitos certainly will."

"We cannot forge ahead forever," Fox replied, her gaze locked resolutely to his. "Unless you sincerely believe we can find more forgiving accommodations before nightfall."

Blade stared back, wishing he had a better alternative. Fox was right. They had no choice. He replaced his swords in their sheaths with a sigh. Fox smiled playfully.

"There, there, that wasn't so hard, was it?"

Blade raised an eyebrow. "I do not see what you find so amusing."

"Of course you don't," Fox laughed. "You ought to smile more, Guardian. You'd look so much prettier."

She continued chuckling and shaking her head as Blade strode off and toward the oncoming throng of thieves. *Strange, infernal woman,* he thought, searching among them for Woldyff. *What reason does she have to be cheerful?*

Perhaps cheerful was not exactly the right word, but something was certainly different. Since the night she had resolved to journey to Elmnas – no longer to hunt the quarry she had originally been seeking, but now to face an old and bitter rival in her sister-in-law – she had changed. Fox trekked through the Aruacas beside him in palpable anticipation, even with their hardships along the way. She was animated, full of something almost like delight the closer they drew to Elmnas. Her ruthless thirst for gold and gain had faded, and a righteous hunger, a warrior's hunger, had taken its place. As a past Guardian of Elmnas, a Warrior in the Way, Blade knew that hunger well. He could not help but admire it when he saw it in others. And over these past few days, as terrible as they had been, Fox proved to be far more than the cruel Coalition mercenary than he had known her as before. Blade saw more of the Fox who had raided Myergo's arena and saved his life than the one who had meant to destroy it. And for the most part, Blade welcomed that Fox. Today, however, he wearied of her.

Do not blame her, he thought. *You are weary of everything.*

Blade caught sight of Woldyff in the middle of the pack, stooped slightly to support a Syndicate member as she limped along. The injuries were piling up, and though Woldyff continued to spend every ounce of his indefatigable, morale-boosting charm, he was receiving diminishing returns. Woldyff looked up, and catching Blade's eye, still managed to flash yet another irrepressible grin.

"Another beaut' of a day, huh, Falky?"

"Truly," Blade said flatly, ignoring the nickname. "I need to speak with you."

Woldyff nodded, and speaking in hushed tones to the group around him, helped the injured thief find another Syndicate member's shoulder. As he weaved through the crowd to reach Blade, the others stopped walking and watched him pass, hope shining in their travel-weary faces that the private conference finally meant rest. Nearly all the group had flopped down where they were standing by the time Woldyff had reached Blade.

"What's the word, then?" Woldyff said conspiratorially as he pulled up to Blade, his charming smile fading into worried exhaustion.

Blade surveyed his old friend with keen concern. Woldyff rolled up the torn sleeves of his shirt once again, baring scratched, scraped, and insect-bitten forearms. Without his usual grin fixed in placed, the endearing crow feet-like lines around his eyes made him look far older than his forty-some years. He wiped the sweat from his brow and pushed back his frazzled braids.

"It seems unprofitable to keep up this pace. Perhaps it is time to make camp. Can you direct some of the better-off of your members to begin clearing brush?"

"That's music to me ears," Woldyff said, placing a hand over his chest in relief. "We'll get on that."

Woldyff turned, but Blade stopped him, grasping his shoulder. "You cannot carry the weight of their worries forever, friend. I fear you'll become quite unwell."

"Aw, no need to concern yourself with little ol' me," Woldyff replied, now smirking. "You should see yourself."

"Jokes aside, you must take care," Blade chided. "I can guide your people out of this jungle, but I cannot lead them. They love and trust you. Stay well."

"Well, ain't that the nicest thing anyone's ever said to me," Woldyff winked, but as Blade's gaze bored into him, he sighed in resignation. "I'll let you know if it's too much, honest. I'm not plannin' on dying. Maren'll kill me if I do."

After a hearty smack to Blade's back, Woldyff rounded on the Syndicate. "C'mere you lot, I got good news. We're beddin' down. Let's get to work."

Blade shook his head, but allowed a small smile as he set to clearing space on the crowded rainforest floor.

Leave it to Woldyff to turn this into good news, he thought, whacking aside sprawling vines and low branches.

He raised *Av'tal* for another pass, but paused. A sound reached his ears; a small sound, barely audible in the midst of the hacking, laughing, cursing, and stomping around him. But it was a *wrong* sound. Blade snapped upright into a fighting stance, *Av'tal* and *Ub'rytal* flashing. His hawk-like eyes scoured the jungle. Out of the corner of them, he saw Fox as alert as he. He met her gaze for a moment. She nodded slowly, her own two blades quivering in front of her.

An energy rifle blast screeched through the trees. Fox bounded forward, meeting the jet before it buried itself in the midst of the unsuspecting thieves. The blast bounced off her blade, hissing into a tree and narrowly missing Woldyff's face. He staggered back, pulling his own pistol from his waistband with a look of horror.

"What—"

"Ambush, ya morons!" Dane shouted, shoving a few Syndicate members to the ground by their heads.

Chaos erupted. People screamed and jumped for cover. Some, like Woldyff and Dane, had the sense to begin shooting, albeit wildly. Blasts came in all directions as Blade ran to join Fox in the center. The air hissed and steamed. He wielded *Av'tal* and *Ub'rytal* in a frenzy. The shots pinged off his swords, ricocheting back into the thick jungle. Screams of pain answered him as a few blasts returned to their unwitting owners. But Blade could not pinpoint their attackers. He could only hear the sounds of battle, see the rush of shadows and the rustle of leaves as figures approached and receded. Blade parried another volley. He could hear Fox at his back, doing the same.

"We're surrounded!" she shouted over the din. She sliced the air, knocking away a blast headed straight for her heart.

"Can you see them?" Blade asked, searching the rainforest through the haze of smoke and light.

"Hardly!" Fox yelled. "But it cannot be Myergo's men. Too coordinated! Their firepower is overwhelming!"

Blade swung his swords feverishly, but the volley of blasts still had not ceased. He could see the silhouettes beginning to close in now, their black-barreled rifles gleaming. Red and black uniforms swerved in and out of view. Gruff voices with Gormlaean accents shouted out military commands behind the trees.

"Coats!" Blade roared. "They're Coalition!"

Dane cursed loudly as he sprayed the rainforest with pistol fire.

"Come on, Jackals!" Woldyff yelled hoarsely, firing shots of his own. "We need all the help we can get! Fire!"

The bravest of the thieves popped out from cover, aiming blasts where Dane and Woldyff directed. Between parries, Blade glanced around. They were not succeeding. Some of their number had already fallen. Scorch marks burned the earth and trees around them. Maren was dragging her twin, Raim, behind a rotted log. He screamed as he clutched the smoking hole in his leg. All around, others found themselves in similar disarray. And Blade could not deflect the relentless fire of the Coalition from them all.

"We're goners!" Dane shouted, and cursed again.

"Not yet!" Fox replied. "The fight does not end until the last of us falls!"

"Won't be long!" Dane shot back. "You can't keep swingin' those things forever!"

Fox flashed forward, knocking away a rifle with one sword and slashing through the overly bold Coat, shoulder to groin, with the other. The soldier had scarcely fallen to her feet before she had hopped back, deflecting the blasts of his angry comrades.

"Watch me!" she growled.

But the tide of Coalition attackers still had not abated. Blade surged into the enemy line, striking down a soldier of his own. He searched the vegetation quickly before jumping back, but to no avail.

"How many are there?"

"Too many!" Woldyff shouted in reply, followed by a snarl of frustration. He threw down one pistol and wrenched out another. "Blasted, sopping air! All our guns'll be done for soon!"

He was right. Blade deflected another blow before chancing a glance at the others. Everywhere, Syndicate members had stopped firing. Fear, anger, and disgust registered on their faces as they shook or tossed away silent pistols. No doubt the weapons could not withstand these terrible conditions; and the longer the battle continued, the more weapons would die.

But the Coalition offensive plowed on in full force, superior in accuracy and firepower. Blasts continued to tear through the rainforest toward the Syndicate, showing no signs of slowing. The thieves huddled under whatever cover they could find, and it wasn't enough. Blade and Fox both circled around them. They fended off each blast with all their strength. But Dane's fateful words were ringing true even as they fought tooth and nail. They could not hold off the worst of it forever.

It went on, and Blade lost all sense of time in the fiery haze. The jungle smoked. It was even beginning to burn. Blade's ribs ached, and every breath brought a sharp jab of pain beneath them. He concentrated hard, drawing on *Av'tal* and *Ub'rytal* for the vigor he needed to survive. Again, they responded, flaring brightly as they poured of themselves into his desperation. Bellowing, Blade charged. He struck another Coat down and retreated, smashing away a renewed volley of blasts.

Still, *Av'tal* and *Ub'rytal* had their limits. A blaze of light pulsed from them, but Blade felt its strain. Like him, their strength was waning. Like him, what they gave now, they could not give for much longer. His fingers grew numb, and his arms shook. Jolts of pain ran from his clenched hands and into every inch of him like screams of agony from the blades themselves. Blade looked back. Fox fought like a demon, but he could see the torment in her contorted face. Her own blades flickered, as if in the last shudder before death.

It is too much, Blade thought hopelessly. *They will never stop. It is how they destroyed us all the first time.*

The Syndicate's covering fire ceased completely. There was nothing to be done.

"We cannot... wait..." Fox panted, parrying a rain of fire. "For death... Must... attack. Into the rainforest."

"We leave, they die," Blade rasped back. "We'll die."

"No choice," Fox replied hoarsely. "Save... some of them."

Blade gritted his teeth, pulling the last ounce of strength he could muster.

A worthy death, he thought. *I accept this end.*

"Now!" he shouted.

Fox vaulted into the trees at Blade's back; he sprinted forward. He crashed into the dense undergrowth, jumping and kicking out. His foot found a soldier's chest. The soldier went down, and *Av'tal* gave the final blow. Blade could hear confused shouting among the Coalition force, and some of the shooting stopped. He ran on, ducking beneath vines to find the next soldier.

The next soldier, however, could not be found. Blade slowed, trying to listen as the blood rushed in his ears. He took a steadying breath.

Where are you? he thought uneasily, weaving a stealthy path through the jungle. As his breathing and pounding heart slowed, voices drifted toward him. They were scattered, farther away than they should have been. A harsh command barked closer by.

"Regroup! Keep your eyes open. We're not alone!"

Blade crouched lower and moved toward the voice. A smattering of rifle blasts met his ears.

"Hold your fire!" the commanding voice shouted again. "Where's it coming from? Don't just stand there! Look, you idiots!"

Vines hung like a thick curtain before Blade, blocking the Coalition soldiers from view. Slowly, he inched around the vines and peered past them. Shining armor and flashes of red and black moved through the trees, fanning out away from where the Jackal Syndicate waited defenselessly in the jungle. Blade counted the soldiers as they moved: at least a dozen or more.

They could have us easily now, he thought, readying *Av'tal* and *Ub'rytal* as he drew nearer. *What is stopping them?*

But just as Blade straightened, something whistled past his ear. It burrowed into a tree behind him with a distinct metallic thud. He whirled around, flattening himself against another tree. Blade understood what the sound meant in an instant. A new contender had joined the ambush. With caution, he sidled to the tree's other side.

The sleek barrel of a weapon landed squarely against his chest.

12

In an instant, *Av'tal* and *Ub'rytal* stretched forward, finding the weapon bearer's throat. Blade looked up, defiant in the deadlock with his opponent, expecting to meet the murderous gaze of a Coalition soldier. Blade's eyes widened in surprise. There was nothing Coalition about the stout warrior before him.

The warrior, a woman at least a head shorter than Blade, stared back. She stood stock still, her light woven cloth of jungle greens and flowering reds giving the illusion she was a very part of the Aruacas itself. Swirling tattoos covered her skin, and Blade recognized how quickly she would fade into shadow with their aid as well. Perhaps that was why he did not see her until she was right in front of him. Red paint streaked over the warrior's nose and around her dark eyes, and a feathered band crowned her head of black hair.

A deep forest dweller, at last, Blade mused.

He could not place this warrior's Aruacan tribe, but he did not presume he should be able to. Never before had he ventured so deep within the rainforest. By now, they had gone far enough to have wandered into claimed Heibeiathan territory itself. Only Dane had come this far before, and it had been his strong counsel that they did not pass this way again. The danger of entering the forest's depths and so close to its fearsome inhabitants was far too great.

It is too late for that, Blade thought grimly.

The warrior did not speak, but she had no need. Her lip curled in a fierce sneer, and she pressed the barrel threateningly against Blade's chest. He hid a wince as a sharp pain shot through his ribs. *Curse this slow healing,* Blade thought with irritation. He would be paying for today's battle for the next week, assuming he lived that long.

The two warriors looked at each other, neither yielding. Blade considered his new Aruacan foe. She could have killed him by now, and if Dane's tales held true, she *should* have killed him, but she didn't. Her stony face had not changed, and the pressure behind the weapon meant business. Still, as formidable as she remained, Blade had the distinct impression that she was not expecting *him* behind the tree, either.

Slowly, Blade lifted his swords from her throat and held them, spread aloft, in a gesture of goodwill. The warrior's eyes darted to each sword, tracing the glowing runes with a concentrated frown, and then to Blade himself. She appraised him, her critical suspicion plain as she did so. But the pressure lessened, and after a moment of consideration, she too pulled back. Blade nodded appreciatively as she swayed the weapon away from him.

But the sound of rustling undergrowth and hissing energy rifles brought Blade back to the present. He gestured to beyond their tree, where the voices of the Coats searching for would-be attackers drew even closer than before. Blade lifted his swords defensively, ready to edge around the tree to attack. The warrior shook her head.

"Why?" Blade said, his voice low enough for only her to hear.

She did not reply, but with a knowing smile, held a finger to her mouth. Blade paused, lowering his swords as he listened. He could hear the Coalition force moving, any spoken words a whisper. They stopped, and the jungle air grew thick with their apprehensive silence.

Blade distinguished that same metallic whistling sound again, followed by a fleshy thwack and a pained scream.

"Attack! We're under attack!" a Coalition soldier cried.

Rifles discharged into the jungle, but it seemed none hit any marks. Their continuous crackling slowed, replaced instead with the sound of strangled shouts and the thud of falling bodies. In moments, the raucous report of rifle fire ceased. Bird calls and animal chattering echoed tentatively in the renewed silence.

The Aruacan warrior nodded to Blade, then ducked out from behind the tree, her weapon in front of her. Blade rounded the other side. *Av'tal* and *Ub'rytal* blazed for battle; reinvigorated already after their brief rest. Through the trees, Blade spotted a clearing, and from it issued some faint sounds of struggle. The Aruacan warrior rushed toward it. Blade joined her, converging on the Coalition force. He burst through, blades shining.

But no foe met him. There were, to his surprise, none left standing. Blade and the Aruacan warrior jumped into view just as the last Coat toppled, clutching weakly at the metal spike protruding from his neck. Blade looked around. The Coalition force had spread themselves into a loose circle, keeping each of their comrades at their backs as he and Fox had done in their defense of the Syndicate. They lay sprawled on the jungle floor. Metal spikes punctured their flesh and had even punched through their armor. Blade searched the jungle for their assailants as he replaced *Av'tal* and *Ub'rytal* in their sheaths, expecting to see other Aruacan warriors glaring back at him through the leaves. But no one did. He peered back at the Aruacan woman with a quizzical look.

"Where are your people?" he asked.

The warrior frowned and shook her head. She spoke, but it was in a language Blade had never heard before.

"I see," Blade nodded, replacing his swords in their sheaths. "Regardless, thank you."

She blinked, slinging her weapon over her shoulder.

Blade watched as the warrior pulled a broad, short, machete-like blade instead, and then kneeled down beside one of the Coats, her fingers on his throat to check for a pulse. She moved around their circle, searching for life among them. He wondered if it would be wise to return to check on the Syndicate. Blade still did not know where the other Aruacan attackers were, and that concerned him. The tribes he knew from his beast hunting days had warned of these recalcitrant deep forest dwellers. They recognized neither Gormlaean Coalition nor Heibeiathan military as authorities, and even among the natives of the Aruacas, treated very few as friends. This warrior had spared Blade, despite his being an obvious outsider. But would her people be just as gracious to the rest of them? He and his companions were, after all, intruders on their land. These warriors had every right to defend what belonged to them.

And clearly, they know how to do it, Blade thought, gazing down into the wide eyes of a dead soldier.

He looked up as the warrior straightened, her legs still tense and bent even as the machete tip pointed at the ground. She squinted shrewdly back at him. Blade did not like that look. He lifted his hands plaintively.

"I still mean you no harm." He spread his hands again in a gesture of peace before pointing over his shoulder. "But my own people need my aid. Let me go to them."

The warrior did not budge. Without warning, she pulled her weapon off her shoulder and leveled it at Blade. Just as quickly, his own hands found *Av'tal* and *Ub'rytal* and withdrew them. As they flared to life, the trees shook violently. Blade snapped his gaze upward, angling his swords to defend against the new danger. Ropes flew down from the tree branches. There was a flurry of tan, red, and green, and suddenly, a dozen Aruacan warriors dropped with almost effortless ease to the jungle floor. They faced Blade, all wearing the same fierce, unyielding expression, all raising weapons of their own. He saw now why the Coalition soldiers had so miserably failed. They never guessed their attackers would come from above.

Blade raised *Av'tal* and *Ub'rytal* as a voice echoed out behind him.

"*Hu'pacz!* Peace!"

The warriors did not move, but a few tilted their heads ever so slightly. The voice continued with a few other words Blade did not recognize. He did, however, recognize the voice, and chanced a glance behind him to confirm.

Dane's shining head came into view. He wiped it profusely, panting as he came into the clearing. Two warriors flanked him, their own weapons upright. They neither held him nor pulled him along, and other than the blood stain on his shirt, Dane seemed unharmed. He did, however, seem tired and annoyed. He puffed into the clearing with the two Aruacan warriors, hands on his knees as he caught his breath.

Blade exhaled slowly as those facing him relaxed, their weapons lowering. Some even smiled as their fellow warriors joined them. Taking their cue, Blade lowered his as well and stared around curiously.

"I'm gettin' too old for this," Dane grumbled, eyeing the standoff and the dead soldiers with something between appreciation and apprehension. "Well, at least they weren't shootin' you. How'd you manage that?"

"You can speak to them?" Blade said.

"Not much," Dane muttered. "I know just enough to keep from getting run through."

"The others," Blade said quietly. "How are they faring?"

"Most are still alive, if that's what you're asking," Dane replied with a snort. "No thanks to their battle instincts. We have the Chychan to thank for that, and I mean to do that now, *before* they change their minds."

Dane searched the warriors, his gaze landing on the woman who had cornered Blade before. He bowed to her, his right arm crossing his chest and his fist resting against his shoulder.

"*Kau'e.*"

She stepped forward, quickly confirming Dane's assessment of her as the leader. Blade compared her to the other warriors, finding that none of the others wore a feathered band or carried quite so many distinctive tattoos. The Chychan leader looked from Dane to Blade, that same shrewd, fierce look on her face as she judged them, but finally, she relented. Returning Dane's gesture, she repeated his greeting. The warriors with her also bowed. Blade could almost feel Dane relax as he straightened from his bow. The Chychan leader replaced her weapon and, with a slight smile, put her hands on her hips.

"Our words don't suit you, do they?" she said, switching easily to Heibeiathan. "I hope this tongue is better. I will speak in no other, and never in the words of the *Co'atyti*."

At this word in Chychan, the other warriors spat on the ground contemptuously.

So, they have a greater enemy in the Coalition than in us, Blade thought, replacing his swords in their sheaths.

"Yes, it suits us well," Dane agreed nervously. "Um, thanks."

"Then you can understand me plainly, and shall give me an answer when I demand it." The Chychan warrior's nostrils flared. "Why are you invading my jungle? Why have you brought the stain of the *Co'atyti* among us?"

"We sure weren't tryin' to do neither, I assure you," Dane said quickly. "And we thank you for your patience with us. We are just... refugees. Just passin' through, that is."

"Lies," she hissed, pulling the machete and pointing it at Dane. "Your so-called refugees are fighters. They carry the *Co'atyti* blast guns. You share faces with our enemies. You would have killed us had they not found you first. And why should the Chychan care if the *Co'atyti* kill one another? I say, it is good. The less *Co'atyti*, the better!"

Grunts of agreement rose from the Chychan leader's ranks, but it seemed only a handful of them understood Heibeiathan. The ones who did whispered hasty translations to their neighbors.

"Uh... um..." Dane stammered.

"But I am not *Co'atyti*," Blade said, stepping forward. "You see this easily. Perhaps it is why you did not strike me down. And I would have once said the same about them. The *Co'atyti* are indeed murderous conquerors. They ravaged my home, my people. I am one of very few left. Your fierce protection of your land is wise and just."

The warrior's gaze snapped up at Blade. Her eyes narrowed judiciously, but she said nothing.

"Not all who share faces with them approve of their ways," Blade continued. "This, I have learned. These fugitives are not *Co'atyti*. Indeed, if the *Co'atyti* prevail against them and others like them, you may find yourself like me. A warrior with no war, a protector with no people, a man with no home."

The Chychan whispered among themselves for only a moment before falling silent. Their leader watched Blade, her face inscrutable.

"What are you called, warrior?" she asked.

Blade's expression darkened. "Many things, and some of which I am not worthy."

"Thus you shall be, Warrior-of-Many-Names," she answered reflectively. "But I witnessed your fight against your enemies, for a tribe not your own. Never before have I seen anything like it, nor with weapons such as those. Is that not worthy?"

It was now Blade's turn to say nothing. The corner of her mouth lifted once again in that knowing smile as she went on.

"I am called Yasi, the mother of the Chychan. Your skill caught my attention, and now your words have caught my ear. It is fitting for you to be rewarded. What do you ask of me?"

"You are gracious and kind." Blade bowed slightly. "We request safe passage out of the Aruacas. I would also impose upon your great patience in offering any help you can in attending to the ill and wounded among us. Our journey is long, and we seek a way into a broad, empty valley still west of here, a place the Heibeiathans call the Desolation."

"Ah, the *Tyeraka*. Yes, I know of the place." Yasi raised a hand to her chin, her brow wrinkled in thought as considered Blade's request. After a moment, she gave a curt nod. "To this, I can consent. Let us go gather your tribe to you, and we will see what we can do. But now you must hear me. This request I grant, but I also give you a warning. Once my warriors lead you out of Chychan jungle, it is fulfilled. Should you return, or send others into our midst, there will be no promise of safe passage. We protect our land to the death. Let it be known."

"It is understood," Blade replied with a nod.

Yasi turned on her heel, speaking quickly to her warriors. As she did so, Dane leaned toward Blade.

"You made that look easy," he muttered. Even speaking in Gormlaean, he barely raised his voice above a whisper. "The Chychan are cold-blooded killers. They'd spear ya as soon as look at ya any other day, maybe even serve you up for supper when it's said and done. Or so I've heard. Complete savages. Totally isolated from the rest of the world. Surprised any of them know any Heibeiathan at all."

"But they did not attack you or the Syndicate?" Blade asked.

"Those two with me, they came into the clearing just after all the fireworks had died down," Dane said. "As soon as I saw 'em, I put my hands up and started saying whatever I could think of in Chychan. Hoisted me off my feet and dragged me out here. Left the others. To be frank, if you and Fox weren't there to begin with, I don't think they'd have cared much for anything I said, Chychan or otherwise."

"What of Fox? Has she returned?"

Dane shook his head. "She went after the Coats, same as you. That's the last I saw of her."

Blade's thoughts went back to their brief battle with the Coalition. Had the Chychan been in the trees all along, watching their slow progress through the rainforest, patiently waiting for the perfect moment to strike? *No doubt they would have attacked, had the Coalition not found us first*, Blade thought. *And even now, they have only stayed their hands because of their leader's fascination with my novelty.*

In even his recent past, Blade would have written the unfolding of these events off to coincidence, and their survival, to luck. But with each moment of unlikely perseverance, moments that seemed to happen far too often these days, giving mere chance the credit was becoming harder to do. Creeds of a distant past were once again ringing in his ears, filling his mind with words and truths he had once known.

I have forgotten, Blade thought. *What a foolish old man I've become.*

Yasi finished conversing with her people by pointing into the jungle and giving a few brief commands in Chychan. Some of the warriors broke off from the group, several running in the opposite direction with a handful of others fanning out from their location. Two shimmied up the ropes and back into the overhanging branches of the jungle trees, disappearing from view with astounding speed. The ropes followed them, and within moments, there was no evidence of human activity above. As for the remaining cadre, they followed Yasi as she marched into the tangled thicket of vines. They moved as one through the jungle, back toward the clearing.

Blade followed in their midst as Dane hurried close behind, treading on the narrow footpaths that each of the Chychan seemed to find instinctually. They melted into the jungle with a stealth so natural that even Blade could have lost them, were he not paying attention.

"Crafty devils, aren't they?" Dane puffed as he trotted to keep up with Blade.

Blade nodded appreciatively. "It is no wonder I never saw them before the attack. Indeed, I hardly sensed their presence at all. But I am now convinced the Chychan have been watching our progress about their territory, for at least the day."

"Huh," Dane grunted. "You reckon they'd have hit us tonight if the Coats hadn't first, don't you?"

"It seems the most natural conclusion," Blade answered darkly.

He watched as a Chychan's head and shoulders bowed beneath a low limb and disappeared into the undergrowth. Blade lengthened his stride. He slid underneath the limb just as the sudden sound of shouting voices caught his ear.

Dane cursed. "What now?"

Av'tal and *Ub'rytal* flashed from their sheaths once more, and Blade rushed toward the commotion. Light dappled the jungle floor beneath his feet, revealing a brief but familiar thinning in the trees ahead. *The Syndicate*, Blade thought. The shouts grew louder.

Blade burst through the trees. With her back to him, Fox stood in the center of the small clearing where he had left the Jackal Syndicate. Her arms were raised, spectral blades glowing with a threatening green glare. Around her, and hidden behind rotted trunks, boulders, or thicker trees, the Syndicate huddled. He could see the plain terror on their faces, although some, like Maren, still aimed energy pistols at the jungle. Their eyes turned to him, first with worry and then with relief and recognition. He entered, his own swords stretched before him.

"Nice of you to show up," Fox said, not even sparing a glance over her shoulder.

Blade looked around. The clearing was surrounded, no longer by Coalition soldiers, but another detachment of Chychan warriors. They were not firing at the moment, but Blade could see the glint of steel embedded in the dirt and the trees from the attempts that Fox must have deflected. From his vantage point on the edge of the grove, he could see the warriors' positions: both in the trees and on the ground, surrounding Fox on nearly every side. Some turned as he arrived, pointing their weapons at him as well.

From the other side, Yasi also entered. Fox glared at her, and she glared back, pointing her weapon.

"Stop!" Blade shouted. "You were to help us! You gave me your word!"

Yasi did not answer him. She eyed Fox contemptuously.

LION

"Some of my people are missing. Where are they?"

"Ah, so you *do* use civilized speech when it suits you," Fox replied in Heibeiathan.

"Civilized," Yasi repeated, hissing. "You keep your civilization, it shall soon be the end of you. I will not ask again. Where are my people?"

"Fox. Did you kill any of them?" Blade asked sharply.

At this, Fox turned her head, incredulity etched on her face. "What, are you on *her* side? Such a question, at a time like this."

Blade gazed around, uneasy at the tension around the grove only heightened by the presence of their leader.

"Answer me," he said tersely.

"You do me a dishonor, Guardian. Though bounty hunter and assassin I may be, I am not a rash, wasteful killer," Fox answered indignantly. "I follow *some* code, you know. At the time, they were not attacking me, so I kicked one in the face and knocked another two out cold. It was enough to return and defend our charges. And if only *some* could exhibit a little faith and patience, they should see the unaccounted for arriving even now."

Fox pointed with her sword. A few glowering warriors emerged from the thicket at her right. One stared with unsubdued animosity as he passed his forearm across his nose, which still streamed blood down his neck and onto his chest.

Even so, Yasi lowered her weapon. The others followed suit. Slowly, Blade did the same, and carefully approached Fox and Yasi to position himself between them.

"You are lucky today, brash fighter," Yasi said coldly. "Should their spirits have been sent to *Jara*, you and two others among you would have repaid the blood debt with your own."

"By all means," Fox sneered, replacing her swords in their sheaths. "You would have been welcome to try."

"Enough." Blade passed a hand over his face, wearily rubbing his eyes and wiping the sweat from his brow. With a sigh, he looked pointedly at both women. "Yasi, this is Fox, my fellow warrior and also a noble defender of a tribe not her own. Fox, this is Yasi, leader of these warriors and the Chychan people into whose home we have trespassed. They are also our rescuers, gracious hosts, and guides through the remaining part of our jungle travels."

With a snide curl of her lip, Fox replied: "My apologies. Next time, I shall remember to curtsy."

13

Night fell heavily upon the Aruacas, and the jungle trees and vines that Blade had grown to despise melted into darkness. Though still too close for his comfort, they had been pared back, and in the torchlight that lined the muddy lane into which he now gazed, he could not see as much of the jungle as he had before. Instead, he stared out at something he had never witnessed in all his long years of life: an entire village on stilts.

The home of the Chychan, never before seen by an outsider's eyes, spread out before Blade and hung suspended some twenty feet above him. Dwelling places had been built into and around living trees, as well as on top of the sawn-off trunks of massive, ancient ones. Spindly supports stretched down to the earth and anchored the more precariously perched of the dwellings. It conjured in Blade's mind the image of a host of giant spiders, legs confused and intermingled, scurrying through the jungle.

A network of bridges ran from the buildings to the trees and back again, spanning the multi-level village like a great web. Strange lanterns hung on the rope-arms of the bridges and emanated a faint, blue light. The ghostly glow illuminated ladders and bridges that stretched even higher in the trees, but whatever lay above disappeared into the foliage and out of Blade's sight. He imagined lookouts and treehouses stationed atop the great trees themselves, forever giving the Chychan a bird's-eye view of all the world below. No longer did Blade wonder at their swift, silent movement through the Aruacas and their agility in the safety of its many branches. Life in the treetops was the Chychan way.

Still, for the feeble, the injured, and for whatever was too large or heavy to make the trip up the ladders and into the trees, the Chychan had erected another stilted building far closer to the ground below. Yasi had told him that this, the village center, served as a gathering place for the people. Tonight, they used it as a triage. Blade peered into the village center, watching as silhouettes held vigil by lantern light or bustled around the cots laid out on the building's floor. There, he knew, the less fortunate Syndicate members convalesced. The least fortunate of all were laid to rest elsewhere. Four new mounds had been added to the Chychan burial grounds that day.

Once again, and to no surprise to Blade, the leaves overhead rattled with the threat of impending rain. In moments, it fell to the ground in torrents, beating rhythmically against the village center's roof and pouring off every exposed surface in streams. With a wave of gratitude for the Chychan, Blade saw the center's roof held, and all its inhabitants remained dry.

He hurried through the downpour, his boots squelching in the rivers of mud already running down the village's traveled lanes. Fires still blazed in metal basins on clever stone platforms, all placed strategically beneath the cover of the tree houses feet above. People cooked or talked around them, unbothered by the flash flood and the roar of rain as they lounged on chairs or perched on tree stumps rolled up for the unanticipated visitors. Blade continued on, his eyes on the fire farthest from him.

He caught glimpses of both thieves he recognized and Chychan individuals he didn't, sitting together around the flames. By now, much of the tension had faded, and the uninjured Syndicate members walked freely among the village, helping tend to the wounded, gathering water, and preparing food alongside their hosts. And though it was no place Blade would ever want to call home, he could appreciate the villagers' homey comforts and their ingenuity in making the Aruacas habitable, even hospitable.

Indeed, this was a wonder. Despite all Blade had heard and experienced at first meeting with the deep forest warriors, the Chychan possessed uncommon hospitality. Frightened suspicions melted quickly into kind welcome after Yasi had gathered and spoken to her people. The tale she shared must have been fascinating, and perhaps spoke a little too glowingly of Blade, for the villagers seemed to regard him with increased respect and interest afterward. He could only suppose this. Naturally, Yasi addressed her people in Chychan, as none of the villagers and a few of the warriors spoke anything else.

Blade walked on, approaching a platform with three figures framed by the firelight. Two sat hunched together by the basin of flames, with the other relaxing on its opposite side. Shaking the excess water from his shaggy head, Blade swung up beside them.

"There he is!" Woldyff turned from the fire, flashing a big smile. "Man o' the hour. We were just talkin' about you, weren't we? What d'ya say? Another lovely, dry evening stroll, I see."

Blade scoffed softly, but could not muster the energy to acknowledge Woldyff's remark with any quip of his own. He glanced around the platform instead. Beside Woldyff, Dane leaned forward in his chair, offering a perfunctory nod before continuing to gaze into the fire. Across from them, Yasi stared back unblinkingly. She inclined her head in greeting, her eyebrow raised slightly in question. Woldyff's smile faltered, and despite his best efforts, the mood around the fire remained sober.

Noticing one member conspicuously absent, Blade scanned the trees around and above. Sure enough, in the supporting tree next to the platform, a figure rested in the crook of one of its lower limbs. Fox stared down at him with an annoyed, haughty air, her arms crossed over her chest and a leg dangling from the branch. Far enough from Yasi as she could manage, Blade surmised, without missing whatever news he would bring.

He stepped closer to the fire, ready to shake the cloud of mosquitos still trailing after him. Yasi gestured to the seat beside hers as he did so, where a plate full of food waited for him. Blade eyed it with anticipation. He had not eaten since that morning.

"Kuimbe helped you meet the Dusty One, then." Yasi stated this as fact, but the others leaned nearer to Blade, faces turned toward him with questions or worry in their eyes.

"Indeed, he did," Blade replied. "We made contact just before dusk."

Blade paused before continuing. His clothes were still dripping, and at the moment, he wanted nothing more than to remember what it felt like to be comfortable and free of wretchedly sodden fabric. He pulled off his shirt and boots, and with a quick shake, laid them on the platform before drawing up the plate of food and sitting. A sarcastic wolf-whistle met him from the crook of the tree.

"Show-off," Woldyff muttered, but he was grinning again.

"Your captain led me to the stone tower, and we lit the fire as you explained," Blade continued to Yasi, ignoring the others. "But the nomad was cautious, slow to arrive. He was not pleased to see me when he finally did. He was expecting you. Still, we came to an arrangement."

"How much did we lose?" Dane asked.

Blade sighed. "All the undamaged armor, the energy rifles, and almost anything else of value that the Chychan stripped and did not keep. But I withheld the sidearms for the Syndicate."

Dane muttered a curse, but said nothing more. Blade knew it had been a raw deal, and he wished he could have retained more of their plunder. Optimism had flooded Blade when the Chychan showed no interest in the Coalition-made weapons or armor: they only wanted their silver, gold, and one spare bidnythine crystal in the Coalition captain's pocket. The Syndicate had full ownership of anything else, and that included an expansive arsenal of the latest model energy rifles and pistols, top grade armor, and waterproof boots. All sorely needed items for the battered guild of fugitive thieves.

And yet, the Syndicate sorely needed one thing more, if they were to survive, and it was for this reason Blade sought out the Heibeiathan trader whom Yasi called the "Dusty One." All agreed only Blade could speak on behalf of the Syndicate, both as a show of their seriousness and strength, and because, for once in his life, being an Elmling and not Gormlaean was an asset instead of a liability. But this "Dusty One" proved a shrewd and difficult buyer.

If only Yasi came with me, instead of Kuimbe, Blade thought, but even as the thought crossed his mind, he knew it would not have helped. It was on Yasi's recommendation that she sent her captain in her stead, for she believed the nomad would find Chychan approval of a foreigner like Blade suspect. Perhaps he might back out of any dealings altogether. It seemed overly cautious to Blade at the time, but given the nomad's chilly reception and uncompromising demand for payment, he grimaced to think how it would have gone had they not followed Yasi's lead.

Still, the Unseen knows we could've used the rifles and the armor, Blade thought ruefully. But it had to be done.

From her branch, Fox scoffed loudly. "And what have these nomads promised in exchange?"

"They will provide transport, horses or some other beasts best suited for the journey, and disguises for the Syndicate, as well as an escort to Errdoga. Thanks to Dane, we know the Syndicate's sister guild, the Abynawa, have a safe house there. It should still be operating just outside the Coalition's reach. I have also arranged that those of us who wish to go on can keep their animals and disguises. And with that, we have a hope of reaching the Kamarians in one piece."

"Well, if we must lose everything else, at least we have a ride." Fox eyed Yasi. "But can we trust him?"

"Yeah, how long have you been trading with these Heibeiathans?" Woldyff asked.

"Long enough to know his mind." Yasi flashed a grim smile. "He and his people hate the *Co'atyti* as we do. The Dusty One will keep his word, if only for a little revenge."

"Won't matter much to either of us if we're ambushed on the way out," Dane muttered. "Any idea what we're up against, Blade?"

"I will go with the Chychan patrol to confirm again in the morning, but by all accounts, we should have a clear path out of the Aruacas," Blade answered. "There is no sign of Coalition activity within ten miles."

"They will not come any closer," Yasi said, nodding her approval. "The *Co'atyti* know. There is only death for them here."

"Even so, Yasi, do not underestimate them," Blade said. "If the Coalition hates anything, it is hubris. I fear the Chychan and any of your neighboring tribes will face their wrath after what happened today. Is that not so, Fox?"

Blade glanced up at Fox, who shrugged.

"They have burned lands and peoples for less," she admitted. "But only if it will be expedient and efficient; tearing up the rainforest would be neither. No, the Supreme Chancellor ensures his minions are not rash or foolish. They know time is on their side, not ours. They need only be patient. Wait for us to poke our heads out of our fortuitous hidey-hole. In the end, I expect the Coats shall believe today to have been only a minor setback."

"Then they'll be waitin' for us on the other side for sure," Woldyff grimaced.

"Perhaps not," Blade said thoughtfully. "The Coalition force that found us had been very unlikely to fail. It may be that others will come to investigate their silence, and they will have to come into the Aruacas on foot, like us all. It may be we have bought a little time."

"And it ain't likely they'll expect us leaving the forest so far south," Dane said, and then added with a grumble: "It's the best shot we have, even if it's a long one."

For a few moments, they sat in silence together around the fire, listening to the loud spitting of the fire and the roar of the ever-falling rain. Blade stared into the dancing flames, rehashing all the details of their journey for the next morning. The others brought up serious flaws in their escape, risks and dangers that had already begun to swirl in Blade's mind before he even returned to share the final plan. He knew the Coalition must be waiting, just as Fox supposed, on the Heibeiathan side of the Aruacas. Even if they expected the Syndicate to emerge farther north, surely they would have hovercrafts patrolling the wastes and the sands along the rainforest's boundaries. The Heibeiathan nomads may have ways of sneaking under the noses of the Coats in normal circumstances, but could they do so now, with scores of hunted fugitives? And how could they get them as far as Errdoga, with so many of the thieves injured from the attack and weakened by the jungle?

Indeed, it seemed they had only a fool's hope of getting out alive. But no other options remained. As sure as the sky boiled red each morning, Blade knew the Coats would never stop scouring the Aruacas for them. Maybe, in Errdoga, the Syndicate had one last chance. And maybe, if Blade and Fox could break away, they could get to Elmnas by way of the unforgiving sands. And once there, maybe, they could do something to stop its final calamity.

That was far too many maybes for comfort. It had been a while since Blade operated with an air-tight plan, but this one had holes that a hovercraft could fly through.

At the very least, thank the Unseen that the Coalition will never find their missing detachment.

Blade had helped Yasi and her warriors with the dirty work of disposing of the deceased. The Chychan had a burial pit for their enemies, a deep crevasse in the darkest jungle where no man could find their resting place without making it his own. The less the Coalition could gather from the struggle in the jungle, the better for the Syndicate as well as the Chychan. Moreover, the loot they garnered already proved invaluable. Before they cast the Coats' bodies within, Blade had the foresight to remove the signature Coalition cloaks. No doubt more than one disguise would be needed along the way.

Yasi shifted, placing her fist under her chin as her eyes narrowed in deep thought. She turned her hard face toward Blade, and by the light of the fire he could see the war paint of earlier had worn away. She appeared more human now, though no more approachable if one only judged by her stony expression. Her shining black eyes flashed in his direction.

"You have made powerful enemies, Warrior-of-Many-Names. Will they pursue you long, even into the sands of Heibeiath?"

"Indeed, they will pursue some of us to the ends of the world," Blade nodded to Fox, and he thought he saw the shimmer of a smirk.

"Why is this?"

"Because my people block the *Co'atyti's* path to total victory, and as broken as we are, the survival of our ways will always be a threat. My existence is a reminder that they do not yet claim all of Reidara for their own," Blade said quietly. "They will not stop, not until none of Elmling blood remains."

Blade's words hung in the air as Yasi pondered them, but not for long. In a low grumble, Dane added, "And the rest of us are just morons. We've gone ahead and turned traitor, and gotten into the middle of war that's gonna kill us all." He jerked a thumb up at Fox. "I should've died the first time someone tried to kill me. I'd have been happier."

Yasi raised an eyebrow as Fox sniggered. Woldyff chuckled, too.

"Buckets o' sunshine, this one."

Dane pointed a stubby finger at him. "Speaking of Sunshine, you idiots owe me a new horse. All that trouble of finding her again after Thunder Run, and then I had to sell her, just to get to this wretched jungle and end up dying, anyway."

"Come on, Dane, you'll get a nice new steed from our nomad pals in place of that tired old draft horse." Woldyff grinned. "You might actually outrun the Coats on whatever they've got. Anyone who's

LION

ever seen that lazy, temperamental mare would know she would've gotten you killed well before *we* could!"

Woldyff continued laughing as Dane muttered to himself, but it trailed away as Yasi suddenly stood.

"What, was it something I said?" he whispered as she moved to the edge of the platform.

Yasi stared out at the jungle, arms crossed over her chest. Their small camp fell once again into somber reflection, the mood around the Chychan fire shifting just as quickly as the wind's whims shifted its flames. Blade looked at the others as they sat in the renewed quiet, feeling once again the weight of all things. *Perhaps*, he wondered. *Yasi feels it too.*

"Do you mean what you say?"

Yasi turned back when she finally spoke, and her hard gaze flicked from Blade to Fox. He inclined his head toward her, watching her in his hawkish way. As he studied the warrior chiefess, he sensed that even now, some burden had begun weighing upon her since their first intense meeting of that day. He could see it in the tautness of her back and arms, in the strain and worry he found hidden behind the ferocity of her glare. *She believed her people free*, he realized. *She believed they were safe.*

Yasi did not lower her gaze. "Will the *Co'atyti* come for the Chychan?"

He considered the question, allowing it to hang there as the silence stretched on between them.

"Yes," he finally answered. "Now that they know you are here, they will come."

She stared back, her expression inscrutable, but if he had to, Blade could venture a guess at what she was thinking. It would be the same thoughts of any leader, every leader, outnumbered and outgunned by the relentless, duplicitous, merciless Coalition. Hard and risky choices lay before her, ones that determined whether her people would survive or be trampled beneath Coalition boots. She would carry the weight of the world, her world, crashing down upon her. If only Blade did not know. If only he had not seen it all before.

Blade held her gaze. He sighed, seeing the storm brewing there, ruing the cynical wisdom of his long years. Without a word, Yasi pivoted and leaped off the platform. Blade could only watch as she trotted off, disappearing beyond the curtains of black rain.

14

The low mist creeping along the jungle floor shimmered as light rose from the horizon and poked through the mass of jungle trees. Morning's arrival stirred the mists themselves, and they shifted, revealing the damp but no longer flooded paths of the Chychan village. The now gone rivulets of rain had carved up the muddy avenues, leaving behind alien patterns in the soft earth. Bedewed leaves above and vibrant flowers around twinkled with the rising daylight. For one breathless moment, even below the ever-clouded sky, the Aruacas swelled with simple, wild beauty.

Blade could see it then. He could understand why so many peoples loved her, worshiped her, and called her home. She was terrible and proud, enrapturing and cruel, like any goddess of which Blade had once heard or read. He stared, one last time, into the rainforest's depths, before shouldering his belongings and turning back toward the center of the village.

Here, the spell of the jungle was broken. People hustled in and out of the village center, hurriedly preparing bundles and helping the less fortunate of the Syndicate members into carts or onto makeshift crutches. Boots stomped and wheels creaked, flattening the stream beds into an indiscernible muck and filling the air with the sound of squishing mud. And that air, thick with the threat of more rain later, was as hot as ever. Blade suspected the journey to the rainforest's edge would be just as miserable as every other day in the Aruacas. Even with the danger that promised to find them once they left the jungle's stifling bounds, he nonetheless had no qualms about doing so.

"Mornin' Falky," Woldyff said, appearing beside Blade to slap him between the shoulders. "I expect we're ready, then."

"It is about time," said Fox, joining them on his other side. "At this rate, the Coalition will have won the war before we get out."

Blade said nothing, but strode into the crowd amassing around the village center. They parted as he, Woldyff, and Fox slipped through, finding Dane and Yasi at the head of the loosely formed column. She nodded as they approached, slinging her weapon across her back by its leather strap and bouncing a long, deadly spear against the ground. Blade glanced up at the spear point, which caught the light with a metallic glint. On the outskirts of the Syndicate throng, her Chychan warriors did the same, some sporting spears, others compound bows, and still others the rifle-like weapons that had proven so fatal against the Coalition onslaught the day before.

"My warriors will escort you as far as the edge of the jungle," Yasi said. She glanced up, and Blade followed her gaze, where he saw others running along the bridges and disappearing into the trees. Yasi bared a fierce smile. "Your people have nothing to fear from around or above until the edge of the *Tyeraka*. And there, let our oath to you be fulfilled."

Blade dipped his head in thanks. "Then let us no longer delay in fulfilling it."

Raising her spear, Yasi shouted something in Chychan, ending the rallying cry with an echoing trill. From above and around, the warriors cried back, punctuated with trills and whoops of their own. And with that, Yasi set off. Chychan villagers watched quietly from the sides as Blade, the others, and the Syndicate column followed her.

Blade could keep up easily with Yasi's motivated stride, but he slowed enough to keep a watchful eye from the middle of the column. They plunged into the jungle. Chychan warriors melted into the surrounding vegetation. Blade glanced back, glad to see a few of the Chychan shoring up the group from the rear. Just a few paces behind him, Dane puffed along, grimacing as he caught Blade's eye.

"Well, she sure doesn't mess around, does she?" he rumbled with annoyance.

"No doubt she wants to be rid of us," Fox said from in front of Blade, smirking. "Our lingering here only spells trouble for everyone involved. If I were her, I should regret not killing us or simply abandoning us to the elements."

"Take it *easy*, scary lady!" Woldyff said, aghast. "What's wrong with you?"

Fox flashed a sinister grin.

"What's wrong with me? My, my, Woldyff, where to start?" She sighed and tapped a tin mug hanging from her belt. "Of course, it *could* just be the lack of qava. I never quite know what to blame these days."

For the better part of the morning, they marched on, following Yasi on a well-beaten Chychan trail. Cleared of the close-growing vines and stamped down by years of traffic, the trail wound through the rainforest in which two or three could walk abreast comfortably. That was a mercy, for Blade had no doubt that the exhausted, battered Syndicate could not have managed another day of forging their own path through the unforgiving jungle. Still, the group stretched along it and straggled behind Yasi, each Syndicate member keeping up as they were able. Blade had spent the last hour striding up and down the column of travelers, watching for trouble and checking their progress. But the Chychan carried out their task well, for wherever Blade heard an unsettling sound or caught an unfamiliar sight, a camouflaged warrior streaked into the forest to investigate its source. He also knew that other warriors roamed far and wide of the main company, for occasionally one would emerge from the jungle and nod to Yasi. At other times, bird-like calls echoed across to the jungle. Yasi would pause and incline her ear to listen.

"No *Co'atyti* within a day's walk," she would then say. And as they got closer to their destination, "The *Tyeraka* is still clear. We go on."

By midday, just as the sweltering heat of the Aruacas reached its apex, Yasi broke off from the main trail. Blade directed traffic onto a smaller path, this one narrower but no less used. He jumped into line behind a few of the more eager Syndicate members, and suddenly found himself in an open place in the midst of the jungle. Oohs of delight whispered behind Blade as the rest followed him into the clearing. They spread out to take in the scene. A brook babbled at their feet, and its grassy banks sloped upward and ended beneath a cascade of boulders. From thirty feet above, water rushed down a split in one of the massive rocks and spilled into a silvery pool. Mist went up from the churn, but everywhere else the water invited them to enjoy its clear, refreshing calm.

"Your people may stop and drink here." Yasi gestured to the pool as Blade strode toward her. "But walk lightly. *Mboi* like to gather here, too."

She placed her hands flat against each other. With a hiss, she moved them in a slithering motion, and Blade caught her meaning.

"We have a few moments to rest and catch our breaths," Blade announced as the last of the Syndicate poured into the clearing. A few grateful but markedly toned-down whoops went up from the group. Some, standing by the brook, flopped down where they stood and reached greedily into the water. Others tossed aside boots and splashed right into the pool up to their knees. Among them, Maren plunged in up to her chest and splashed a friend with a loud laugh.

"Watch for snakes!" Blade added, cupping his hands over his mouth.

With a horrified grimace, Maren scrambled back to the bank. Raim, easing himself down at the water's edge, pointed and laughed.

"Watch it," Maren grumbled. "Go ahead, keep on like that, and see if I don't knock that crutch out from under you."

Blade allowed a rare smile as he came to the water's edge himself, gazing down into it as he unscrewed the top of his canteen. The pool sparkled like glass, and, where the silt had not been disturbed by enthusiastic travelers, was clear to its sandy bottom. He found it a refreshing change from the majority of the waterways they had encountered in the Aruacas. The murkiness of the other channels promised aching bellies as well as other dangers, namely, those filled with teeth. They had kept to collecting rainwater instead.

He poised the canteen over the pool, but paused as he caught sight of his own reflection. Hard eyes and a pale, hollowed face looked back. Disheveled black hair and a thick, wild beard seemed to sprout in all directions. Even in the reflection, Blade could see all the touches of gray in both. He had forgotten that face. He never did spend much time looking at it, and in these last years, he had no desire or much need to do so. Had he really grown so old?

Gingerly, he dipped his hand into the pool and combed wet fingers through his beard and hair. As he smoothed down the hairs below his chin, a voice reached out of his memory and echoed from the past.

Please, tell me you're not keeping that.

Still, he remembered it, turning from the mirror, where he had been running a comb through a sparser and far blacker beard, though no less wild or easier to tame. There, Theana stood behind him, hands on her hips. How he drank her in, from her long, golden hair to the curves of her body beneath the simple but elegant betrothal dress. A halo of sunlight fell over her through the open window. A vision, a goddess, an angel – whatever she was – graced him with her presence. It had been ages, and the memory alone made his breath catch in his chest. Here he was, in his prime, one of the strongest

Warriors of the Way, but still, the mere sight of Theana made him weak.

Blade stared into the surface of the pond, but saw only what followed in that dream from years ago. He could not stop it if he had tried, and he did not want to. The memory went on, as if it had only been yesterday. There was Theana, giving him that faux critical gaze. There was the smile, that perfect smile, the one she could never hold back from playing on her perfect lips.

It is distinguished, Blade had said, straightening to face her. *It is what all the men wear for such occasions.*

Falkir.

She moved toward him, her arms reaching up over his shoulders. Blade folded her into his embrace, breathing in her scent, coming undone by the warmth of her touch. She tilted her face up toward his, her bright eyes locked on his own.

You know I love you, right?

Yes.

Blade drew her in tighter, brushing his lips against hers. She kissed him back, but pulled away with a giggle.

Well, I'm not marrying you with that thing on your face.

She grinned, tugging on his cheek. Her eyes danced with mischief.

For a moment, Blade closed his eyes, recalling the feel of her hand against his cheek. He felt again the hint of mischief in his own smile as he whirled her around. Theana's squeal as they landed in a heap on the couch beside the dressing room mirror, the feel of her chest against his, the scent of her hair, the light caress of her fingers over his shoulder.

Anything. Anything for you. I shall shave it right now.

Agony swelled inside Blade alongside the bliss as he remembered what came next. When she pressed against him, the kiss was deeper, and still he had not forgotten. It was misery to remember, yes, but still more misery to forget. How could he forget? The lips that grazed his ear, that whispered:

It can wait, just for a little while longer.

"Do not tell me you have already found one of those horrid creatures," a voice said, shaking Blade out of moments long since past. "I have had enough of snakes, as well as everything else that lives in this wretched place."

In the reflection of the pool, Blade saw Fox standing over him, her arms crossed as she scoured the bottom with a sour expression. He blinked, realizing his canteen was still poised above the water.

"No," he said slowly, dipping the canteen in an almost mechanical motion. "All is well."

Blade rose from the spot, turning with effort. He looked at Fox, still not quite seeing her or anything else. *That memory. When was the last time I recalled it?* The moment faded into darkness. It had been years, perhaps decades, since he had allowed it to surface.

"Are you... alright?" Fox asked, appraising him critically.

Blade lifted the canteen to his lips. They felt as parched and thick as the Heibeiathan sands. What could he even say? What words existed to encapsulate a lifetime of loss, of joy stolen, of agony deeper than the trenches of the sea? How could she understand? How could anyone comprehend it?

And yet she does comprehend.

The thought jarred him out of his own self-pity. Indeed, the bounty contract she had shown him had made her understanding all too clear, and if he had not believed the ink dried to the page, he believed what he saw in her eyes: the longing, the sorrow, the torment, the regret. With the flourish of his quill, the Supreme Chancellor had taken from Fox everything that had mattered. Blade had suffered under the cruel impersonality of an act of war. Fox had been crushed in the hand of an even crueler father.

Blade lowered the canteen, staring, he soon realized, in his most uncomfortable, hawkish way. Fox did not shrink, as most did, but bristled with restless discomfort. But he could not help it. His stare intensified.

"What was his name?"

Fox stepped back, and for the first time in a while, looked as angry as the day Blade met her. Her eyes grew dangerous. "Pardon?"

"The letter. It did not name him."

Fox opened her mouth, but for once, no fiery words came. Blade waited, incapable of relenting, unwilling to bury everything forever, desperate to no longer bear his grief alone. He could share it, if only this once, with someone whose grief was as great as his own. Blade's gaze flicked to the scar on Fox's cheek. Out of the corner of his eye, he saw movement; her hand flinching upward, as if to hide the old wound. Her fist balled instead. Blade braced for the inevitable swing, perhaps the one he deserved for prying.

But it did not come. As she released her fingers, so did the anger fall away. Fox's face softened, and her unfocused eyes wandered from his. She paused, her jaw clenching and unclenching. And when she spoke, she whispered, all the sharp edges of her wit and her words gone.

"He was called Reylas."

For a long moment, she stood that way, her thoughts as far away as Blade's own. She returned, her gaze falling on the withered flower still pinioned to his shirt.

"And hers?"

Blade offered a wry smile. "Theana."

Fox smiled, blinking away something and shaking her head as she looked away. "We do not forget."

"Never," Blade replied.

Neither spoke anything further. For Blade, there was no need. To be seen, to be understood; it was enough.

They remained that way, Fox's gaze elsewhere. Eventually, Blade followed it. Some paces away, Maren crouched at the pool's edge, her own canteen stretched tentatively over the surface. But just as she dipped it in, she froze in horror.

"Augh!"

She jumped back, throwing the canteen as hard as she could at the water. It broke the surface with an anticlimactic splash. Maren looked around furtively, and seeing Fox and Blade, her fear melted into sheepish embarrassment. She peered down at the bobbing canteen, and her face reddened.

"Um, whoops," she chuckled uncomfortably, pulling in the bottle. "Just a fish, I think."

15

An oppressively hot afternoon came and passed before Yasi halted their stumbling procession. Blade stood close behind her, his damp skin prickling as the breath of a stiff breeze rushed past him. After their detour at the waterfall pool, they had traveled hard up steep trails and through crowded jungle paths that seemed to grow darker with every step. Their perseverance, however, was rewarded. They reached the rainforest's edge.

Blade stepped out and searched their new setting, where the branches of the trees above fell farther apart and larger swathes of the sky roiled between their boughs. Ahead, the trees grew scant and abruptly, at the bare edge of a precipice, ended. A rust-colored gorge yawned back at him, and from beyond that, its bottom melted into shadow. Across the gorge, the world turned a dusty, lifeless brown. It stretched endlessly across the horizon, and nothing but squat, black shrubs broke up its monotony.

The Desolation. We meet you at last, Blade thought. *And what new peril shall you bring us?*

The breeze gathered strength, becoming a warm, blasting wind as it whistled over the emptiness to meet them. With a growing sense of unease, Blade glanced back at the dense, dark trees of the Aruacas spreading out in the valley behind them. Low-hanging misty clouds rolled over the treetops, adorning the great, green expanse in a sense of breathtaking awe and mystery. Despite the relief of finally escaping the jungle, he could not help recall its beauty and, once the Chychan became their guides, its relative safety. Given the prospects the Desolation offered, he almost missed it.

Blade lowered his gaze, now scanning the shadowy thicket just behind him. In weary heaps clumped the footsore Syndicate, fanning themselves or rubbing aching calf muscles as they awaited whatever came next. Lingering deeper still in the jungle, Chychan faces moved in and out of shadow. No warrior but Yasi approached the rainforest's end, but Blade caught the glint of a spear and heard the hushed rattle of a full quiver as they paroled from within.

"Will they come no further?" Blade turned to Yasi, who scanned the Desolation with narrowed eyes beside him.

"They have done what honor required," Yasi replied, her tone clipped. She gave Blade a sidelong glance. "Would you demand more?"

Blade looked down at her with the hint of a shrewd smile. "I would not presume upon their already generous aid. But I am curious about what dangers they have foreseen that we have not."

"There is a saying among the Chychan," Yasi said, crossing her arms. "In this tongue, it goes something like 'do not gamble your hands for what the eyes want, should you lose both.' We know how to face the dangers of the Aruacas, we know what is worth risking life and limb for. But the *Tyeraka*? There is little here worth that, and as you have learned, our greatest strength is in our secrecy. No wise enemy dares to fall upon those he can neither judge nor see. Out of sight, we have survived."

"Then how did your dealings with the Heibeiathans begin in the first place?" Blade asked, surprised.

At this, Yasi smirked. "I said there is little here worth the risk, but not nothing. And the Dusty One took the risk first. He was lucky that his treasures pleased us."

"And what does he get from you?"

"Enough to keep him returning."

Blade cast another backward glance, catching once more the shining tip of a spear between the fronds.

"I see," he said.

A rustle beside the two caught both of their attention. Fox, followed by Woldyff, and then Dane, stepped through a gap between the shrubs to join them.

"Alright," Woldyff said, rubbing his hands together. "What's the plan?"

"We wait," Yasi replied, already back to scanning the gorge.

"Well, how long, then?" Woldyff pressed.

"Until he arrives," Yasi said.

"But–" Woldyff began, but Dane elbowed him. "Ow! Alright, we wait. Beats walkin' all day, I guess."

Smirking and shaking her head, Fox settled on a fallen tree trunk on Blade's other side. Resigning himself to hours of watching and waiting, Woldyff sighed and leaned up against another tree. Dane muttered something as he wandered off in the other direction, scouring the Desolation for any sign of movement.

No one spoke as they all watched the expansive emptiness together. Blade could feel their tension as they did so, even as the time wore on. Woldyff fidgeted and Fox thumbed the grips of her pistols in their holsters. Dane had long disappeared into the undergrowth, as Blade knew was his custom as a smuggler. Not too long ago, he had watched the pass to Thunder Run from the cover of the Swaying Forest, a practice which had, no doubt, kept him alive and in business. Only Fox had managed to escape his vigilant gaze, and that was hardly fair. Few could outwit a bounty hunter trained in the Way, especially one who trained under Hiraeth himself.

And here Blade was, watching and waiting with this motley crew; trying to shepherd an entire guild of city-wise thieves through Reidara's most hostile wilderness, with that same ex-Coalition bounty hunter, the smuggler she nearly killed, and the rakish thief who lost everything for rescuing Blade. All this, while being escorted by the chief of the most feared people of the Aruacas. Blade stroked his beard, wondering at the increasing absurdity of his circumstances.

It has been said, Blade mused. *The Unseen works in the most unusual ways.*

The wind whistled on as they lingered, bringing with it the dry desert heat of the wasteland. Already Blade could imagine what a furnace it would be to cross it during the day. If the Heibeiathans were wise, as he judged them to be, they would wait until closer to night. Then, the constant cloud cover would shield their movements, as well as keep them from freezing to death. Blade might have snorted at this if he were so inclined. *One small benefit of never seeing the sun again.*

By now, Woldyff had sprung back onto his feet, busying himself by picking up fallen seed pods, tearing them to pieces, and tossing them back to the ground. As he paced along in front of the other three, he cast nervous glances at the gorge. Suddenly, Woldyff stopped in front of Yasi, and pointed at her weapon.

"I've got to ask," Woldyff said as he eyed it warily. "What's that you got there?"

"It's a glorified blowgun." Fox rolled her eyes, stretching out along the fallen tree as she offered a lazy, dismissive wave of her hand. "Certainly you've seen something like that before."

Yasi's gaze snapped toward Fox. She scowled, her hand straying to her machete. Fox, largely unbothered, plucked at fungi stuck to the side of the log and examined it without interest.

"Oh, but it's a beaut' of a thing, isn't it?" Woldyff spoke quickly. He gave a stupid wave of his hands, as if by directing Yasi's attention to him, she'd forget Fox altogether. That much did seem to work as

Woldyff had hoped, for she turned her sharp gaze upon him. However, Blade did not miss the murderous look she shot at Fox on his other side. Woldyff continued talking, far louder and more rapidly than usual.

"I mean to say, no doubt it's deadly. You took down a whole bunch of Coats while our lot could hardly touch 'em. What's the secret? Do you mind if I have a look?"

"We call it a *boka*. The *bokas* are much quieter than the rifles the *Co'atyti* carry." Yasi shrugged, handing the weapon over. "They do not overheat or stop firing when damp. And in the hands of a Chychan, they are lethal. You have already witnessed our marksmanship, our stealth, our superiority against the *Co'atyti* in the Aruacas. I need not speak of it further."

"And what are these made of?"

Woldyff slid a sharp metal projectile from its holding chamber and turned it over in his hands. A smooth, cylindrical base attached seamlessly to a teardrop shape, terminating into something like a spear tip. Woldyff held it up, and it sparkled as he turned it in the fading light. Blade studied the projectile with interest as well. The metal craft was deceptively simple to the untrained eye. As one who had forged his own weapons, Blade could see the extraordinary skill that went into the projectile's making, a skill far more nuanced than one might expect of a people many considered technologically backward. And for all his knowledge and years of experience, Blade could not place the ore used to craft it. Indeed, it was no common iron or even steel. He marveled as he realized it was something he had never before seen.

"That is a secret art, and it is not for outsiders," Yasi replied, snatching back the projectile.

Sheepishly, Woldyff handed the *boka* back to her. "No offense meant."

"My, my, but that is a pretty piece of work. You must have mines, deep in the forest, for something as special as that." Fox perked up, arching her neck to look past Blade at Yasi. "And it is this metal that you sell to the nomads?"

Yasi glared. "What is it to you?"

"Nothing to me," Fox smirked. "But the *Co'atyti*, as you call them, would certainly be interested."

"They do not know of it," Yasi retorted.

"Do not be so sure of that," Fox replied, and to Blade's relief, she did not say this with an air of gloating relish, but of sincere regret.

Though glowering, Yasi said nothing more. Carefully, she replaced the metal projectile in its chamber and slung the *boka* over her back. With a withering glare, she turned and trekked back through the jungle, passing the groups of Syndicate members and disappearing behind the trees. Blade watched her go, catching sight of her Chychan fellows as she met them.

He turned to face the Desolation, feeling he too was being watched. Out of the corner of his eye, he saw Fox staring at him. He gave her a sidelong, probing glance.

"What?" Fox said, a little defensively.

"Must you provoke her?" Blade asked, without malice but without amusement, either.

"She needs to be provoked," Fox replied shortly, crossing her arms. "She needs to know what is coming for them. There is no use in denying it, and you know that as well. A small tribe like the Chychan are nothing to the Coalition. They will be devoured."

"Ah," Blade nodded. "Today you bedevil with good intentions."

"Sometimes," Fox said with a sly smile. "Increasingly so, I suppose."

"Well, it'll be a shame if you've scared her off for good. I was starting to like her," Woldyff said, snorting as if he had made a joke. However, Blade heard a note of anxiety in his voice.

"Rest assured. She will return," Fox sighed. "And perhaps she will also have heeded my words and made preparation for her people."

"And even if she does not, we have struck a fair bargain," Blade added. "It is the best we can do. Are you alright, Woldyff?"

"Yeah, I'm fine."

Woldyff ran his hand through his hair and shook his head. "No, I 'spose not. It's just this, right? I'd feel a lot better with Yasi dealing with this Heibeiathan than any of us. Seems like they got a good thing going. But with just us? You know how those nomads can be. Not exactly known for their integrity, are they?"

"Neither are we," Fox laughed. "You and yours steal things for a living. I needn't mention my recent line of work."

"We at least got a code, don't we? But nomads, huh," Woldyff scoffed. "They're as shifty as those sands out there."

Blade said nothing, but Woldyff had a point. In all his wanderings in Heibeiath, he had to be more on his guard around the nomads than the run-of-the-mill Coats who tried to control the region.

"They may be opportunists, but I do not believe this group benefits from not keeping their end of the bargain. The Dusty One, as Yasi calls him, was more than eager to get his hands on Coalition armaments. They know as well as we how unmerciful the Coats are when it comes to stolen goods. We have a mutual interest in steering clear of Coalition surveillance."

"I sure hope you're right. We need a break."

Woldyff sighed and sat down against the tree trunk, glancing back at the bedraggled group of thieves. He looked back at Blade and shook his head. "They ain't got much left in 'em."

Blade nodded, but Fox narrowed her eyes.

"They need rest, to be certain, but most did well enough," Fox said. "Now is not the time to sit back on one's haunches and wait. It is time to act."

"Listen," Woldyff sighed again. "A few thugs every now and then? Yeah, the Syndicate can handle that. And if the cards are right, like they were with Myergo, we can even pull off a good ol' fashioned ambush. But you all saw it yesterday. They ain't soldiers. This last fight..." Woldyff stared off toward the Syndicate again, shaking his head. "It did 'em in, it did. No, I can't ask them to go on. This lot needs a proper safe house."

"Have you not been listening?" Fox scoffed. "There *are* no safe places left. And if there are, they will not stand for long. You cannot treat these thieves like children, Woldyff. They need to—"

"Enough." Blade raised a hand, casting a severe look at Fox. Fox's own eyes flashed dangerously, but she said nothing more. That was enough for Blade. He turned again to Woldyff, who was staring at his feet and scratching the new beard growth along his jaw.

"The Syndicate has done all that has been needed, and more," Blade assured him. "I would repay my debt to you in full by getting you all safe to Errdoga. You have my word."

At this, Woldyff looked up, a grim smile on his face.

"Well, mate, hate to disappoint you, but it won't be that easy to get rid of me."

Fox again narrowed shrewd eyes at him. "You are coming with us? To Elmnas?"

"Yeah," Woldyff shrugged. "I'm not too keen on Heibeiath, you see. Too much sand. Gets everywhere."

At any other time, Blade might have chuckled, despite himself, but he could not now.

"Woldyff," Blade said seriously. "The Syndicate needs a good leader. They will not survive without one."

"They'll have a leader. The best anyone could ask for," Woldyff said. "Maren, of course. It's already been taken care of."

"She has agreed to it?" Blade asked, raising an eyebrow.

Woldyff hedged with a noncommittal gesture. "Well, yeah, with a little persuasion. And Dane'll be with her too, obviously. Not that he needed any convincing, but I've asked him to stay with the Syndicate. He's got the best Heibeiathan out of all of us."

Blade cocked his head. "Do you indeed believe Maren is up for it?"

"She will do well," Fox said. "Pity, though, to not have her accompany us. She has a fighting spirit. Would you not agree, Blade?"

"Indeed," Blade said, a small smile turning up the corner of his mouth. "Though I would be wary of her directing that spirit at me."

"True, though you would deserve it," Fox grinned.

Blade dipped his head in acknowledgement as Woldyff laughed. Even Fox chuckled along, and Blade felt his smile widen. He could have stopped it, returning with comfortable ease to his usual staid disposition, but for once, he did not want to. For once, he allowed himself the small luxury of enjoying the company of friends.

The brush beside them rustled, and Blade turned to see a weathered hand shoot through the fronds. Dane's annoyed, scowling face followed. He appraised Woldyff, still chuckling, with a gloomy stare.

"What are you crackpots crowin' about?" he said gruffly.

"Just passin' the time, without cranky smugglers to ruin it," Woldyff replied, eyes twinkling. "What's your grousin' for?"

Dane continued to glower. "Well, that nomad is coming, and he's alone. So that should be enough to wipe the stupid grin off your face."

"What do you mean by that?" Woldyff asked, frowning.

"What else do you think I mean? He's *alone*. As in just him," Dane answered scornfully. "You know what that means."

Woldyff continued to frown. "No, I don't. How else should he come? With all his people in the open? He said he'd meet us, and he did. I wouldn't be bringin' my whole caravan out if I didn't have to, either."

"Dane thinks he is being watched," Blade said, his brow furrowing. "And the nomad knows it."

Dane mumbled indistinguishable but sarcastic-sounding remarks as he made a show of shaking out his handkerchief and mopping his brow. Fox jumped off the log, already reaching back for her blades.

"Did you see anything else?" she asked. "Any sign the Coalition is near?"

Dane shook his head in frustration. "Nothing. But I wouldn't, not if they came in along the gorge."

"So, you didn't see anything," Woldyff said, rolling his eyes as he crossed his arms.

"I don't have to!" Dane growled. He pointed forcefully at his gut. "I trust this. It hasn't steered me wrong. Not once. You know what happened the last time I ignored it?"

Dane pursed his lips angrily as he jabbed a finger in Fox's direction and then back at his shoulder. But Fox did not grin this time.

"What do you think of our bargain now, Blade?" Fox said quietly. "Will it be enough?"

"We will soon find out," Blade replied. "But right now, we need Yasi."

"I'll find her," Woldyff said, his voice low. He walked back toward the jungle without another word.

"Where is this Heibeiathan?" Fox said after a time, scanning the gorge. "I cannot see him from here."

"A little ways south, yet." Dane pointed beyond their line of sight into the trees at their left. "He came up out of a little trail on the edge of the canyon, still about a half mile off, and was coming straight for the jungle. I expect he'll get far enough into the trees so he can't be seen from the desert side."

"What is the problem?"

Yasi spoke in Heibeiathan as she strode up to the trio quickly. Woldyff followed closely behind. She carried her *boka* on one shoulder, and on the other, a drawstring pack. New paint streaked her face and arms, but the feathered headband was gone, replaced by a simpler one. A dagger peaked out of the belt band on her hip, along with a pouch that rattled with a soft, metallic tinkle when she moved. Yasi's eyes met Blade's as she swept over the three, a curious expression in them. She fixed her gaze on Dane.

"Your nomad," Dane replied in Heibeiathan. "He's coming up

the canyon pretty far to the south and making his way to the jungle back there."

"That is not his usual way. The Dusty One always comes up the cliff there." Yasi nodded dead ahead, toward the slope where the head of a worn trail terminated at the gorge's sharp edge. "He stays out of the jungle until he gets to Chychan territory, of which this is the outer boundary. Other tribes do not deal with him. It is not his way to enter their land. He knows it is not wise to wander through alone."

"Well, that sure would've been nice to know before you let me walk off that way," Dane muttered in Gormlaean. Yasi narrowed her eyes, and he quickly reverted. "Well, that's how he's coming. He should be here soon."

"Hmm," Yasi touched her chin thoughtfully. "If that is so, then we shall wait. Tell your people to be ready, but let us remain hidden in the safety of the jungle."

Dane shot a look at the rest of them, one that Blade knew dripped with far more cantankerous suspicion than usual. Woldyff rolled his eyes at Dane, and with a meaningful, pointed flick of his head, indicated what he wanted Dane to do.

"Fine," Dane sighed heavily, readjusting his belt. "I'll talk to Maren."

As the restive group behind them prepared to set off, Blade, Yasi, Fox, and Woldyff watched the southern edge of the Aruacas in silence. Nothing moved along the outside of the tree line, but soon enough, Blade could hear the swish of a tree branch or the snap of a twig underfoot. Fox and Yasi both seemed to hear it, too, but while Yasi only followed the sounds with her stare, Fox waited with her weapons drawn. In time, the stir of movement was unmistakable. Woldyff jumped as Yasi let loose a shrill whistle.

The stirring did not stop, but angled toward them. Blade rested his hands on *Av'tal* and *Ub'rytal* as he arched his neck to search the undergrowth. A dusty, forest green keffiyeh bobbed into view and disappeared before cloth-wrapped fingers reached through branches. The nomad's face followed, all his features covered by the patterned headdress wound across his mouth and draped in a neat triangle over his right shoulder. Dark-lensed, bottle-thick goggles obscured his eyes, and he appeared bizarrely alien as he turned his whole head slowly to observe each one of them. The Dusty One did not remove the goggles, but he wiped a layer of grime off them with his sleeve. He gave Blade a long, hard stare before pulling down the keffiyeh around his mouth and turning to Yasi. He clicked his tongue disapprovingly.

"Turn back while you still can, Chiefess of the Chychan. Your Elmling is a marked man."

16

51st of Sun's Wane
Elmnas

A cold rain drummed atop the roof of the hovercraft as its five passengers sat huddled beside the couch in the central cabin. Mouse peered over toward the cockpit and watched it streak across the windshield in huge, pattering droplets. Outside, it had grown dark, even darker than the shadows that already enclosed them after they had dropped their craft farther into the shelter of the forest for that night. The heavy rain and sudden approach of dusk blackened everything, except for the streaking rain falling with heavy thuds on the glass. *Too heavy for rain*, Mouse noted. She studied the paths of the drops, which dispersed sluggishly and then crystallized as they spread.

"It's actually freezing," Toma shivered, wrapping his hands around a steaming cup of tea. "Don't see that often where I'm from. Glad we're not out there tonight."

"For more reasons than that," Rhavin replied, sipping his own with a knowing, sober look.

"No mist though, thank the Unseen," Fraeda said, pouring another cup.

With a smile that Mouse could only describe as mischievous, Fraeda approached Linnea, the cup of tea held out before her. Their royal runaway positioned herself outside their familiar circle, back turned, arms crossed, and nose pointed at the ceiling, just as she had for the last few nights in the craft together. It was not that Linnea had been completely uncooperative – she offered information when asked and did as she was told – but she gave nothing more to the group than that. For the last few days, she had parked herself on the couch, glaring down her nose at them whenever they gathered, or staring with annoyance out the hovercraft windshield whenever they went anywhere. Of course, the annoyance might have come from the fact that they had not actually *made* it anywhere. Mouse had the worst sense of direction out of the rest of them, but even she knew they had been flying in circles, changing course constantly to avoid the creeping mists on all sides and the ever-frequent presence of Coalition patrols. And each day, as the red dawn rose out of the east, Mouse's optimism sank a little lower.

Will we ever make it out to Titans' Rest?

She watched as Fraeda gave Linnea a gentle prod. Mouse shook her head as Linnea sighed, turning only to give Fraeda an exasperated eye roll. Regardless, Fraeda's smile widened.

Why does she bother? Mouse wondered.

Linnea had little interest in anything like friendship. She had made that clear. But while that was just fine for Mouse, it would never do for Fraeda. The former Ameliorite novitiate saw every snub as a challenge, redoubling her efforts to win Linnea over.

Your patience is unbelievable, Mouse thought with a smirk.

"Come on," Fraeda said, as if coaxing a frightened kitten out from under a building. "It's good, and it's good for you. I promise."

With another sigh, Linnea took hold of the gift and took a polite sip. Whether she liked it or not, Mouse could not tell, but Linnea offered a graceful dip of her head before turning to her corner once again. Mouse raised her eyebrows in some surprise. It seemed even Linnea's best efforts to repel Fraeda's hospitality had its limits.

Fraeda winked at Mouse before settling back down and filling her own cup last. She sipped thoughtfully as she perused the map laid open across the floor. Her lips pursed in concentration as she pointed to a forested area on the map, north of the mistlands they had just escaped.

"If we are here... well, I believe we are. Anyway, we should be safe enough tonight. From Mistwolves, at least."

"I sure hope you're right," Toma muttered. "Would be nice not to run from the mists tonight. I'm getting tired of it."

Mouse shuddered, sparing a glance out the windshield one more time. No mists, but it would not be the first time they had thought they had found a safe haven, only to find a wall of mist barreling toward them. She frowned down at her bandaged leg.

At least I don't have to outrun them on foot this time.

Even after a few days of rest, Mouse didn't think she could if she tried. Still, with Fraeda's steady hand and the onboard med kit Linnea had retrieved for them, the worst of the damage had been bathed, sutured, and dressed. Fraeda also tested the leg for a break, but for as painful and gruesome as it was, she found the injury less severe than it looked. Not that Mouse could find comfort in that distinction. Break or not, she still couldn't walk on it. And as Fraeda fretted over the ever-present threat of infection, Mouse discovered firsthand that the Mistwolf's bark had nothing on its bite.

Not that its bark is anything to sneeze at, Mouse thought, recoiling.

Regardless, Fraeda was optimistic. "We're not clear just yet," Fraeda had said the last time she checked the wounds. "But this kit has the best medicine Coalition coin can buy. What a blessing!"

Well, that's one way to put it, Mouse sighed. *I've managed not to die. At least not today.*

She picked up her cup of tea and tentatively swirled a finger in the clay-colored water. Steam still wafted from the translucent surface, but it didn't burn her as it had her tongue at the first sip. She tried again, grimacing a little at its distinctly herbal taste. Mouse did not *hate* the flavor, but she did not love it, either. Back in the Priory, Sister Raelin had served her medicinal concoctions with a jar of honey, which Mouse had heaped into each cup in exuberant spoonfuls. Fraeda had insisted on continuing Sister Raelin's tea regimen on their journey, but she had regretfully left the honey jar behind. No one else seemed to care, but Mouse was beginning to dread tea time. She kept thinking of that sweet, liquid gold, wishing she had put more spoons of it directly in her mouth instead of her tea.

Mouse frowned down at the cup she had now, chancing a covert glance at Fraeda before daring to set it down again. But Fraeda had caught her eye, a ready smile waiting.

"You'll want to drink that now," Fraeda said brightly. "Before it gets too cold."

Mouse forced her mouth into a polite smile and quickly drained the cup. For someone accustomed to eating gruel packets daily, she was finding it harder not to gag on the bitter dregs. She managed one last gulp without a grimace. Toma grinned behind Fraeda, and Mouse shot him a warning look as soon as Fraeda returned to the map. He sipped with a dangerous smile.

"Anyway," Toma said, working hard to keep that smile from showing. "What's next?"

"We should wait this out," Rhavin nodded solemnly. "And the dark, too. I may be good, but alas, even I am not that good. Though I expect better than any of you."

"Tell us how you really feel," Toma deadpanned, but he grinned broadly. "Anyway, we'll want to leave by daybreak again, so we should get some sleep now."

He eyed Linnea before adding, "Still in shifts."

Linnea huffed.

"It's not going to matter what time we leave if we can't ever seem to get out of here," Rhavin said darkly.

"You're right. It's been too long already," Toma sighed. "We need a plan. A real one."

"That's just it. How do we get to..." Mouse paused, her eyes also darting to Linnea. "Where we are trying to go?"

She touched Fraeda's shoulder. "Any ideas on how do we go from here?"

"I was just working on that. I've gotten a good idea of where we ended up. I was thinking we might try through here." Fraeda traced a path along the outside of the wood that moved north. "Forests are dense in Elmnas. I'm not sure we could get a hovercraft through. But we might be able to go along the edge and find an easier way east."

Linnea turned slightly, glaring over her shoulder with an indignant snort. "You know, I *could* help if you would just tell me what you're up to."

"Why don't you help us, anyway?" Mouse retorted. "You said it yourself. It's your skin as much as ours if the Coats catch us."

"Even you aren't so dim to realize that I cannot. Not if you refuse to be truthful and tell me where you want to go," Linnea snapped back. "Look, Constan told me that any movement through Elmnas needs to be precise if you want to avoid Coalition detection. One wrong turn, one hour too far in any direction, and you will find yourselves in the middle of an outpost or a garrison. Especially as you draw closer to the free north's border. I can only assume that is some part of your plan."

Mouse glowered, but looked to her friends for direction. Seemingly as uncertain as she was, none of them offered much help. Mouse sighed.

"Say we *were* trying to get the free north. How would you get there?"

Linnea rolled her eyes and got to her feet. Toma stood as well, but she waved him off as she depressed a panel embedded in the hovercraft's interior wall. Mouse peered into it curiously as Linnea rummaged through the panel's contents. With a grunt, she tugged out a circular, black device that Mouse did not recognize. Linnea settled once again on the floor and tapped on the device's shining exterior.

Everyone leaned in as it sparked to life, its surface projecting a cloudy orb, smaller than that of a holograstone, but in some way Mouse could not understand, deeper. Linnea tapped again. The cloudy surface settled and stilled, flattening and expanding as it did so. As Mouse squinted into it, trying to decipher the image resolving there, Fraeda squealed with delight.

"Oh, it's a map!" She clapped her hands together. "A map of Elmnas! Why, I've never seen anything like this! It's amazing!"

Linnea smirked, and for a moment, looked exactly like her frightening aunt. "Coalition ingenuity at its finest. This device is directly calibrated to this craft, tracking its movements since we left Pardaetha."

"Would have been nice to know you had that up your sleeve five days ago," Toma grumbled.

"You should have asked," Linnea said smugly.
Toma crossed his arms as she tapped again, enlarging a blinking red point in what looked like a sea of glowing green.

"*Anyway*," she continued. "According to its calculations, this is where we are. And if you look here–"

Linnea tapped yet again, and the blinking red point shrunk as a cartographic landscape sprung up around it. Winding black and blue lines spread amid the trees and mountains, as well as red asterisks that glowed along them. "The blue ones are rivers, black are roads. And the red points are places with a known Coalition presence. As you can see
it won't be what one might call easy to get past them."

Mouse's mouth hung open. At the top of the image, the mapped roads and rivers ended abruptly. Between their blinking red dot and the uncharted area, which Mouse could only assume was the free north, red points stretched and snaked along its border in an almost unbroken line.

149

"That's all... Coalition?" Fraeda whispered.

Linnea nodded. "Grandfather is planning something. He has recently added to the forces here, and every day, more are coming. Father knew this. He had wanted to get me through before the surge was completed."

Despair rolled over Mouse. "We'll never get through. Not now."

"The surge is not finished, not just yet. It could still work."

Linnea dragged her finger across the device, causing the map to speed away from their blinking marker. The image moved west, and as it did so, the red asterisks became fewer. Linnea pointed to an area between two of the Coalition markers.

"I have been told that the western region is harder to manage. It is a rougher terrain, and it appears mostly unpeopled. The Coalition will have to build a supply line before it can begin establishing any real presence here."

"That's it, then. The only way," Toma said solemnly. "How long until we can get there?"

"From where you found me, Constan had said it was only about a day." Linnea frowned. "But I cannot say for certain."

"There's something I don't understand," Mouse said, puzzling down at the red dots along the border. "What's stopping the Coalition from just... flying over the free north's border? They've conquered the whole south without a problem."

"There is something... strange about the border," Linnea answered slowly. "I am not sure what it is. Father does not even know. All he could tell Constan is that we would find an impenetrable barrier. It is what Grandfather has been trying to break through for a century, but the free Elmlings have kept their secret."

Fraeda nodded in solemn agreement. "Not even the conquered tribes know how they have remained free. Many of us have tried to get there to find out. And... many of us have failed."

Fraeda's shoulders slumped as her eyes fell to the floor. Mouse patted her hand with as much assurance as she could, knowing all too well how horrific failed escape attempts could be. Fraeda took a deep breath before giving Mouse a grateful nod.

"So... how were *you* expecting to get in?" Toma asked.

Linnea offered an embarrassed shrug. "Our plan was to, in one sense, knock and see if anyone answered. Father believed they would see our value, even if they kept us under lock and key. It may make no sense to you, but I am safer as a prisoner of the Elmlings than as a traitor in the hands of Mother."

Toma and Mouse's eyes met. *Yikes*, he mouthed.

"I do not mean to interrupt, but this... this is troubling," Rhavin said, his eyes narrowing. He looked at the others. "If these are all military installments, then the Elmlings are not the only ones in for a bitter battle. Take a look. Here. The Coalition is moving into position along Heibeiath's border. Whatever Linnea might be, she was telling the truth about one thing. The Supreme Chancellor is planning an impressive offensive."

Rhavin pointed to the far southwestern portion of the displayed map, which now showed some of Heibeiath and Gormlaen's shared border. Red asterisks followed the curve.

"Of course I was telling the truth," Linnea snorted. "What do I gain from misleading you? You must also know the plan will proceed, with or without my assassination. Grandfather will find a way to make my sudden disappearance Heibeiath's fault. He will find a way to get what he really wants. He always does."

Toma let out a low whistle. "We're all in trouble."

"We need to warn my people, but I do not know how." Rhavin steepled his fingers in front of his lips in thought. His eyes darted to the holograstone. "Perhaps we could use that."

Linnea shook her head. "Too dangerous. Father told me not to, even under the worst circumstances. Mother might be able to find us if we did. Anyway, even if we got through to somebody who could help, why would they believe us?"

"Why not?" Mouse shrugged. "Rhavin is basically Heibeiathan royalty, right? He could explain it to them."

"No, Linnea speaks wisely," Rhavin agreed. His expression soured. "It might seem as if I, a lesser future *Imyr*, were trying to stage a coup by tricking the Grand *Imyr* into an unjust war. Such things have happened before. Also, my father believes me dead, if he still lives himself. He will have chosen another successor. I am nothing."

Rhavin folded his arms across his chest and looked away. Mouse pursed her lips, wishing she had not said anything at all.

"Well..." she cast about. "Would they believe ambassadors from the free Elmling tribes?"

"Huh," Toma scoffed. "That's assuming a lot. For one, that we can even get to them. And two, that they'll want to warn Heibeiath if we do."

He sighed as Mouse frowned back questioningly. "The Heibeiathans got off easy as far as Coalition rule goes. Gormlaean, Heibeiathan... they're all Coats to us in Maiendell. Sorry, Rhavin."

Rhavin shrugged dismissively. "It is understandable."

"Anyway, if *we* don't think fondly of Heibeiath, I can't really see the free tribes of Elmnas ready to buddy up. Am I right, Fraeda, or am I right?"

"I'm afraid so." She nodded soberly. "Our people do not forget the cruelties they've lived through, and all they continue to live through. They keep that memory alive, and I worry it's only for vengeance's sake. If the free north cares for their southern brothers and sisters, they will want... a reckoning. Many will never forgive Heibeiath's part in the Last War."

Fraeda tapped a finger against her teacup and stared past the others. Her brow wrinkled in thought.

"We have been given an impossible task as it is," Fraeda continued, choosing her words carefully. Her gaze returned to the others, first meeting Mouse with deliberate purpose. "But we have continued to overcome the impossible. The Unseen is with us. We have to try."

Mouse wrapped her arms around herself, watching the others as Fraeda's words hung in the air in the silence followed. All the members of the group, it seemed, were busy brooding over their own thoughts on the matter – although Linnea had initially rolled her eyes and murmured something to herself before staring into her tea. *The Unseen is with us.* Not long ago, Mouse would have sneered at that idea as well. But the events of their journey, even from the very day she escaped Misty Summit, had changed everything. The more she thought about it, the less sheer dumb luck could explain her survival through it all. She was convinced now, even if she could not understand it. *There is a reason. There has to be.*

Her fingers strayed to her pocket, once again feeling the familiar grooves and shape of the electronic chip Red had given to her in what seemed like a lifetime ago. Mouse gazed at the faces of those around her, faces that bore the different, proud, and tragic histories of their homelands, the ancestral imprints of their peoples, the marks of suffering both survived and inflicted. They were here for a reason. Even Linnea. Again, that fateful dream rushed into her mind, a voice echoing in the dark.

Will you follow?

"We're going to Titans' Rest," Mouse said.

Linnea frowned in confusion. "And where is that? *What* is that?"

"It's the easternmost point of Elmnas, and, we hope, the place where we have the best chance of reaching all the northern Elmling tribes at once. If we don't get there in time, we're not just looking at another war, as horrible as that will be. We're facing the end of Elmnas. Forever."

Mouse pulled the chip out of her pocket, holding it out flat in the palm of her hand for Linnea to see. Linnea squinted at it. No understanding of it seemed to register in her expression, but she nodded and pursed her lips.

"What does it do?"

"I think it... controls people. But worse. It hollows them out, makes them less than human. Makes them do whatever this thing wants them to do. The Coalition was testing them on the prisoners at Misty Summit."

Linnea whispered, struggling to speak as her mouth hung open. "Are you saying... Grandfather wants to... use these on dissidents? Elmlings? Turn them all into mindless slaves? Everyone?"

"Or kill them trying," Mouse nodded, her face grim. She closed her fist around the chip slowly, squeezing her fingers tight around its edges.

Linnea raised a hand to her mouth. "No wonder he sent the bounty huntress after you."

"I think we need your help, Linnea," Mouse said. "You know what the Coalition is capable of. You have an idea of what will happen if we don't reach the free tribes. I think... you are here for a reason. You can tell the rebellion leaders what you know, and they will believe you. Exactly because of who you are. You can help us save them."

"And not just them," Toma added, nodding toward Rhavin. "Maybe the rest of the world, too."

"I am not sure you understand what you are asking," Linnea said in a low whisper. "I knew you were heading north. That's where I wanted to go, after all, to hide. Even if it meant as a prisoner. But if I speak, if I work willingly to bring down Grandfather... I am no longer a mere runaway. I will be committing treason. I will be a traitor to Gormlaen, a traitor of the highest order."

"Does it matter?" Mouse asked. "Your family was trying to kill you, anyway."

"I know," Linnea said uncertainly. "I mean, I thought I knew what it meant. It is just that... if I go all on my own, without Constan or the others, to take responsibility for me, I have no excuse. Mother may have killed me regardless, but if she catches up with me now... You must understand that death alone will not suffice as punishment. She will do something far worse."

Linnea took a shuddering breath, composing herself before leveling a fierce glare at each of them. "Besides, you may not understand this, but I still have a duty to my people. Father taught me to love them, to govern them well, and to do my best for the good of Gormlaen. Can I be loyal to my people if I go willingly to their enemies?"

"We've spent time with some of your people," Toma said, exchanging a knowing look with Mouse. "I think your common Gormlaeans might feel a little differently about that."

This gave Linnea pause, and Mouse wondered if she had ever even spent time with anyone outside the walls of her palace before. And Mouse was sure no unworthy commoner had been *inside* them with her. All at once, Mouse recalled Woldyff's grandiose bow when she first met him in the sewer dwelling of the Jackal Syndicate. She imagined him doing the same thing in Linnea's presence, the whole of the Coalition Assembly behind her. Mouse couldn't help smirking at the thought.

"And think of what it will mean," Fraeda added. "If you come to offer help and peace. It seems to me you can never return to your life as it was before. Why not try building a better one, a new future, for you *and* for the world? A future far better than the one your grandfather built over a hundred years ago?"

Linnea shook her head in disbelief. "You see that this is simply preposterous, right? All of it. It's impossible."

"Weren't you listening?" Toma grinned. "We're all in for the impossible."

17

Hiiri.

Mouse stirred, eyes still closed and thoughts lost in that drowsy, empty place between sleep and wake. All senses remained dulled, resisting the pull toward alertness. But something pricked at the back of her mind; the memory of a dream, the call of a familiar voice... something. Mouse was already forgetting. She sunk back into the darkness.

Hiiri, it's time to go.

Images resolved in the darkness. Mouse opened her eye, just enough to see who was talking. There was a man above her, a man with one hand on her shoulder and the other lifting her from her bed of furs. But Mouse was not afraid. She knew him. All of her life, she had loved him. Papa.

Don't wake her, Brehn. There isn't time to explain.

Mouse peered up at the other speaker and smiled drowsily. Mama. Mama wrapped her arms around her instead and pulled her gently from the bed. Mouse nestled into her arms, laying her head against Mama's chest. Her heartbeat thumped fast, but it did not bother Mouse. She was safe.

Papa whispered in a low, urgent voice. *She ought to wake. You can't carry her this whole time. Hiiri, you've got to be brave. You must wake.*

Mouse frowned. What was Papa talking about?

They're here. Papa's voice grew stern and scary. *They're here, Niiri. Run. RUN!*

She felt Mama move fast. Out the door, into the cool, night air. But the air grew warm, too warm. Shouts filled her ears. Mouse looked up.

Mama gazed down at her, her brows knitted with concern. *Sleep. Go to sleep.*

Mouse jolted upright, the explosion that always came hurtling her out of her mother's arms and out of her familiar dream. She rubbed her eyes and searched wildly. The searing light was gone, but stars lingered in her vision and her body trembled with its lasting impression. The blinding points faded, and Mouse found herself where she had been when she first fell asleep in the darkened cabin of a sleek Coalition hovercraft. In the soft, yellow glow of its interior running lights, Mouse could also see four people-shaped lumps rising and falling beneath heaps of blankets and bedrolls.

She watched them, glad her nightmare had not awakened them, but unable to shake the uneasy feeling that maybe it should have. Her father's voice lingered in her head. *It's time to go. And what else did he say?* Mouse squeezed her eyes shut to concentrate. *What did he call me?*

Hiiri.

A name, her name, the one she could not remember for so long. Its force hit her like a hurricane, whipping up a frenzy of emotions. It rang in her ears as if her father's urgent voice had just spoken it, calling to her. *Hiiri.* Tears stained Mouse's cheeks. She wanted to shout it out, jump, clap, and cry. She was more than a number in

Misty Summit's endless supply of bodies, more than the iteration of herself she had to invent to survive. Mouse had a name. And she was loved.

But with that revelation, a strange sense of conflict stirred inside her. *I know my name*, she thought, *but is that really who I am?*

It was a problem she kept having. She might have been Hiiri, but she was still very much Mouse. Her life after memory lost had continued, perhaps in a way unthinkable to the life of before. She had become someone quite different from that innocent, happy half-Elmling, half-Samrasine girl. Still, the past kept breaking in on the present, entangling Mouse's understanding of what was true and what had been lies. But *neither* were lies. Her brow wrinkled with concerted effort as she tried to reconcile those realities. Who was she, really?

She could almost believe her identity issue was easier to deal with at the Summit, in the days when the dream never changed and she lived without the burden of knowledge. These days, of course, a new dream seemed to come to her every night, and each brought a chaotic torrent of truth that both complicated and clarified her journey.

And through it, she could more or less piece together her last day and night with her parents. By now, she understood why she was alone: her parents had believed she was the Harbinger, the prophesied maiden who would herald the return of the Phoenix and of Elmnas' restored kingdom. They believed she, not any other girl in her home, the village Shomroh, fulfilled that last oracle of the Guardian Keeper Alvilde. And when the Coalition razed her home to the ground and murdered her people because of it, her parents had done everything they could to smuggle her out alive.

Mouse had survived, somehow. The parts before and after that night still had not surfaced in her mind. As always, she wished more than anything to know the full story, to truly understand the happiness of who she was before, to comprehend how she could have possibly ended up in a Coalition prison and experimental torture facility. And all this, without even the Supervisors of that dreadful place knowing where she had really come from. But even as Mouse longed for her memories to return, she dreaded what each new remnant would reveal, and how she would have to learn to piece herself together anew. Far worse, each night as she laid down to sleep, Mouse knew she would once again relive an unspeakable horror. Each night, she saw what she could only assume were the final moments of her mother and father; every night, an atrocity that changed her and her life forever. And yet she welcomed the nightmare, if only to hear their tender voices, to feel safe – even for just a breath – anything to know their enduring, sacrificial love. And she loved them, too. Fiercely, hopefully, painfully; she loved her parents, her people, and a past that was stolen from her. For them, and for others who had walked with her on the way, she would finish this impossible journey. For them, Mouse would get to Titans' Rest... somehow.

Sleep had fled completely from Mouse. She extracted herself from her blankets and tip-toed past her still-slumbering companions. A growing unease settled in the pit of her stomach, and not just because of the usual traumatic contents of her dreams. Papa's voice was still echoing in her head. *You've got to be brave*, he said. *You must wake.*

She managed to make it to the front of the hovercraft, but not at all as gracefully or as quietly as she had hoped. Her wounded leg had grown stiff in the night, and though feeling far better than it had before, Mouse winced whenever she tried to put weight on it. She reached out for the captain's chair as soon as she arrived, leaning on it for support as she gently massaged her leg above the bandages. With effort, she heaved herself into the chair, and careful not to kick any of the controls, propped her leg up on the dashboard. Mouse stared out at the inky darkness and exhaled a shuddering breath. Her heart raced, and it wasn't just from the little trek across the hovercraft's cabin. Something felt wrong. She tossed a glance over her shoulder, wondering why no one else seemed to feel it, too.

Her companions slept on, huddled together beside the soft glow of the floor-level lights. Someone was even snoring. Mouse squinted suspiciously at them, the ominous foreboding growing. Even the semi-dark chamber of the hovercraft seemed eerier than when they first came aboard. There was a far better reason for that then; they did not know what new danger awaited them onboard. Now they had found it safe, or safe enough at least, but Mouse felt even more uneasy about the lack of caution now. Her friends slept peacefully, comfortably, unaware of whatever danger might lurk in the unfamiliar shadows.

But what is the danger? Why in the world do I feel like this?

Mouse focused once again on the darkened windshield. It had stopped sleeting, but now and then, as the wind gusted and receded, water splattered against the glass from the trees overhead. Far above, the wine-red clouds rolled in and out of each other, always moving but never breaking. Mouse inched closer to the glass and peered out at ground level. The hovercraft rested in a little grove, hemmed in by creaking pines, holly, and juniper bushes. All was quiet, except for the intermittent blasts of wind. Mouse watched as the branches rippled, then paused, then rippled again. She found herself shivering with them.

Hiiri.

Mouse looked around in surprise. *Did I really just hear that?*

Hiiri, it's time to go.

She was hearing it, alright: a voice, a familiar voice, intruding upon her thoughts and rattling around in her brain. And each time it spoke, it grew louder and more insistent.

"I'm going crazy," Mouse whispered, but a pit formed in her stomach. The voice's warning still rang, striking like a clock ticking away the seconds until cataclysm.

Hiiri!

Mouse jumped. Without another thought, she depressed the hovercraft's starter. It purred to life, and Mouse threw switches in an almost trance-like state as it continued to power on. Headlights flared to life, but she quickly doused them. In their brief, blinding flash, Mouse thought she saw something silhouetted against the trees.

Rustling and startled snorts from the cabin reached her ears as Mouse grabbed hold of the steering. The craft elevated, whirring as she maneuvered it backward out of the grove.

Toma's groggy voice groaned behind her. "What's going on?"

She did not answer. Mouse turned the craft carefully, her breathing shallow as the ticking countdown in her head inched closer to zero.

"It would appear we are moving," Rhavin answered. "Now... why is that? That is the real question."

"Thanks, Captain Literal," Toma sighed heavily.

"Mouse!" Fraeda gasped. "What are you doing?"

Feet pounded down into the cockpit. Mouse kept her eyes forward as bodies squeezed in. She could feel her friends beside her, hear their hard breathing and confused shouting. And still, they seemed miles away, voices coming to her as if through the fog of a dream. She could only stare ahead as the craft glided quietly backward.

"She can't hear us! She's in one of those trances again!"

"Well, do something!"

Mouse stared on, slapping away the hand that was reaching for the steering. The craft angled up a slope, and Mouse sped up, klaxons exploding in her brain. Arms reached around her; hands shook her shoulders.

"Mouse, please, you need to snap out of it. Mouse!"

"Yikes, those boulders– Mouse, look out!"

She slammed down on the brakes, halting the craft in mid-air. Her friends rocketed forward, each of them gasping as they caught hold of whatever they could to keep from flying into the windshield. Mouse flicked switches quickly, and the craft drifted down to earth. Its whirring died, and a sudden silence filled the air. Hands trembling and sweating, Mouse rubbed her eyes and temples. She blinked. Slowly, finally, she looked around, gazing into the astonished, bewildered, and frightened faces of Toma, Rhavin, and Fraeda. She had to turn fully around to see a red-faced Linnea, gripping the captain's chair with white knuckles and heaving in agitation.

"Are you *insane?*" she asked, pushing wild, tangled hair out of her eyes.

It seemed the same question was on the minds of everyone else, as well. Mouse clutched her temples again and shook her head. The alarm bells had died away, the voice of her father gone from her recent memory. She looked up, searching for an answer, when Fraeda gasped again.

"Look!" Fraeda pointed out the windshield.

Everyone turned, and Mouse's stomach plummeted once again. Down below, in the little grove where moments before the group had slept soundly, a raging fire blazed. The silhouettes of small figures moved around the inferno, the unmistakable shape of long-barreled energy rifles pointed ahead of them.

"Coats?" Toma asked incredulously. "There's just no way. They couldn't know we were here. In *this*. How did they find us?"

The squadron continued searching the burning trees, looking just as confused as Mouse. She wondered what they must have seen. One moment, their craft was there, lights flashing; the next, they were gone. Mouse's senses awakened, the peculiar numbness that had spread into each limb now receding. She unclenched her death grip on the steering and slumped back into the chair, a trembling weakness taking over.

"I doubt they expected us," Rhavin said ominously. "The Coalition had their fugitive princess and state traitors in mind."

Linnea raised a hand to her mouth. A tumult of terror and amazement filled her large, widening eyes as they turned to Mouse.

"You... you saved us," she whispered. "You saved *me*. How did you know? How could you possibly know?"

Mouse swallowed hard, finding her mouth suddenly dry. "I didn't."

"She is a true seer," Fraeda said in awe. "Just like the Guardian Keepers of old."

No one replied. They watched the flare of flames stretch up into the sky. Mouse's thoughts raced.

Me? she thought weakly. *A Keeper?*

Instinctively, she reached down and grazed the dagger that never left her hip. Heat rose from it as if the fire blazing down the hill was burning beneath her extended fingertips. Hand trembling, she grasped the hilt, covertly pulling the blade from its holster. The runic patterns danced in a shifting sea of brilliant blue-green.

Was that so crazy?

As much as Mouse tried to pretend it was not true, something extraordinary was happening to her. What she had once called dreams had become memories, and those memories were now transforming into something new altogether, something that inhabited the present and even shaped the future. These dreams, these visions... they seemed a living thing, a thing wholly other than herself. They spoke and even acted... through *her*. The thought rattled Mouse. Was an outside force guiding her? Or worse, was it controlling her, forcing Mouse to behave in ways she could not avoid? And if that was true, what purpose did it harbor? Was it an evil, deceiving her, driving her and her friends deeper into danger until they could not escape? Was she wrong... about everything?

The light of the dagger caught her eye once more, its heat no longer a blaze but a comforting warmth. She watched the glow rise and recede, swirling in reflection of her troubling thoughts. But the longer she looked, the stronger and calmer she felt. It settled as she did, its brilliant hue diffusing into a softer glow. And something occurred to her. This dagger, the once-possession of an ancient Keeper, had come into her hands before Thunder Run. *Before* her first trance. And it had begun to respond to *her*; not just her touch, but her thoughts and emotions as well. It was almost as if... this gift from a Guardian of Elmnas had an innate life all its own, and it was sharing it with her.

Mouse did not understand the connection, but it washed over her like a wave that the impossible prescience and supernatural ability must come from the dagger itself. And it had continued to keep her alive, despite her best efforts to the contrary.

It was no accident. The Cardanthium blade had chosen *her*.

Just like a Guardian, she thought. *Just like Blade.*

Mouse drew a shaky breath as she slowly slid the dagger back into place, full of wonder and terror at the idea.

A Keeper. Mouse shook her head in disbelief. *What will the others think of me?*

She looked around, but everyone stared at the grove in flames instead of at her. Well, almost everyone. Toma considered her with unnerving intensity, his face drawn with a mixture of warring emotions. Mouse shifted uncomfortably as he glanced suspiciously at the dagger.

What does he see that I can't? she wondered. *What will it mean... for us?*

Toma lifted his gaze to hers again. The intensity had softened, if only a little, and Mouse saw in his eyes a concern that was not out of the ordinary. A concern, she realized, he had reserved only for her. Toma leaned forward and gently stretched out his hand. Mouse clenched her sweating palms on her thighs as his fingers hesitated above hers.

"Are you... okay?" he asked, his brow creasing. He rested his hand on her arm.

Mouse nodded, finding it hard to speak or to look away. She searched his face, feeling the weakness and cold shock melt into warmth the longer she gazed. Toma, too, seemed to relax the longer they remained that way, the intensity and worry fading into a smile that extended to his angular cheeks and tender eyes. Mouse inhaled sharply, astounded by the sudden urge to reach up and brush her fingers against his lips and his face.

"Ah, well." Rhavin cleared his throat. "What now?"

Mouse blinked rapidly. Rhavin watched her with one eyebrow conspicuously raised.

"Um, I–" Mouse looked at Fraeda for help, who, despite everything, simply looked back with the hint of a smile.

"They cannot remain here for long," Linnea chimed in, still peering intently at the Coalition figures milling below. She tapped an index finger against her lips and frowned. "What *are* they doing? There is nothing in the grove. They obliterated it."

"Maybe they need evidence," Toma suggested. "A piece of hovercraft or something. Some proof to report back. The mission is over and done with."

"They will not find any," Rhavin said grimly. "We must get far from here."

"Not yet." Linnea raised a finger. "Any movement or noise is certain to draw their attention. We have to wait."

A trouble silence settled over them before Toma abruptly ended it.

"Okay, but seriously, how *did* they find us?" He asked.

Linnea did not immediately answer, but her face paled. She turned, scrambling out of the cockpit. Mouse watched her disappear into the cabin, thump around, and then rush back. Linnea held the holographic map device aloft.

"How good is your memory, Fraeda?"

Fraeda took a sharp breath. "Um, above average."

Linnea flipped it over, pried open a small panel with her fingernail, and pulled out its insides. She held up a tiny electronic chip, much like the one Mouse carried with her, before snapping it in two.

"There. That should do it," Linnea breathed.

"A tracking device?" Mouse said incredulously. "You knew it was there, and you didn't tell us?"

Linnea looked like she was going to be sick. "I did not think of it. It was... how Father was to find us, if he could escape. And even if he did not, if he was found out, he had a plan for the link to be destroyed. I hope I am wrong, but..."

She wrung her hands and stared out the windshield.

... but your father is in trouble, Mouse thought, and it hit her like a punch in the gut. *Another loss, another sacrifice. How much more can we endure?*

Mouse slumped into the chair, watching as Fraeda reached over to pat Linnea's arm. Linnea flinched, but she gave Fraeda a curt nod of acknowledgment at the proffered comfort. Together, they watched the grove burn, orange tongues of fire reaching up to the red sky. Linnea wiped at the corner of her eye and breathed.

"I hope against hope I am wrong."

18

At least an hour ticked by before the Coalition detachment receded from view. Mouse, Toma, Fraeda, Rhavin, and Linnea crowded into the front of their own craft, all that time watching as dark figures searched the forest and hills around the smoldering grove. They spoke few words in the last hour, instead waiting as rigidly and silently as soldiers before the battle begins.

But even as the Coalition search party roamed the area, climbing and scouring their hill, they never made it to the ridge where the craft waited in hiding. All of this, Mouse understood quickly, was a verifiable miracle. She had blindly piloted the craft through a rocky outcropping, avoiding the sharp teeth of angry rocks and navigating into a crevice among the slope's boulders. And quite a park job it was: less than two feet separated the craft from each of the solid walls of rock. An overhang jutting above them offered even less clearance. But it had been the perfect place, perhaps the only place, the Coalition would not see. The difficult terrain and darkness of the night blanketed them from view, at least for now.

Yet as the flames in the forest below died down and the deep shadows of the late hour wore on, the search party wearied. In groups of two and three, the Coalition soldiers struggled back toward the forest and disappeared behind puffs of smoke and intact trees. Far off, the glaring headlights of a Coalition hovercraft streaked through the limbs of birch, ash, and pine, but these too soon faded, leaving everything once again in darkness.

A collective sigh filled the cockpit. Mouse exhaled shakily and finally dared to look around. Toma and Rhavin, who had been leaning against opposite sides of the cockpit chairs, stretched aching limbs and rubbed sleepy eyes, but grinned at each other in the dark. Having moved to Mouse's left, Toma reached down to give her shoulder a friendly, reassuring squeeze. Fraeda leaned over from the other chair, her arm extended for an exuberant side hug.

"You did it!" she said enthusiastically, although her voice quavered.

"She did," Linnea added, her tone more subdued. Sharing the other chair with Fraeda, she leaned forward to offer Mouse an impressed nod. "I can hardly believe it. Indeed, if I was not a witness, I would not have believed. I have never seen anything like that in my life."

"Don't get used to it," Mouse grinned. "I don't think I can just turn it on whenever I want."

Linnea frowned in thought. "I don't understand. Is this why the Coalition is after you? Because you have these strange... abilities?"

Mouse shook her head. "No, I... I wasn't anyone special. I just know things. Things I'm not supposed to know."

At this, Linnea raised an eyebrow, but said nothing more.

"Stop selling yourself short," Toma said, sounding both annoyed and proud at the same time. "And this isn't the first time this has happened. I think it's going to keep happening. We need to figure out why."

Mouse's cheeks grew hot as she looked up in surprise at Toma.

"Uh, I- well–" Mouse stuttered. Flustered, she looked down at her hands and jammed them into her pockets. "It only seems to happen when we're in real trouble, right? But we can't count on that, can we? At some point, our luck is going to run out."

"It's happening because you *are* the Harbinger," Fraeda said pointedly. "It isn't luck. The Unseen is guiding us."

"You don't know that," Mouse muttered. Sudden anger sprang up inside her. "And even if I am, it doesn't mean we're safe. It doesn't mean a whole lot to me if all these people... all my friends... if they all keep dying. Does the Unseen care about that? Sure doesn't seem like it. Sure doesn't seem like the Unseen is much good for anything."

The words tumbled out of Mouse, her fears and hurts tumbling out with them. She could not stop the unbidden wave of bitterness that followed. First her parents, then Red, Blade... who else would meet their end because of her? A new guilt, that of the fate of Linnea's father, now hounded her. She knew everyone would say she wasn't responsible – how could she be responsible? But that didn't matter. Terrible things kept happening when she was around. Death trailed her like a vulture. Everywhere she looked, it was there. How could she believe that there was something *else* out there, something good, something walking with her, caring about her, after all that had come to pass? It seemed the next loss was only a matter of time. Who would it be next? Rhavin? Fraeda? Even... Toma?

Mouse crossed her arms, covering her fear with pointed defiance. She glared at Fraeda, expecting a platitude, but it did not come. Pain clouded Fraeda's face instead. Mouse lowered her arms slowly.

She's got just as many fears and hurts as me. The realization brought a wave of shame. *More than me. She remembers everything she's lost. But she still believes in something, and I've gone ahead and made a point of mocking it.*

Mouse now wished she could suck those frustrated words back in, but the damage was done. Fraeda chewed her lip and looked down at the floor.

"Whatever it might be, we ought to be more careful," Rhavin said with a flippant shrug. "And perhaps that means it is time to go on."

Mouse nodded and extracted herself from the captain's chair.

"You're right. You should get us out of here, Rhavin. I'm not so sure I'm actually any good at flying."

Rhavin flashed a rakish smile as he took to his post, immediately getting the hovercraft online as he hopped into the seat. Mouse squeezed past and dragged herself out of the cockpit, now suddenly aware of just how hot and stuffy it was getting in there. Linnea followed close behind, yawning.

"Yeah, most of us should get some sleep," Toma said. "Fraeda, you want to lay down? I can help Rhavin navigate."

"That's okay," Fraeda said quietly. "I'd rather stay up for a bit, I think. I know Elmnas better than anyone else, anyway, and it seems I'm the only one who has Linnea's map in her head. I think I'll be useful and help Rhavin avoid more trouble for now."

Mouse tramped back to her sleeping bag and slumped onto the floor, pangs of guilt hitting her hard. She tried not to make eye contact as Linnea and Toma followed, but at the very least, she needn't worry about Linnea. Gliding past and on to the back of the hovercraft, presumably to use the latrine, Linnea did not acknowledge anyone. Whatever worries she had earlier, Linnea once again concealed them beneath her usual air of haughty confidence. Even so, Mouse knew better. The fault lines were showing.

Give it another day, Mouse thought. *She can't keep that act up forever.*

Toma plopped down next to her as the hovercraft engine purred. It rocked slightly as it lifted, and over the sound of whirring Mouse could hear Fraeda advising Rhavin on how to exit the tight alcove without further scraping up the sides of the craft. Mouse sighed, grimacing as she arranged her blankets.

"It's your leg, huh? Still bothering you?" Toma asked.

"What?" Mouse looked up to find him sitting cross-legged beside her, watching intently.

Her leg felt mostly fine and had little to do with why she felt terrible. She nodded anyway, trying to mask her guilt as she stretched the wounded leg out atop her blankets and rubbed above the calf.

"Oh, um, yeah. A bit."

"That was the scariest moment of my life," Toma said seriously, leaning forward.

Mouse smirked despite herself. "Really? You wouldn't rank Thunder Run or our romp with Eris above that? Or how about that time in that alley in Lilien with the Sentinels after us? That was just as bad, right?"

Toma shrugged, looking down at hands that fiddled nervously in his lap. "Yeah, that was all pretty terrifying. But... those other times... I didn't see you almost die. There is nothing worse than that."

Mouse couldn't think of anything to say. She just stared at him, her heart thumping as she tried to work out exactly what he meant. In that death-defying moment, or any of the others they had experienced together, Mouse had never once thought Toma would be more concerned for her life than his own. But *he* had been the one to pull her up into the hovercraft just as the Mistwolf had closed in, hadn't he? He was there, struggling without a hope, as the monster ripped into her and tried to drag her once again into the mists below. But Toma had saved her. Somehow, he managed to get her free. Against all odds, he staved off those nightmarish jaws, expelled the horrors from the cabin and even closed the hovercraft door. She was alive because of him.

Mouse took a deep breath as she picked at the stray threads of her blanket. "I can't believe I never thanked you. For saving my life, I mean. Well, you keep doing that, don't you? You don't know what it means, really. But I wish..."

Toma looked up, gazing at her with glassy eyes as she searched for words. *I wish you wouldn't waste your time on me*, was what Mouse wanted to say. *I'm not worth it, Toma*. But she couldn't bring herself to say it, not when those same glassy, beautiful eyes watched her with such concern, such... admiration.

"You don't need to thank me. I'd be a pretty poor friend otherwise," Toma grinned. His grin faded, however, and he cleared his throat. "Listen, I've been meaning to say something. And now is as good of a time as any. Mouse..."

Mouse leaned toward him, her heart now jumping into her throat. She tried to swallow, to push down the lump there and keep the frantic beating of her heart in her chest. Toma inhaled slowly, avoiding her eyes as cast around for words.

"Uh," he croaked.

Mouse would have said the same if she could speak. Her mouth had gone dry, and she had to strain to hear Toma over the thumping in her ears. Toma took a sharp, steadying breath, and this time, looked directly at her. Determination etched his features. Mouse felt all the world had stopped around her.

"It's just this, okay? I–"

But Toma stopped short, snapping his head toward Linnea as she returned to the cabin. Confusion spread across Linnea's face as he stared at her.

"What?" she said, tossing her now sleek, fully brushed hair. Self-consciously, Linnea hid something small behind her back. Mouse squinted at what she thought was an old stuffed lion, the ragged fibers of its ruddy mane still poking out guiltily from Linnea's concealed hand.

"Nothing," he muttered, missing Linnea's scowl as she plopped into her sleeping bag. He turned back to Mouse. "I, um, just want to say you need to be more careful. What you did out there was really brave, and it probably saved our lives, but... it was also really dangerous. Just... just be careful, okay?"

A stab of disappointment went through Mouse, but she nodded understandingly. "Yeah, okay. I'll try."

"Good. Great. Okay. Awesome." Toma clapped his hands together and sighed. "Well, time to sleep."

And without another word, Toma dropped down onto his bedroll and curled up on his side, facing away from Mouse.

"Right," Mouse ventured tentatively. "Yeah. Good night."

She turned over, her thoughts a confused muddle as she gingerly nestled herself in the blanket nest she had made on the hovercraft floor. The nervous knot that had formed in her stomach as she and Toma spoke was untangling, but it wasn't making her feel any better. A nagging sense of words left unsaid, of business unfinished, of desperate longing replaced it instead. Her heart ached, and she was beginning to understand why. Mouse sneaked a glance over her shoulder, watching the contour of his side rise and fall as he drifted to sleep. Watching, and wishing he'd turn over and speak to her once more. Why did she feel so differently about him than she did about anyone else? Why did his gaze make her fall to pieces, his touch strangle the breath out of her, his laugh lighten every dark place she had ever gone? And was it really possible that he felt the same way? For a moment, it had seemed so... and for a moment, Mouse dared to hope.

Don't be stupid, she thought. *You don't know what he meant to say. You don't know anything about boys. You barely understand yourself. Or even your friends.*

Fraeda's crestfallen face flashed through her mind, and the guilt began anew. The stomach knot returned, along with a sick feeling that only stirred the muddy uncertainty filling her. *Why can't I get anything right?*

Mouse cringed and buried her face in her bedding. The floor vibrated and whined beneath them. With her eyes closed, Mouse could feel the swaying movement of the craft as it sped and weaved down the slope. From there, she hoped, it would be straight on to their next destination. The craft rocked. She imagined this was what journeying by sea must be like, bobbing along the waves as the wind pulled the ship where it willed. Mouse had never seen an ocean; she could only cobble together an image from the vivid descriptions Rhavin and Toma had offered from their own experiences, and even then, all she could ever imagine was a hazy body of water; deep, dark churning with great flecks of foam, staring back at her with its ominous beauty, swallowing her in exhilarating incomprehension, a majestic terror.

Each day outside of Misty Summit felt like that swirling sea in her mind. The world beyond those prison walls brimmed with darkness; a darkness so deep and bewildering that Mouse wondered why she had bothered jumping into it in the first place. And yet she could not ignore the beauty she had found – conviction, hope, and friendship – the light that shimmered over those tempestuous waters and perhaps showed its depths not as deep as she had believed.

The hovercraft whirred a little louder but in steady progression as it gained speed. Mouse supposed they must have come to more even ground, for it no longer rocked from side to side or nosed slightly downward. Weariness crept in, heavy now as the interruption to her sleep and the excitement of the night had passed. In the quiet space between consciousness and dreams, Mouse felt once again the stupidity of her sharp words to Fraeda. She yawned, resolving to apologize when she woke. Another thought edged in with that resolution. Mouse drifted off, Toma's searching gaze in her mind.

In the morning, she thought, succumbing to sleep. *I'll speak to him then.*

19

67th of Sun's Wane
  The Desolation's Edge
  Heibeiath

"What is this, desert dweller?" Yasi said, her gaze shifting to Blade. "Speak."

The nomad appraised her in an emotionless, insectoid fashion, his bug-likeness only heightened by the reflective goggles. He shook his head.

"You have no part in this," he replied. "My business is with the Elmling."

Yasi's gaze hardened as she rolled the *boka* off her shoulder and gripped it upright, its butt resting on the ground. "His business is now mine. The *Co'atyti* has made it so. Now speak."

What does she mean by that? Blade thought. His brow creased in confusion, and as he glanced at the others, he could see surprise registering with them as well. The Dusty One, however, simply shrugged.

"So be it," he said, turning his bug-like lenses toward Blade. "The deal is changed."

Blade stared into the lenses as Woldyff and Fox bristled. He knew what it meant, given the nomad's first words to Yasi: a new, far higher price and another devastating problem for the Syndicate. His own frustration rose, but Blade pushed it down, his face and demeanor unmoved.

"Why?" Blade asked.

The Dusty One cocked his head. "Do you know what is waiting for you in the canyon?"

"I have my suspicions."

"A Coalition squadron. High-quality soldiers. Even nicer armor than the ones you sold to me. Their captain met me on my journey here. He asked if I had spoken to an Elmling carrying two green swords."

His face tilted toward Blade's hands, resting on the pommels of *Av'tal* and *Ub'rytal*, before looking up again.

Blade thought he knew the answer to the question, but he asked anyway. "And what did you tell him?"

At this, the nomad's mouth quirked. "I said yes, I had. That I was contracted to escort him across to the Desolation."

"Why you–" Woldyff lunged forward, but Blade threw his hand across his chest.

"Wait," Blade growled, but his own ire was rising. He took a sharp breath before turning back to the nomad. "So, he offered you much gold to betray us."

The Dusty One smirked. "Double the worth of what you sold me. And if I brought in your companions, Cardanthium on top."

"Ah," Fox spoke, her unsheathed blades glowing threateningly. "So now you want us to call the bet?"

Blade lowered his voice. "You must know we have nothing left with which to bargain."

"You do not have what I want," the Dusty One replied coolly. "But the Coats do."

"Enough empty talk!" Yasi snarled. "Speak to us plainly."

Unfazed, the nomad continued to stare at Blade. "Given the events, our former contract is insufficient. But it can be amended. Get me the Coalition hovercraft in which your pursuers have come, and my people shall bring yours to safety. Refuse, and I leave you here."

"We gave you a fortune," Woldyff said through gritted teeth. "What about that, eh?"

Once again, the nomad shrugged. "It is the price of risky business."

Fox swung her swords with menacing prowess, a smile that meant murder on her lips. "And what comes of the deal if I strike off your head where you stand and we take our chances?"

But the Dusty One did not flinch. The goggled eyes turned slowly toward Fox.

"Do not be fooled by appearances, wrathful stranger. The odds are against you."

The nomad gestured toward the gorge, where, as if on cue, something slinked out of it. Blade squinted at the shape rising from its edge, which could have been the red stone itself had it not been moving. Only after its whole body emerged, now visible beneath the saddle of its Heibeiathan rider, did Blade begin to comprehend it. A reptilian head swerved from side to side, its copper irises with long, black slits for pupils unblinking in their direction. Its lissome body stretched on and on, finally terminating in a strong, whip-like tail. The creature crawled low to the ground as it came out of the canyon, and its great dagger-like claws punctured the earth and crumbled rock at the cliff's edge. But as the creature came level, the squat legs lengthened, and the creature lifted. Both body and rider stood as high off the ground as if it were a horse. A forked tongue slipped between its sharp rows of needle-like teeth. Involuntarily, Blade recoiled.

"*Shalas* are faster than horses and can scale hundreds of feet of canyon wall," the Dusty One continued. "Only my people prefer them. It takes great courage to ride a *shala*, for they do rather like the taste of human flesh."

"How many of them you got?" Woldyff asked, looking at the creature with open horror and disgust.

"Enough to take your people across the gorge. Much of our herd. They wait here, where the Coats do not see."

Fox sighed and pulled back her swords. "Point taken, I suppose."

Blade rubbed his beard as he turned back to the nomad. "Even if I were to agree to the new terms, how do you propose I fulfill it? A squadron of specialized Coats against the three of us and whatever people you are willing to spare gives us little hope of success."

"Four of us," Yasi corrected.

Fox inclined her head with a sly smirk. "And yet another joins our little band of warriors. Are you certain, forest dweller?"

Yasi gave a curt nod. "If it is as you say, then I must. To protect the Chychan, and preserve my home. Perhaps I die, but I would not do it cornered like a common rat. Small though the Chychan be to the *Co'atyti,* though they swat our peoples like wasps... Still, they shall feel my sting first."

"Even so," Blade said, giving Yasi an appreciative nod. "We are outnumbered."

The Dusty One again gestured to the *shala.* "My people keep their word. You shall each have mounts, as we agreed. I shall also be with you. I know where the Coats have set their trap. We can spring ours before theirs."

Woldyff threw up his hands angrily. "This is suicide, is what it is. Not a single one of us will make it! What do you take us for, nomad?"

Again, the Dusty One only shrugged. "You need to cross. I need the craft. I am offering a deal."

Blade threw his arm across Woldyff's chest again as his friend surged forward. Woldyff fought against the restraint, eyes bulging as he jabbed a finger toward the nomad and shouted.

"You're offerin' nothing but a fraud! You don't give a mite what happens to us! Who's to say you ain't in with Coats even now? You're tryin' to make us come quietly, herd us into that canyon like a big ol' lot of stupid cattle, eh? Well, I ain't buyin' it, and I'll throttle you before you take me in! Gerrof me!"

By now, Blade had twisted to stand in front of Woldyff, pushing him back with the flat of his hand. Woldyff pushed back hard, with force enough to cause any other man to topple over or stumble. But Blade stood firm. Woldyff gave an angry snort and threw up his hands in frustration.

"Fine," he grumbled, crossing his arms over his broad chest.

The nomad watched the altercation unfold, his head tilted as if he had simply found the events mildly curious. Woldyff huffed as the Dusty One stood in silence, only watching. Finally, the nomad spoke.

"I did not have to come," he whispered. "It would have been far easier to leave you to your fates. Or I could have brought you to the Coats and collected my easy prize. Still, I did neither."

Woldyff did not reply, but looked sulkily at the ground. Blade turned to fully face the nomad once again, his gaze flitting to Yasi and Fox as he considered the proposal. He touched his chin thoughtfully before answering.

"We need to discuss this," Blade said after a moment. "Shall we call for you when we reach a decision?"

The Dusty one nodded, turned, and walked toward the thinning trees closer to the gorge. The *shala* and its rider had come to the last sparse row of jungle vegetation, and Blade watched as the Dusty One hailed the rider and stroked the monster's hide. Blade shook his head and turned back to his own companions, who had already drawn together in a close circle.

"Well?" he said.

"We-ell," Woldyff drew out the word sarcastically. "We do *his* deal, and we'll be breakfast for his lizard friends or full of smokin' holes before the day is through. That's what I think."

Yasi shook her head. "You do not know the Dusty One. He is hard, but he is not a liar. The others will get your people to safety, even if we do not survive."

"Regardless of his honor or intentions, I cannot see another way,"

Fox added. "What other way can there be should the Syndicate ever hope to escape the Aruacas? It is as we feared. The Coats suspected and now know we are here. They will not leave the border unattended, and what is worse, if we do not emerge, they will come for us again. This time, the Chychan will not take them by surprise. You have said so yourself, Woldyff. The thieves are not up for this fight, not yet. I am sorry to say that if it comes to us, it will be a bloodbath."

Woldyff snorted again, but did not argue. Fox pressed on.

"We know what we are walking into. A handful of Coats who believe us uniformed and ill-prepared, leading a group of liabilities. But now it is we who have the element of surprise, and perhaps, with these Heibeiathans and their horrible mounts, there is yet a chance."

"It is well said," Yasi agreed, nodding. "It is the only path forward."

Woldyff pursed his lips and looked expectantly at Blade. "You've been awful quiet. What about you?"

Blade stared out at the nomads as they continued speaking to one another. He thought he saw a few other monstrous lizard heads poke up from the gorge, but nothing else climbed over its edge. Past the gash into the distance, the Desolation remained forlorn. The orange sky was reddening rapidly. Already wine dark behind them, the light spilled in a vermilion haze out beyond the endless stretch of forbidding emptiness in the west. When night fell, it would be impossible to see anything in the gorge. It might already be nothing but shadows. And perhaps that was no disadvantage to them.

"I understand your fears, Woldyff, and I, too, see them," Blade said. "The Syndicate is indeed in grave danger. But that danger only grows the longer we linger here. I have no love for the nomad's devices, for only he and his people stand to gain from this arrangement, regardless. Still, for the sake of the Syndicate, agreeing to the Dusty One's deal is our best hope for success."

Woldyff ground his jaw in annoyance as he mulled over Blade's words. Finally, he rubbed his hand across his face and sighed. "Well, seems like I'm overruled, at any rate. Fine, it's what we'll do."

Blade nodded and clasped Woldyff's shoulder. "Whatever happens, I would sooner die than see harm come to any more of the Syndicate. You have my word, and I know Maren will do the same. Besides, what better diversion for their escape than two of the Coalition's most wanted?"

"Indeed," Fox smirked. "What a lovely prize we make."

Woldyff's weak smile was a shadow of his normal jovial self, but for Blade, it was better than nothing.

"Then it is settled," Yasi said. As the others nodded in agreement, she let out a piercing whistle. Woldyff clapped his hands to his ears as the nomad's head turned in their direction. Yasi waved him up. With one parting word to the *shala* rider, he trod back into the jungle.

"Now... how to do it," Fox said, watching the nomad approach. She sighed. "If only I had any of my charges left. A few well-placed detonations would serve us well."

Fox tapped her long fingers against her lips as she eyed Blade ruefully. "Ah, yes, I handed my last one off to you. And you wasted it on a mangy, half-dead Mistwolf."

Blade raised an eyebrow. "Had it been you in the arena, I am certain you would have believed it no waste."

20

The *shala* beneath Blade moved less like a horse than even he thought it would. Despite initial appearances, the creature hardly ever walked at its fullest height, moving instead with reptilian legs bowed out from its body and giving its gait a distinctly serpentine plod. Over the open patch of land between the Aruacas and the gorge, Blade found it more of an absurd oddity than anything as he waggled from side-to-side upon its middle. But then, they re-entered the jungle, using the thick trees as a shield between them and the prying eyes of possible Coalition scouts. Here, the *shala* had no qualms crawling along, leaping over, and even scaling the various natural obstacles in their path. At the first leap, Blade learned that the clips upon the Heibeiathan-style saddles and stirrups served far more than mere ornamentation; more than once, he had almost slipped off the creature's back. And, more than once, Woldyff had been less lucky.

A rust-colored tail lashed back and forth in front of Blade, knocking aside vines and leaves as the Dusty One's *shala* slithered over moss-covered rocks and slippery, rotting tree trunks ahead of him. Blade reined back his own eager mount, sure to keep a tail-length between them as the nomad had instructed. An annoyed hiss punctuated by strange clicks and squeals escaped between its teeth. Blade's *shala* turned a disturbingly intelligent eye back at him.

"Easy," Blade said softly in Heibeiathan, pulling the reins with a firm but gentle pressure.

The *shala* obeyed, even as it announced its displeasure with a forceful snort. Blade goaded it forward with a stiff prod of his heels, just as a loud curse erupted on his left.

"Why- in all- Reidara–" Woldyff puffed beside Blade, each word punctuated as he fought a losing battle against his *shala's* will. "Did it- have to be- giant- bloomin'- lizards?"

"Would giant spiders have been better?"

Fox held the reins loosely in one hand as she leaned forward to smirk at Woldyff. Initially, Fox too had grappled with her *shala*, but she had clearly mastered it. Woldyff glowered.

"If I've asked it once, I'll ask it a hundred times," he grumbled. "What's *wrong* with you?"

Fox shrugged and leaned back into the saddle. She pulled a piece of meat from her pack, and waving it in front of her mount's flickering tongue, tossed it forward. The *shala* snapped its jaws and caught the meat greedily. Blade watched with some fascination as she patted the creature's long, scaly neck, a loving admiration in her eyes he could only compare to the way a child might look at a puppy.

"There, there," she cooed. "That's a good beastie."

"You have a way with monsters," Blade said, raising an eyebrow.

"It takes one to know one," Fox replied, grinning.

"Hey! How 'bout a little help here, eh?" Woldyff said tensely. "Yeh scaly devil! Stop that, won't you?"

His *shala* swung its head angrily and arched its neck to look at him, taking hissing snaps at his fingers. He drew his fingers back with a muttered obscenity.

"Oh, for gods' sake, Woldyff."

Fox produced more meat from her pocket and lobbed it over Blade at him.

"What-hey, no!"

Woldyff bobbled it, too afraid to let go of the reins, and instead smacked the morsel to the ground. He moved to rein the *shala* in, but it was too late. His mount dived headfirst toward the fallen snack. Woldyff let off another string of curses as he clung to the saddle horns.

"Master yourself!" Yasi hissed from behind them. "Do you want all the *Co'atyti* within a hundred miles to hear you? You squeal more than a suckling pig."

Blade turned to look at her as she brought up the rear on a *shala* of her own. She slowed her *shala* and gave Woldyff an icy frown. With her new streaks of warrior's paint and the formidable *boka* jangling upon her back, it was a look that would have chilled even Blade had she directed at him. Woldyff gathered up his reins with a hasty tug and regained control of his mount. He chanced a sheepish glance backward before tugging a satchel of morsels from his belt. The *shala* nosed toward Woldyff's fingers, tongue flickering, but before it snapped, he offered it some cheese and a handful of venison jerky. Yasi clicked her tongue impatiently before pulling around Woldyff and falling in beside Blade.

"Oh, hold your horses," Woldyff muttered behind them, but he goaded the beast forward. It complied this time, and Blade thought that if it could, the *shala* would have smacked its lips in satisfaction.

Yasi took a deep breath, her dark eyes fixed on the trail the Dusty One forged before them. She held her position in the saddle rigidly, and beads of sweat rolled down her temple. Her tension was as palpable as the humid jungle air. Blade could only wonder at what she was feeling right now. *To leave her home, the people she leads, to embark on a journey that seems to go only to death...*

"Why do you watch me like that?" she snapped.

Blade cocked his head in confusion. "Like what?"

"Think little of it, Yasi," Fox interjected with a loud sigh. "That is just the way he looks at people."

"You mean that look where you ain't sure if he's deciding to snap your neck or smile?" Woldyff said behind them.

"Indeed!" Fox chuckled. "The look of the consummate hunter."

Blade rolled his eyes up to the sky and gave a little sigh before turning back to Yasi.

"I apologize," Blade said. "I was simply observing how well you ride. You said you had never ridden a *shala* before, but for all your repose and ease upon its back, I could have been fooled."

"Ah." Yasi relaxed, if only a little. "No, not a *shala*, but I have had some practice in the art."

"Hmm," Blade said thoughtfully. "I did not see any horses in the village."

"That is because there are no horses," Yasi replied.

"Are there then other mounts that the Chychan use?"

Yasi cocked her head and smiled. "For the bravest among us, yes. There are other mounts."

Blade faced forward again, his brow crinkling as he pondered her cryptic reply. But he had little time to think of it. In front of him, the Dusty One's *shala* halted. Blade pulled up short on his reins, causing his mount to rear. It climbed halfway up the nearest tree, hissing. He guided it back down as mildly as he could while the nomad brought his mount around to face them.

"We are here," the Dusty One said, gesturing to the thinning trees to his left.

Blade peered in that direction, now able to see clearly where the jungle ended and the gorge began. The Aruacas came far closer to the edge here, leaving them to cover only a few of the *shala's* natural strides in the open. A worn, dry trail snaked away from the jungle and tumbled into the canyon. From this angle, the way down seemed impossibly steep.

No mule or man could make that descent without losing life and breaking limbs, Blade thought.

"It is time," the nomad continued, pointing to his goggles.

Blade, Woldyff, Fox, and Yasi pulled on the sets of Heibeiathan goggles the nomad had given to each of them. The gathering darkness became infinitely darker at first.

"Oof, how does this help?" Woldyff said.

"It is on the daytime setting," Fox said wearily. "Do you not listen?"

Blade could imagine her rolling her eyes. With a small smile, he felt around the edges of the lenses, searching for the button the Dusty One had shown them how to use earlier. He found it, and with a single tap, the darkness fell away. The deep shadows of the Aruacas shifted into vibrant, sharp lines of green. He adjusted the straps to fit more snugly before pulling the hood of his cloak up over his head and low over the top of his goggles. They might have a slighter edge of advantage with the night-sight goggles, but in case the Coalition had their own ways of seeing in the dark, Blade deemed it wisest to conceal as much of his identity as he could manage.

The nomad pointed to the canyon, indicating a spot in the direction from which they had just come. "The Coalition soldiers should be waiting north of the bend, where they have expected me to bring you. I left them stationed along the trail we last passed. But these ones are clever. I would not be surprised if they have scouts hidden at the other canyon trails."

"So, they are spread thin," Fox said, still adjusting her goggles. "Good. It shall be easier to pick them off."

The Dusty One offered only the merest hint of a smile. "So we can hope."

He clucked softly at his *shala*, arranged his keffiyeh back over his mouth and nose, and guided the creature out of the trees. Blade and the others followed, falling into single file.

"Atta boy," Woldyff murmured behind him. Finally, Fox's food trick had helped his mount to warm to him.

Blade focused as the Dusty One emerged from the trees ahead, his *shala* gaining speed as it tasted the open desert air. They raced toward the precipice. All was cast in reliefs of green now, but Blade could imagine the dim haze of coppery-orange along the horizon, far beyond the miles and miles of the Desolation. Dusk settled down upon them, and Blade knew that in the shadows of the canyon, it would be pitch-black without their goggles. The nomad's *shala* dived over the cliff's edge head first. His straight back and scarf-draped shoulders teetered oddly there for a moment, and then his body plummeted out of view. A puff of dust and a whipping tail took his place, and then he was gone.

Us next. Blade gritted his teeth, clenching the reins and the double horns as his legs gripped his mount with all his strength. The *shala* scuttled forward. Wind whistled in his ears. He willed his eyes to remain open as he felt the clawed forelegs stretch down. They lurched, and before Blade's stomach could register it, they had tipped over the canyon edge.

The *shala* only moved faster, flying down the sheer wall of rock with terrifying speed. Its claws grasped impossible holds as its belly slid along the surface, and this appeared to be only slightly impeding their irrepressible momentum. Blade, now perpendicular, leaned back as far as he could against the flank of the beast. He was only assured they were not plunging to their deaths by the rhythmic catch of claws on rock. But his gut had caught up with him by now, and the falling sensation brought bile to his throat and pumped adrenaline to his rigid limbs.

And yet, just as quickly, the *shala* found purchase on a narrow path carved into the canyon. Blade felt the creature right itself, if only a little, and he leaned up straighter in the saddle. No longer up and down, the *shala* once again stretched taller and resumed a pace Blade could withstand down the winding, steep decline of the narrow path. He exhaled, and with a displeased glower, finally dared to look around.

Their expedient descent brought them some way down into the gorge. Perhaps a hundred feet above, the edge of the cliff cut against the rolling clouds. Woldyff, Fox, and Yasi followed behind Blade, their *shalas* weaving on the dangerous path with necks extended and sweeping low to the stony ground. None of them, not even the *shalas*, emitted a single sound, although Woldyff's mouth was wide open in a frozen, silent scream. No sane person could blame him. Claws scraped the unyielding rock mere inches from the bare edge, and even then, the sides of the beasts brushed up against the canyon wall. One slip or misstep, and an unlucky rider might tumble to his doom.

*And how far would he tumble fo*r? Blade tried not to satisfy his curiosity, but despite himself, he looked down. With the night-sight goggles, he could see the bottom far below. A shiny sliver of water snaked along it, so small that he could have mistaken it for nothing more than a trickling stream. The white froth of rapids, as tiny as they were from here, brought to mind the roaring fury of Thunder Run instead, and Blade knew there remained hundreds of feet to the bottom. His stomach gave a tremendous flip.

Blade swept his gaze away, above the bottom, away from the *shalas* and riders, out past their unbelievably narrow path and over the canyon itself. Even with the surge of queasy discomfort and the growing disquiet that preceded a battle, a sense of wonder also rose within him. At another time, the view would be nothing less than majestic. The striated cliff wall on the opposite side stretched on and on, rising like an endless monolith into the night sky. Wind whooshed through the gorge, cooling the hot sweat dewing Blade's brow. A great horned owl swooped into sight nearby, and out from the small openings in the cliff face above buzzed and flapped all manner of nocturnal winged things. Their reptilian mounts scurried downward, leaving the sky above farther and farther behind and trekking ever deeper into the new world waiting below.

Time ticked on as they descended, and the canyon walls blotted out the last gasps of daylight. Blade could see everything in hues of green behind his goggles, but even so, he could almost feel the impressive depth of the gorge's darkness. Curious, Blade lifted the edge of his goggles. Impenetrable shadow blackened everything below. Above, only a dull, reddish streak of sky illuminated anything, and that light did not stretch past the cliff edge. Blade lifted his hand before him, and only vaguely did he see its shape in that utter darkness. Carefully, he gripped the saddle horns again, the only thing that anchored him as he floated on. He chanced one last glance in the dark before replacing his goggles. The crimson orbs of his *shala*'s eyes reflected what little light there was in the canyon with a devilish gleam. Blade snapped his goggles back in place and his sight returned. It was a welcome relief.

The *shalas* needed little prompting now as they wended along the precarious trail, and each followed the other as if it had made the journey hundreds of times before. They had settled into a brisk but comfortable pace, and Blade's insides no longer churned with their descent. His thoughts turned to what lay ahead, and the churning threatened to resume.

Though the Dusty One had given his best appraisal of the situation, Blade wondered if the nomad might have been a little presumptuous. Did he know the Coalition like Blade did? And if he had underestimated their opponent, what really faced them at the bottom of the gorge? All the possibilities with their potential outcomes spun through Blade's mind. And while the *shalas* gave them some advantage, their approach had its drawbacks, especially for Blade. He glanced down at the sidearm he had acquired from their last victory over the Coats. His prowess in stealth had always served him well, but long-range combat, especially with a foreigner's weapon, had never been a strength of his. *Av'tal* and *Ub'rytal*, his unfailing brothers in battle, could not serve him here, and even if he needed to call upon them, he could only use one or the other. Given the unpredictable ways the *shala* moved, he would need at least one hand to secure himself upon the creature's back. The thought of being limited to one of his trusted swords brought revulsion. Never before had Blade felt so laid bare and exposed.

The increasing sound of rushing water met Blade's ears. He shook away his thoughts and looked down. Below, the ribbon of water had grown into a roaring river, and it was now only several dozen feet beneath them. His mount crept along above it, and the steep path under its reptilian claws had leveled into something like a shelf in the rock. They moved in a northwesterly direction, following the curve of the canyon. The waters surged past, thundering on southward. It was, Blade realized, the river known as the Wamble, which flowed between the Aruacas and Heibeiath's Southern Plains. It would empty into Khiset Bay, a great harbor and shipping lane of Hurdu, the even greater Heibeiathan port city. There, the Wamble was broad, gentle, and easy to navigate, but here, at its source, it gushed forth with all the intensity of a geyser.

If one fell in here, he might not resurface for miles.

Blade squeezed his mount's sides a little tighter.

At long last, the trail descended once again, and this time, it broadened. The Dusty One urged his *shala* faster, and the other three riders kept pace. Faster and faster they went, when suddenly, the rocky path dropped out paces ahead. Blade gripped the saddle horns, ready to dig in to slow his careening mount. But as the shelf fell away, the Dusty One's *shala* sprang into the air. Its claws found purchase on a rock shelf twenty feet away. Blade's own beast gathered itself, and before he could do anything, it leaped. Air whooshed past him for only a moment. The *shala* landed with a great thud, bouncing Blade up from the saddle. Its back feet scrabbled up the edge of the shelf and propelled it forward, just in time for another *shala* to crunch in the rock behind them. Two more subsequent thuds followed, and Blade heard a rather shrill squawk nearby. It had not come, he deduced, from either Fox or Yasi.

This shelf broadened even more, and overhead, the canyon wall jutted out above them. The Dusty One guided his *shala* deeper into the hollow beneath the overhang. Blade and the others followed. The nomad stopped. With a nod, he dismounted, and the rest did the same. Blade slid off the side of the *shala*, his legs bowed more than usual. He never particularly relished traveling by horse, but that was worlds better than what had just transpired. Blade glanced at the others, who looked as he felt. A peaky Woldyff banged his fists against his thighs to gain feeling in them; Yasi grimaced as she rubbed her backside.

The Dusty One did not shout over the roar of the Wamble, but beckoned them toward him. Blade and the others drew near.

"It is best to speak here," he said, as loudly as he could without his words being lost to the river. He pointed ahead. "The Coats are waiting there, below. We shall leave the *shala* to rest here, but first, let us reward them. We shall need them at full strength for what is ahead."

The nomad went to his *shala* and unhooked a pouch from the saddlebag. He dumped its contents, what appeared to be a pail's worth of dried fish, on the ground in front of his mount. As the *shala* began to eat, the other mounts looked on enviously. Blade strode over to his animal, finding a similar pouch in his own saddlebag, and shook it out before its flickering tongue. He patted its scaly shoulder as it inhaled the offering.

Before the *shalas* had curled up in the alcove, satisfied, the five riders crept quietly to the shelf's next edge. They drew close, and the Dusty One signaled for them to halt. He dropped to lie flat on his stomach and slowly inched toward the edge. Blade dropped beside him, with Fox at his right, Woldyff beside the nomad, and Yasi beside him. They crawled, the smell of dust in their nostrils, the river roaring in their ears. The edge drew nearer. Finally, the Dusty One stopped just before its brink.

"There," he said, pointing.

The canyon basin spread out below them, where the Wamble ripped through at the very bottom. Vegetation sprouted along the banks of the river, but grew sparser and yielded altogether to the dusty, rocky ground some twenty yards away. The gravelly banks sloped away from the riverbed until they stopped abruptly against the canyon walls, except at the place where a wide path interrupted the flow of monolithic rock. Massive, flat steps, worn but clearly hewn out of the canyon, approached the Wamble.

And it was there, close to the canyon wall and partially obscured by a large boulder beside the steps, a hovercraft hull rested. Blade scanned the bank, and sure enough, he found also the soldiers who had manned it. As the Dusty One had predicted, two soldiers waited on either side of the steps. The others pressed themselves into concealed places below, or patrolled up and down the river bank. Blade squinted toward the boulder, where several of the soldiers congregated in silent conspiracy. The crest of a Coalition captain's helmet bent low among them.

"I count ten," Fox whispered. "But there will be two in the craft at the least, and perhaps three or so more lying in wait elsewhere."

"Even if we each pick off one with our first shot, it will be grim battle with the rest," Blade said. "Our chances are slimmer still if those in the craft are quick to the draw."

"Yes," Fox mused. "As soon as its lights go on, we shall not last long."

Woldyff muttered a curse.

"Peace," Yasi said quietly, and she pointed. "Look, see these two at the steps? They are far from their fellows. We can take the two quickly enough, and with little sound if we use *bokas*. As long as they are felled together, we shall have surprise on our side."

"I suspect I am the next best shot with a *boka*," Fox said. "Hmm. Yes, the river will drown out any sound of their demise. Once they are down, we work inward, starting with those below, hitting the patrolmen along the river, and ending with the soldiers nearest the craft."

Woldyff blew out a shaky breath. "Well, at least that evens the odds a smidge before we're fightin' hand to hand."

"The *shalas* will be a help then," the Dusty One nodded.

"It is not impossible," Blade agreed, but still, the plan did not sit well with him. He turned to the nomad. "Are you certain that this was the only craft in the canyon?"

"I can only tell you what my eyes have seen," the Dusty One replied.

"Thanks, that's helpful," Woldyff grumbled.

The nomad did not reply, but stared down at the hovercraft. "Leave the ship to me."

Woldyff scoffed. "Even ol' King of the Shadows here can't get down there and inside without being seen, and then you gotta fight whatever's waitin' inside."

A sly smile turned up the corner of the nomad's mouth. "Even so, leave the ship to me."

21

As the Dusty One slid back from the edge, crouched his way beneath the overhang, and began striding purposefully to his *shala*, Woldyff turned toward Blade. Even beneath his night-sight goggles, Blade could make out the look of incredulity.

"What do you suppose we're to make of that?" Woldyff whispered.

"He means what he says," Yasi replied solemnly.

"Yes," Blade nodded. "Come. We must act when he does."

The four returned quickly to their *shalas*. Blade mounted his *shala* as the Dusty One finished securing himself to the saddle. He turned toward Blade and nodded.

"A distraction, I think, would be welcome."

And without another word, he spurred the creature with a sharp kick. *Shala* and rider made straight for the shelf adjacent to the Wamble. Down they went, out of view. Blade secured himself as fast as he could, goading his mount forward to see what the nomad was doing. He peered over the edge. A blur of green registered in his night-sight goggles, rushing over the loose stones and into the sparse undergrowth.

"He is attempting to ford it," Fox said, pulling her mount beside Blade and shaking her head in disbelief. "They shall be swept away."

"No, they will not. Look–" Blade pointed just as the great lizard leaped and scrabbled for something in the river. "He makes for the boulders."

They watched as the nomad and his mount zig zagged across the river, hopping from stone to stone. It was a dangerous game. The loose collection of boulders rose only just above the rapid flow of the Wamble. Churning spray made slick their exposed, uneven surfaces. The *shala* had to keep moving, lest it slip and be sucked beneath the foaming tide. Its tail and back leg splashed into the water, but with a powerful lash, it broke free of the Wamble's hold. If the Dusty One was concerned, he did not show it. He had untied the length of the reins, using the excess to slap the sides of the *shala* and goad it on. The beast made one last great leap. Blade breathed easier as its claws dug into earth on the other side.

"How does that help?" Woldyff asked as he and Yasi joined them.

"He shall have to cross again, but then he will approach the hovercraft from behind." Fox nodded with appreciation. "Clever. Perhaps, if we time it well, we might pull off this ambush after all."

"Let's get in position," Blade said.

They came once again to the edge. With a nod, Yasi dropped over it, followed by Fox. Their *shalas* found another narrow path along the canyon wall. Blade watched them creep along it, single file, his eyes flitting back to the Coats. Feeling unusually useless, he reached for his sidearm and aimed at those passing closest to the women. Beside him, Woldyff did the same, muttering about their range.

Blade searched the other side of the river for any sign of the nomad. He found none. Yasi came within feet of the trail, the *shalas* pressed against the canyon wall. From what Blade could tell, they remained undetected. The canyon wall jutted up over the step, hiding their approach. It appeared, ironically, that this was the tactic the Coats themselves had planned to employ themselves. Anyone coming down the steps could easily miss the snipers crouching on either side.

Yasi dismounted. Swinging herself up, she clambered up the protective boulder. She flattened as she reached the top and readied her *boka*. Stealthily, she peered down at the soldiers. They had not moved nor indicated suspicion. Yasi crawled forward. Fox followed, *boka* in hand, blades carefully hidden in their sheaths on her back. They set up, side by side, and Fox turned to look back at Blade. He held up a hand as he searched the far bank.

Far up the Wamble, the smallest hint of movement caught his gaze. A green blur streaked toward the river. Blade signaled.

"Now," he mouthed.

Fox leaned toward the sight on her *boka*, mirroring Yasi. A pause. Blade held his breath. No sound met his ears. He had to imagine the fleshy thud as the first soldier stumbled backward. The unfortunate Coat disappeared behind the boulder. Blade snapped his gaze toward the other. The other jumped into a posture of alertness. Moving out of cover, he stretched across the boulder to see the step below, rifle at the ready. His body jerked. The rifle clattered beside him.

Fox mouthed a curse, but Yasi was already reloading her *boka*'s chamber. Blade aimed as another soldier trotted forward, rifle pointed at the step. He stopped short, and his body shuddered. His fingers grasped weakly at his neck, but with another thud and shudder, the soldier crumpled. Indistinguishable shouts rose over the din of the river. Soldiers came running, and this time, they were ready. The crack of energy blasts echoed around the canyon. Intense light streaked across Blade's vision, blinding him. He heard the shattering of rock in the distance, the rumble of blasts ricocheting everywhere. Blade blinked, his vision clearing in time to see Yasi and Fox bounding down from the boulder. A blast exploded over Yasi's head, missing her by inches.

"They are discovered! Find marks!" Blade said roughly, but Woldyff was already firing.

Blade ripped down his goggles, returning the world to flashes of searing light and shadow. Woldyff's blast pinged off the armor of a soldier below. The soldier looked up and spotted them. Blade fired. He cursed as the blast went wide. The soldier took aim, but Woldyff was quicker, and the soldier fell.

The remaining Coats jumped into cover, but Woldyff and Blade continued to fire. He could hear the hovercraft whirring to life. *Hurry*, Blade thought, watching Yasi and Fox jump onto their mounts as he and Woldyff continued their suppressing volley. But energy pistols, even good ones, do not fire forever. His sidearm grew hot in his hand, a warning sign of overuse. Woldyff's fire slowed as well. Coalition helmets popped up, rifles leveled toward them.

"Move!" Blade shouted.

He kicked his *shala* hard. It hissed a warning as it rushed forward, an energy blast searing by Blade's shoulder. The creature plunged straight down the small precipice. Out of the corner of his streaming eye, Blade saw Woldyff's mount leap vertically. It bounced sideways along the canyon wall.

Another blast seared past Blade. His *shala* screamed in fury; Blade looked back, seeing the shot severed the lashing tail. The beast reared. Blade hung on with both hands, now at the mercy of the enraged mount. Fire came in every direction. The canyon resounded with crackling energy. Hot streaks of light tore by on every side. He hung on.

They hit the canyon floor with a thud. Blade unhooked from the *shala*. He need not jump; it pitched him right off as it swerved to meet the first attacker it found. Blade rolled, pain shooting through his shoulders and screaming across his ribcage as he met the dirt. Still, his hands found *Av'tal* and *Ub'rytal*, and the sharp agony receded beneath a flood of battle fury. The swords shone bright in the darkness. He righted himself before his foes. Their cries of recognition met him as he rose to his full height.

"The Guardian! It's him!"

Another scream, this one muffled, also reached his ears; the *shala* had found its foe, crushing the soldier's body beneath its talons and renting limbs from sockets with its teeth. But Blade had no time to think on this horrible sight. He parried blasts now concentrated on him. The glow of *Av'tal* and *Ub'rytal* surged, bathing everything around Blade in their emerald light. He could see the faces of the soldiers, the glittering rush of the Wamble beside them, the *shala* retreating into the shadows with its prey. Blade whirled his swords against the onslaught, the crackle of ricocheting energy rolling around him like a fiery tempest. He labored to breathe as the air grew hot and his sweat fell.

Where are the others? He wondered and worried.

But the report of an energy pistol and flashes of neon green answered his anxious thoughts. The volley lessened, if only for a moment, and Blade jumped to cover. A blast narrowly missed him as he rolled behind a bolder. Clasping his ribs with painful breaths, he gazed around.

A few battered Coats still stood, including their captain. Fox faced off against him and two others as Woldyff fired at two others. Blade searched for Yasi, unable to find her in the new darkness. A thud and cry from one of the soldiers nearby told him she had found a new vantage point instead.

Though it was agony, Blade took a deep breath and raised his swords. He flitted out of cover, slapping away a stray rifle blast as he returned to the fray. Woldyff, still on his *shala*, galloped past him, cursing at his no longer functioning weapon. A soldier stood up and quickly took aim as he passed, but Blade was faster. The man's face froze in an expression of surprise as the light of *Av'tal* and *Ub'rytal* fell upon him. And as the soldier collapsed on the ground, the surprise remained there forever.

But Blade was already running, leaping over small boulders and showering the riverbank with loose shale to reach Fox. Locked in deadly combat coming from both sides, she held off the advances of the now one remaining soldier and the Coalition captain. Another streak of green met one of her swords.

A Master's saber, Blade realized, as the sickly green glow cut through the darkness. Rage rose in his chest as, behind the sword, the eyes of the captain gleamed with despicable glee. Blade sprinted forward with a roar.

"Always back-to-back lately, aren't we?" Fox panted as Blade smashed through the hail of rifle fire.

Blade said nothing, but with a quick surge, pounced upon the lower-ranking soldier. *Ub'rytal* sliced upward, cutting the rifle barrel in two, as *Av'tal* fell, smiting the soldier at the neck. Blade spun with the momentum, turning just in time to catch a blast from the sidearm in the captain's other hand.

He and Fox faced the captain alone.

"That does not belong to you," Blade said, a righteous rage flaring through his swords.

A hateful sneer curled the captain's lip. He leveled the saber and the pistol at his foes.

"Go on an' try to take it," the captain mocked. "You're not leavin' this canyon alive."

Blade stepped forward, but the sudden drone of an engine stopped him. A panic-stricken voice echoed off the walls of the gorge.

"The hovercraft!" Woldyff shouted. "It's coming! Get outta the way!"

But it was coming far too fast. The craft rose into the air, whirring to life in mere moments as it glided out from behind its resting place. Floodlights bathed and blinded them as the craft's mounted guns swiveled in their direction. Blade and Fox turned to face it, knowing that running was no use. The captain leered at them in triumph.

The hovercraft screamed to a stop only yards from them. Blade stared down the barrels of its turrets, guns too large to be held in the hands of a solider. Even if he blocked the blast, its sheer force promised a death blow. Blade raised his swords anyway, if only for the last time. The Coalition captain raised his saber in salute and laughed.

A deafening explosion came from the craft's massive gun barrel.

Light blinded Blade. He braced, but the searing heat careened wide and to the left. It slammed into the captain instead.

The captain flew backward, saber clattering, limbs already limp as he tumbled through the air. He went over the banks of the Wamble and splashed into its current. For a moment, the crest of his helmet flashed above the surge, and in the next, it was gone. Blade lowered *Av'tal* and *Ub'rytal*. The sounds of battle died away, replaced once again by the thunder of the Wamble and now the low drone of the hovercraft. Despite himself, Blade stared at the place where the captain disappeared. It would have been a worse fate to drown in those inescapable waters, but Blade knew the captain was dead before he had hit the surface.

He turned to face the glaring lights of the transport craft instead. As he shielded his eyes, the lights dimmed. The transport's door hissed open. A familiar dusty, goggled head popped out. Woldyff laughed loudly as he joined Blade and Fox in spotlights.

"I wouldn't believe it if I hadn't seen it myself," Woldyff said, impressed. "Actually, I'm not so sure I believe it, anyhow. Hey there! Dusty One! How'd you manage *that*?"

The nomad hopped down from the craft, approaching the other three. He cocked his head.

"I knocked."

"You what?" Woldyff choked.

"I knocked," the Dusty One replied with a shrug. "They expected someone else, I am certain."

Woldyff shook his head, chuckling, as the Heibeiathan turned to Blade.

"It was a timely distraction." He nodded. "You have held up your end of the bargain."

"We did it," Woldyff said, shaking his head. "I can't believe it. We did it."

Blade opened his mouth to reply, but a shrill whistle cut across the canyon. Replacing his goggles, Blade searched for the source of the sound.

"There!" Fox said, pointing.

The others looked. From a perch high above where the hovercraft had waited, Yasi gazed down from the back of her *shala*. She waved her arms, pointing ahead as they found her.

Blade followed her hand, and all the elation of their victory fled. Lights pierced the darkness, illuminating the gorge to the north. A telltale hum reverberated along the walls of rock. Blade tensed as a dark shape followed. Another Coalition transport was roaring around the bend.

22

They only had minutes before the craft would bear down upon them; less before it locked them in weapons range. *No time at all.*

"Come!" The Dusty One turned and sprinted back toward the hovercraft. Blade, Fox, and Woldyff exchanged glances.

"Go!" Woldyff said, turning his *shala* to the canyon wall. "I'm with Yasi!"

Without another word, Blade and Fox sheathed their swords and bolted after the nomad. The craft was already whirring to life and lifting from the ground. A rope ladder twisted in the whirling dust. Blade leaped for it. He caught hold and hoisted himself up. Fox grabbed the ladder as he rolled into the open bay door. The craft began to turn. Blade thrust his hand out. Fox grasped and pulled up, rolling in after him. Blade punched his fist against the hatch button. It closed just as the craft rocketed forward.

His body slammed against the secured door. Pain ripped so fiercely through his ribs that Blade had no breath to even groan. Fox hit the hatch beside him, cursing.

"Guns!" the nomad shouted back at them.

Fox heaved forward, cursing again as she righted herself as the craft rocked side to side. Blade peered past her as she stumbled into the cockpit. Three seats stretched across the front of the craft – a pilot's seat in the middle, with two gunner chairs on either side. Fox dragged herself into the righthand seat. She turned to glare at Blade before strapping in.

"Do you wish to explode in a ball of flames, or shall you give us a fighting chance?"

Blade wrapped one arm around his ribcage and used the other to pull himself upright. Gritting his teeth, he took a leaping stride and fell in beside the Heibeiathan on his left. He threw the buckles over him, clipping in just as the nomad sheered left over the Wamble. A streak of light screamed over the starboard side.

The hovercraft weaved over the tumultuous waters, crossing to the bank on the Heibeiathan side as the other craft shot by on the other. Fox swiveled in her chair, the turret controls and scope turning with her as she squeezed the trigger. Her attack missed; the turret slammed to a stop, unable to rotate any further to the craft now behind them. Blade leaned toward his own scope, twisting the turret for a view of the outside. Equipped with night sight like the Heibeiathan's goggles, the scope cast the canyon outside in hues of green. He swiveled as far as he could, catching a glimpse of the nose of the other craft just before their own craft banked right. Blade followed, facing the sight forward.

On opposite banks of the Wamble, the crafts aligned with each other. Blade depressed his trigger. A surge of energy ripped from the turret. It glanced off the side of the other craft, already swerving away. Their own craft jerked. The nomad pulled the steering as two jets of light answered Blade's attack. One found them with a sizzling crack. Their craft shuddered violently with the impact.

Still, the Dusty One managed to avoid the other. He accelerated southward along the bank. The walls of the canyon flew by, but Blade knew the Coalition remained close behind. Glancing blows skimmed off the hull of the ship as their attackers gave chase. Their hovercraft threatened to spin out of control with every impact.

"One direct hit and we shall be splinters," Fox said through gritted teeth. "And I cannot even get them in my line of sight!"

"We cannot get behind them," the Dusty One said calmly. "It would appear they are better at this than we are."

Fox stared daggers at the nomad. "Obviously. Do you happen to have any helpful ideas?"

"Perhaps," he said, and he pulled up the craft and accelerated with stomach-wrenching force.

The hovercraft upended, nose to the heavens as it shot into the sky. Blade kept his eyes to the scope, even as bile rose in his throat. Below them, the sleek profile of the other hovercraft shot beneath them. Their ship rattled, the whirring power cells guttering. Blade knew little about the operation of hovercrafts, but he was certain that they did not work this way. The nomad wrenched the steering again, easing off the accelerator and powering down. Their craft somersaulted mid-air.

Blade held his breath as it careened back toward the earth, bracing for the inevitable crash. It did not come. With a sudden whoosh, it whirred to life, and they became level with the ground beneath them. Once more, they accelerated, rocketing back to where they had laid ambush to the Coats from the backs of the *shalas*.

"Impressive," Fox gasped. She swallowed hard, presumably, like Blade, to keep the contents of her stomach where they should be. "But they will not be fooled for long. And we cannot run from them forever."

"Nor can we outgun them," Blade said, watching as the Coalition craft once again roared toward them.

He aimed the turret and released a stream of fire toward their pursuers, but none made contact. They navigated each attack with almost effortless ease. Blade grimaced, feeling again his insufficient combat wisdom in situations like these. Still, the attacking craft remained at enough distance that they could not make easy contact, either. They held their fire, unnervingly patient as they creeped closer.

"Do not despair yet, wild strangers," the Dusty One said. "We may yet have one trick up our sleeves."

"And what would that be?" Fox asked, exasperation straining her voice.

She aimed and blasted, but the shot went wide and struck the canyon wall. Their pursuers accelerated, catching up enough to return Fox's unsuccessful volley. Warning lights flashed on the dashboard panel in front of them. One blast ricocheted off their port side. Blade gasped in pain as their craft lurched.

"We force it back from where it came," the nomad shrugged, as if this were the most obvious answer.

Blade stared at him. He had never been prone to panic, but even he was finding it hard to comprehend the unnatural calm that the Dusty One persisted in, despite their dire circumstances. The nomad said nothing more, but swerved along the canyon drunkenly instead. It was working. Though ferocious, the renewed attack had failed to anticipate their random movements.

The craft drifted partway over the Wamble as the canyon began to constrict, and the strip of sandy land between the river and rock wall narrowed. They passed close beside the wall, the pursuing craft screaming close behind them. Suddenly, the Dusty One pointed his chin to their right, somewhere above in the darkness. "Here, on this side of the gorge. Look."

Unable to see with his scope, Blade leaned forward to gaze out the windshield. He peered up at the side of the canyon. It was flashing by at dizzying speeds, stark reliefs of stone illuminated by the beams of hovercraft headlights. He pulled his goggles back up over his eyes, staring into the night at the place where the wall seemed to end. At the bend, shapes scurried around an overhang set in the wall.

Shalas, Blade realized. They leaped from ledge to ledge, clinging to the rock with their great, curved claws. Riders held onto their backs, most of them doubled up on each of the creatures. Blade squinted, trying to comprehend what they were doing. The front riders directed their mounts, but the back riders each carried large staves. They were thrusting the staves hard into the ledges. Portions of the rock cracked beneath the force.

He grasped all these details in an instant, for as soon as he took in the scene, they roared past it, the Coalition in hot pursuit. The Dusty One made another spectacular turn, and spun them away from the approaching, and once again firing, Coalition craft. They sped out over the widest part of the river, its waters frothing menacingly below. Still, they found ground again on the other shore. Blade ripped down the goggles again and refocused on aiming his turret. His shot hardly clipped their attackers. It streaked through the canyon and hit rock in a spray of rubble.

"The other riders," Blade said quickly as Fox looked at him and the nomad inquiringly. "They are attempting to bring down the wall by the bend."

"On top of the other hovercraft?" Fox replied with a scoff. "Impossible! Even if they manage a rockslide, it will not be big enough or fast enough! It will accomplish nothing!"

The Dusty One gave a sharp shake of his head. "It will fall. Quickly. We must corner them there."

"They'll shoot us to bits first!" Fox exclaimed.

"Not if we help the others," Blade said.

The entire scene stretched before him, frozen in the long moment between his breaths. They faced their attackers, too close to dodge the next volley effectively, and perhaps too slow to escape them yet again. The Coalition craft idled, pressed close to the canyon wall, sensing, it seemed, that victory was near at hand. But the rock was beginning to crumble.

Blade aimed the turret. *Shalas* scurried away from the ledge as his first blast struck below it. A warning. But it did what he had wanted.

Cleared in moments, his consecutive blasts loosened boulders. They shouted their freedom as they cascaded down the incline.

Fox needed no further explanation. She fired rapidly at the Coalition craft, this time striking one of their turrets before it could strike them. It did not fall, but the blast jammed its maneuvering mechanism. It shot wildly to their left and no closer.

But the other turret took full aim. Blade saw the jet before he felt it as it cracked across their bow. Wobbling from the blow, the hovercraft squealed in protest. It keeled toward the river. Blade kept his finger on the trigger, spraying blasts above and at their attacker. The Dusty One threw levers and switches as system warnings beeped loudly in their ears. It was little use. Blade abandoned the turret, and he grasped the chair arms instead. The hovercraft dropped, scraping the gravelly bank with a screeching thud. Blade groaned in pain as they came to rest with a terrible jolt. The lights flickered and dimmed. Red emergency lighting flared in the interior.

Blade shook his head, droplets of blood dribbling out of his mouth from where he bit off a piece of his tongue.

It will not be long now, Blade thought, hastening to undo the straps on his chair. *They shot us down. They want us alive.*

He looked over at the nomad, whose head lolled on his chest, his hands limp against the steering. Blade fumbled for *Av'tal* and *Ub'rytal*, the only sound now the ticking of the dying engine.

They will have no such opportunity for prisoners.

The swords blazed to life.

"I am sorry to say you won't be needing them this time, Guardian," Fox said.

Blade looked over at her sharply, realizing that she remained her seat, unconcerned. She stared out the windshield and shook her head.

"Unbelievable," she muttered under her breath.

"What is it now?" Blade said.

Fox sighed, waving her hand dismissively. "See for yourself."

With a sharp look, he stared down at the Dusty One. "And what of the nomad?"

She placed her fingers against the nomad's throat. "He lives. Do not fear, I shall set to work on him. You look out there and see."

Blade frowned, still holding his swords in defense as he bent to gaze out the windshield. No hovercraft headlights beamed toward them across the river. Their own lights had gone out. It was dark, and above the rush of the Wamble, he could hear nothing. Confused, Blade replaced *Av'tal* and *Ub'rytal* and fitted his goggles in place.

An enormous hill of boulders lay heaped upon the canyon floor and spilled into the river. Blade looked up along the canyon wall, where massive sections of sheer rock face had once been. Hundreds of feet of the bend had fallen, and Blade could speculate upon what was crushed beneath the rubble. There was no sign of their attackers, but above and around, the great lizard mounts of the Heibeiathan nomads crawled down the surrounding ledges and hopped atop the heaps of stones. Riders lifted their arms and staves in celebration. Blade passed a hand over his sweat-soaked brow, a silent prayer of thanks on his lips. Not even the persistent ache of his ribs could shake from him the awe of their victory.

The sound of rummaging brought Blade back to the present. He turned and kneeled beside the nomad as Fox retrieved a vial from the small bag on her side. She uncorked it.

"Other than a likely concussion, I see no other injuries," Fox said. "But I daresay he shall be sore. Pull down his scarf."

Blade obeyed, and Fox passed the vial beneath the nomad's nose. The Dusty One shuddered and coughed as his head wobbled. He lifted it gingerly before turning slowly to each of them. With a wince, he brought a hand to his temple. To Blade's surprise, he looked sorely disappointed.

"So, this is how it ends," the nomad said quietly. "Indeed, I have died and failed to reach paradise."

Blade grasped his arm. "No friend, you remain in the land of the living yet."

A broad smile curved across the nomad's face. He pulled off his goggles, squinting up at the Guardian with a warm mirth that Blade had assumed him incapable of expressing.

"I meant that with no offense," the Dusty One said. "But there are other faces I should rather see in the afterlife."

Fox laughed. "And yet, you are not the first to express that sentiment. I have to admit, I am beginning to take it personally."

23

Blade stood at the edge of the gorge and gazed down into its yawning black abyss. Without the goggles on, he could make out nothing. It might as well have been bottomless, for he could not even hear the echoes of the Wamble as it rushed far below. The fact that he and his companions fought a bitter battle against the Coalition and won there already felt like a legend, as far in the past as the canyon floor was far below.

Well, except for this, Blade thought, wincing as he brushed his hand against his tender side.

It was not the first time he emerged from a fight sore, and no doubt it would not be the last. Especially since there were now plenty more fights to be had. Blade could only guess at when the next fight for his life would begin. For the sake of his ribs and the realization that age was slowing him, he prayed it would not be soon.

The crunch of rocky soil stirred Blade from his thoughts.

"We'd have never made it without these hissin' horrors, would we?"

Woldyff walked up beside him and paused, staring down into the canyon with Blade. One hand rested on his hip and the other patted the flank of his *shala*. Blade observed his friend. Their journey through the Aruacas had certainly treated Woldyff unkindly, but their last adventure had done even worse. Scrapes covered most of Woldyff's exposed skin. His proud, long hair sat matted and frazzled atop his head, and his well-groomed face overgrown with wild, curling hairs. Much of it had grown out gray, and it made him look far older than Blade ever remembered him being. Blade grasped Woldyff's shoulder and nodded in agreement.

"No doubt the *shalas* are a necessity in this strange land. We must be generous in our thanks."

Blade looked back over his shoulder, where a score of the nomadic Heibeiathans, who called themselves the Bedua, spread out. In the dark, he had trouble spotting them, but he knew they busied themselves with preparation for the journey to Errdoga. He replaced his goggles to see that they had nearly finished packing supplies and the Syndicate's belongings on the camels that would take them the rest of the way.

The Syndicate also busied themselves among the Bedua, making fast and light work of the exchange from *shala* to camel. Blade counted heads for perhaps the third time that night, just to be sure every Syndicate member that had survived the rainforest remained. After their altercation with the Coalition, and the life-saving help of the thieves and Bedua alike, Blade thanked the Unseen that they had made it this far. Even so, he eschewed shallow optimism at their current success. The Desolation had received its name for a reason; and the journey, even with expert guides and on the backs of animals well-suited for such a task, still possessed untold dangers.

The Coats won't be long to arrive here, at any rate, Blade thought, and grimaced. The Dusty One and a few other brave souls among the Bedua still remained on the canyon floor, working to repair the damage done to their prize. Blade knew too little about Coalition technology to make even an educated guess at how long such repairs should take, but the Dusty One and his comrades appeared unconcerned with such details. He shook off all of Blade's warnings about the Coalition's inevitable return to investigate with a shrug. Perhaps the Bedua were willing to risk all for such a treasure, but Blade was not. He itched to be off, with so many miles between him and this gorge that he no longer remembered what the great canyon looked like. And if the empty leagues of Heibeiathan desert claimed his life, it would be a better death than the one he would find waiting here. Blade hoped the Bedua understood that.

May the Unseen help anyone the Coalition catches near this place.

Blade sighed, resuming his duty of lookout while the journey preparations continued. He did so with impatient resignation. Already packed and prepared for his next quest, and having done as much as he could to help the others without being a nuisance, Blade did the next most helpful thing. He watched. Blade scanned the horizons before and behind once more. Nothing moved across the Desolation's great expanse, and no stirrings in the Aruacas or in the canyon below gave Blade pause. He looked back, relieved to see the Syndicate members dispersed among the camels. Some of the Bedua helped them finish packing and began mounting camels themselves, while a handful of their number returned to the *shalas*. There, a few of the younger nomads tended the monstrous creatures with surprising confidence. It was no small thing that these young Bedua could garner the obedience of the *shalas*, all without the sullen hissing and snapping Blade and his companions met with instead. These creatures waited patiently for their riders to return, feasting upon slabs of some animal carcass that Blade did not readily recognize.

What work it must be to keep these monsters fed, Blade thought. He looked at his own mount, curled up on his other side by the edge of the cliff. It flicked its tail, the nubby end missing about six inches of its original length. Blade wondered if it would grow back. For its trouble, he had offered it what morsels he had after recovering the beast in the canyon, but he had his suspicions it had eaten its fill. Little remained of the unfortunate Coalition soldier to bury with the others. And while Blade was no sentimental man, still he could not repress the shudder at the first sight of the creature's stained snout and blood-soaked claws.

If the choice is between my skin or that of some other poor creature, then the work of feeding it is well worth doing, Blade thought somberly.

More footsteps crunched up behind him. Blade turned. Maren and Dane approached, with Fox following, leading her *shala*.

"We're ready about," Maren said, rubbing her hands together nervously. She gave Woldyff an intense, somber look. "Are you really sure about this?"

Woldyff grinned, and with a little laugh, extended his hand. "Come on, Mar', when have I ever been really sure about anything?"

She gave Woldyff an exasperated eye roll before grasping his forearm in return. But with a shake of her head, she allowed a small smile and chuckle of her own. Maren sighed and looked directly at Blade. "Yeah, well, you were pretty sure about the King of the Shadows here, weren't you?"

"Yeah," Woldyff said. "I 'spose I was. And am."

Maren let go of Woldyff's arm and extended her hand to Blade. Blade shook it, and looking into her eyes, saw the disgust, anger, and frustration had finally gone. Respect and even a hint of appreciation came forth instead, and Blade felt it in the strength of her grasp as she searched him.

"Take care of 'im, alright?" Maren said. "I want this idiot back in one piece."

"You have my solemn word," Blade replied, as she let go.

"Hey!" Woldyff said with mock indignation. He pointed to his chest. "This idiot and this idiot alone gets to decide how he comes back, don' he? Besides, a missin' ear or being short a few fingers could score me points elsewhere, if you know what I mean."

Woldyff winked at Maren. "Maybe even you'd let me take you out to dinner, if only out of pity."

Maren scowled. "You stop that, or you'll be short a limb sooner than you think."

Woldyff laughed and threw his arms around her in a bear hug. "I'll miss you, too, dear."

Blade thought he saw a flush rise in her cheeks as she thumped Woldyff on the back.

"Alright, alright," Maren said, pushing him away and reaching for Fox's hand. "The night's not getting any younger. You best be off."

"And the rest of us, too," Dane added gruffly. "Time's wastin', and those Coats won't be happy when they find what's been done here. Can't believe that ol' Dusty One is still tinkerin' around at the bottom of the gorge. I say, the sooner to Errdoga, the better, and even then, I ain't feelin' optimistic."

Dane stepped forward and shook hands all around, although Woldyff also pulled him in for an enthusiastic hug. Wriggling free and dusting himself off, Dane paused when he got to Fox.

"Never woulda thought we'd wind up as... well... whatever we are, but like you're all so fond of sayin', stranger things have happened."

"Why, Dane, are you suggesting that we have become friends?" Fox said with a little smirk. "I am touched, truly. You might imagine I do not make so many of those."

"You'd make a few more if you didn't shoot at them first," Dane replied, but for once, he was grinning.

Fox batted her eyelashes with a mischievous pout. "Oh, but where is the fun in that?"

Dane opened his mouth to retort, but paused as Yasi and one of the Bedua rode up on *shalas*.

"The Bedua are ready," Yasi said in Heibeiathan. "It is time."

Woldyff took a deep breath, shaking out his hands and bouncing with nervous energy.

"That's it then." Giving Maren and Dane one last mournful salute, he spoke the Syndicate farewell with uncharacteristic solemnity. "*A lak krataman wan mim bli'hhab.*"

Maren replied with a sad smile. "*A lak tikkh nan shi sulnye.*"

Woldyff turned to mount his *shala*. With a final nod to Dane and Maren, Blade spoke. "May the Unseen watch over you."

"Yeah, you too," Dane said with a nod of his own.

Yasi pulled up beside Woldyff as Fox and Blade jumped on the backs of their mounts. The *shalas* snorted and got to their feet, scratching the dirt with anticipation. Blade watched as Maren, Dane, and the Bedua rider turned to join the others. The column of travelers had already moved westward. They joined the throng and soon disappeared from view.

"Well, off they go," Woldyff sighed. "S'pose we're next."

Blade nodded, bringing his mount around to face north. From here and even with the night sight goggles, he could see no hint of the Kamarian mountains rising over the horizon. Only the vast flatness of the Desolation stretched on and on before him. They had weathered so much, had fought and won impossible battles, had traveled incredible distances, and still, they had many, many miles to go.

Can we endure it?

Blade looked at his companions, surprised by the gratitude and affection that swelled in his chest. It served them far less than Blade surmised it was worth to go to the extremities of Reidara, even to the far east of Elmnas, all to fight a hopeless war on the side of those already once decimated and conquered. But as he looked at their faces, set and stern to the north, he knew nothing now could change their minds. Nor did he want to try. These three brave warriors, their mettle proven against foes greater in strength and number than they had won Blade's respect and friendship. Even those who were once enemies now became the only companions Blade would choose to have by his side. Perhaps, one day, he would find a way to say it; to tell them that in all his long, lonely years, he had forgotten the incomparable worth of loyal, courageous friends until he had met each one of them.

But he had no words or time for this now. The task ahead called louder.

Blade kicked his heels into the *shala's* sides. It shuddered beneath him as it shook out the stiffness from its limbs and broke into a reptilian run. Sand and sky rushed past, and the world blurred. Swiftly they went, deeper into the Desolation, into the night, into the great horizon. Whoops went up from beside Blade as the three other beasts joined his own, riders low upon their backs.

"To Elmnas?" Blade shouted.

The others answered, their voices fierce and strong in the rushing wind.

"To Elmnas!"

24

60th of Sun's Wane
Elmnas

"Mouse? Are you there? We're getting close. If ever there was a time to wake up, it's now."

The voice spoke quietly by Mouse's head, stirring her from the blackness of a dreamless sleep. A hand gently shook her shoulder. Mouse opened a bleary eye, finding a blur of brown freckles and red hair. She wanted to shut it again, burrow into the soft blankets, and drift off once more to the sound of the hovercraft's soothing whir. But Fraeda's gentle shaking was insistent, and Mouse suddenly remembered what she meant by her waking greeting.

Mouse sat up groggily, rubbing her face and running her fingers through a mass of tangled locks. They caught in the knots, and she had to wrench one finger out, taking a bit of hair with it. Mouse grimaced and blinked sleepily at Fraeda.

"Close already? I was sure it would take a lot longer to get there."

"Well... it did," Fraeda said. "You've just slept through most of the trip."

Mouse looked around, realizing with a start that she was no longer lying on the hovercraft floor. Instead, she found the bare but considerably cozy bedroom of the craft. The door hung open a crack, and a springy mattress sank beneath her fingers. Fraeda sat on its edge beside her.

"That night really took it out of you. You stirred every now and then, enough for me to get some food and drink in you and get you to the latrine, but it's like you were sleep-walking. We even stopped a few times and everything. You didn't budge. Toma moved you the first morning when we got going again."

Mouse blinked incredulously. "How long has it been?"

"Well, we've traveled on and off, mostly in the dark. We've stopped around dawn each day once Rhavin found a good place to hide," Fraeda said. "Let's see... when we started out again at dusk yesterday, it was 59th of Sun's Wane. We flew most of the night, and it's mid-morning now... So, I think it's been about a week."

"A week?" Mouse replied, now rubbing her eyes vigorously. A powerful exhaustion still clung fast to her, and she was finding it hard to focus. But if they were finally nearing the border to the free north, she and everyone with her would need all their wits about them. "I'm sorry. I must have missed so much... we could have been in trouble, and I could've helped, really, I–"

Fraeda lifted her hand to quiet Mouse in a way that was reminiscent of Sister Alba. "No need. There was nothing for you to do. You saved everyone's lives, remember? You had done enough, and the Unseen has blessed our journey. Truly. We are all fine."

Mouse sighed. Knowing Fraeda, Mouse doubted that she meant to allude to her outburst of the night of their latest escape. Nonetheless, the pang of guilt returned to Mouse's stomach.

"Well," Mouse ventured sheepishly. "Don't let me off the hook. For anything... like, for example, being a rude jerk. Anyway, I'm sorry."

Fraeda exhaled through her nose sharply with something like a laugh, but it wasn't a derisive or unkind one. She looked at her hands, now folded in her lap, with a sad smile.

"I had forgotten all about that. Oh, Mouse, it's no wonder you feel the way that you do. You've been through an awful lot. And here you are, being asked to carry even more. I thought to encourage you by calling you the Harbinger, but I realize now it was another weight to bear. That wasn't fair."

"No, I wasn't being fair," Mouse said quietly, shaking her head. "You've been through just as much. And even worse, you remember it all. You're here talking about what I've got to carry, but you? I still forget sometimes. I'm sorry. It's easy to forget, because you just seem so..."

"Positive?" Fraeda supplied with a wry smile.

"Yeah, I guess that's it." Mouse extricated herself from the covers and sat next to Fraeda. "You're almost normal."

Fraeda laughed, a real, happy laugh that made Mouse smile herself.

"She said to the deaf and formerly mute child prisoner-turned-acolyte," Fraeda said, still laughing.

"Still," Mouse said seriously. "I think you know what I mean. You have every reason in the world to be miserable toward people. No one would have blinked if you'd have thrown Linnea out the door the moment we knew who she was."

Fraeda's eyes widened with shock. "Throw her out the door? To the wolves? I wonder if I *could* do that, even to a true enemy."

"I mean, don't tell her, but that's what I wanted to do," Mouse said guiltily. "Anyway, I just don't understand it, I guess. How you can be so kind, so giving, after all you've been through?"

"It's not always how I feel, of course," Fraeda replied. "But I've had a lot of help. I spent years learning from the Sisters how to heal, to forgive, to trust that the Unseen meant these evil things for something more than senseless pain... even when I couldn't see it or figure it out. Actually, if I am honest, I don't understand it all either. Not totally, anyway. But I know my hurt is no reason to hurt others.

And well, when I choose a different way, I think that kindness is honored. It *is* meaningful. I've found peace enough in that."

Mouse breathed in slowly. "You know, back in Misty Summit, when I couldn't remember... I had no reason to dream that I was a part of anything. That I made any difference. All of us there, we were just forgotten, hated people. We suffered, we died, we lost all the things that made us human... just because. How could I believe anything... how I could *hope*... and even now..."

She clenched her knees as she exhaled, searching her mind for the words she wanted. It was impossible to voice every tumultuous thought inside her. Mouse could not help but feel crushed between two paradoxical realities, one in which nothing cared about or stopped the cruelties that she had lived and seen, and one in which something, someone, did. Neither made perfect sense. Neither could fit neatly in the box of her experience. Both explained so much, and at the same time, never enough. What else could she do except choose one and try to live with it? Finally, she turned inquiringly to Fraeda.

"But how you can believe those things? Those oracles, all that stuff about the Unseen... everything, without doubting?"

"Whoever said anything about not doubting?" Fraeda smirked, but her face quickly sobered. "But if anything cast aside my doubts, it was you, wasn't it?"

Mouse scoffed. "Me?"

"Mouse, how many times should you have died or been captured before you even got to Elmnas? I don't think I need to convince you that your luck, if that's what you want to call it, has been... astounding. And then you showed up at the Priory, and you brought with you visions and dreams. You brought me a mission and finally, after so long, hope. Can't you see it? I am surer than ever. I meant what I said before. And nothing you could say will convince me otherwise."

There certainly was not anything Mouse could say in answer to that. She passed a hand over her mouth, pondering Fraeda's words, and another thought popped into her mind.

"This might seem like a strange question right now," Mouse said. "And I'm not sure you could know much about it. But..."

Mouse sighed, her fingers already wrapping around the hilt of her dagger. Fraeda waited patiently, watching as Mouse slowly slid the blade from its sheath. She laid it across her thighs, tracing the runic patterns as the glowing hues shifted with her touch. The way its glow pulsed, Mouse swore it looked like it was breathing. She looked up at her friend.

"Ever since Blade gave this dagger to me, I've felt this kind of connection to it. Like it understands me, reacts to me, and lately, I think, it even guides me. It's got this... this presence that I don't understand. I don't know what to make of it. Blade didn't explain a lot about it, but it sounded like this special Guardian thing. The way they used Cardanthium... it sounds like magic. And then, when we were at the Priory, all the Sisters had their own Cardanthium gems. What does it all mean? What is it with the Cardanthium?"

Fraeda nodded in understanding, but a frown knitted her brow. "Yes, there is something special about it, isn't there? I wish I could tell you more about that connection, but the Sacred Writings are frustratingly vague. What I do know is that for a Guardian hopeful, the forging of a Cardanthium blade marks the end of their training in the Way. It is a rite of initiation to have such a weapon. The twin blades for the Warrior, the saber for the Master, and for the Keeper..."

She gestured at the dagger in Mouse's lap. Fraeda sighed as she continued. "But I must say my knowledge of the intricacies is lacking. As you know, none of us ever met any living Guardians, so the understanding of Cardanthium's place in the Way has long since passed. Even Sister Alba, who is the best studied in the lore among us, said it was difficult to decipher. But this is what I do know. There *is* a power in Cardanthium that does not belong to this world. It is a power that binds to its bearer, like in the Guardians, giving them their special strength and long lives."

Mouse nodded in agreement. "Yeah, I can feel that power. It's... something else."

It's terrifying, is what Mouse wanted to say. She brushed the thought away, frowning.

"Is that the purpose of the Cardanthium at the Priory, then? Do the Ameliorites keep the crystals to... well, harness that power? Like a Guardian might?"

Fraeda shook her head. "The crystals don't grant abilities to the bearer like the ore does, but something of Cardanthium's deepest, truest power resonates in them. Not power in the way the Coalition has used it, you know– as fuel– but something else, something... holy. We've discovered through the Sacred Writings that the crystals had a place in worship during the Golden Age of Elmnas, to aid common people in meeting the Unseen. It is why our order has kept the crystals hidden, safe, not misused like the Coalition had done for a century. We have passed them down as... hm, what did Sister Alba call it again? 'An echo of the Divine.' We see them as sacred things, relics that connect us to the spiritual world we cannot see."

"Do you have one?" Mouse asked eagerly.

"No, you only receive it upon becoming a full initiate," Fraeda said, and Mouse detected a hint of regret in her words. "But if I can ever go back, I hope to steward a prayer gem for the order."

Mouse slipped the dagger back into its sheath before patting Fraeda on the shoulder. "Don't worry. We'll get you back. I'll walk you there myself. I promise."

"Okay, but you better let that leg heal all the way first," Fraeda smiled. "Anyway, we ought to get moving. From what Rhavin and Linnea were saying, this next part of our trip could get pretty tricky."

"Yeah, I think I'm finally feeling awake now."

Mouse hopped up, stretched, and yawned. Fraeda slid open the door and held it back for Mouse with a smile. Mouse sneaked a glance out of the compartment, seeing an empty cabin before her. Everyone else appeared to be in the cockpit. She paused, and looked at Fraeda in what she hoped was an innocent, inconspicuous way.

"So," Mouse said as casually as she could. "You said, uh, Toma carried me back here?"

Fraeda raised her eyebrows knowingly. "Yes."

"Did he... did he, uh, stay long with me? What I mean is, I hope he wasn't worried. You know how he can get sometimes."

A little smile quirked up the edge of Fraeda's mouth. She lowered her voice.

"Come to think of it, we were all a little worried. It was his idea to sit with you every day, just for a bit, to make sure you were okay. I thought it was a good one. I would have happily done so, but I think Toma knew Rhavin, Linnea, and I needed the rest a bit more. You know how he is."

Mouse's stomach fluttered, the same eager hope of the night before blossoming inside her once again. *He stayed with me*, she thought, and her heart soared. Her mind raced toward the words Toma had left unsaid, and she wondered what he might have whispered to her when she could not hear. Mouse tried and failed to recall any inkling of awareness of when he carried her, of any secrets shared that made their way into her dreams. Nothing came to her, and for a wild moment, she longed for the next night, when she could pretend to sleep and hear every precious word.

But why should it be more? Wouldn't he do that for anyone? Wouldn't he be perfectly gallant and care for any one of his friends in the same way? Mouse paused at the voice of doubt, but as quickly as the thought came, she found it easy to push away. She could not imagine Toma sitting at Fraeda or Rhavin's bedside, and the idea of him sitting beside pretty Linnea made her insides churn with anger.

No, she decided, *he wouldn't. This is different. This is... something else.*

And even the passing, bitter thought of Toma and Linnea together could not temper the sudden surge of elation, the marvelous hope that he felt for her as she now knew she had grown to feel for him.

"Yeah, of course," Mouse said, shaking herself back to reality and finally replying to Fraeda. She tried not to smile as she self-consciously rubbed the back of her neck. "That makes sense. I'll have to thank him, and uh, let him know he didn't need to. I'm okay. Great, actually."

"I am glad to hear it, and I am sure he will be, as well."

Mouse sidled out the door in front of Fraeda, ignoring the now plain grin dimpling Fraeda's cheeks. *Is it that obvious?* Mouse thought, feeling the flush rising on her own face. It might have been as red as Fraeda's hair, but she was finding it hard to worry about it. In stark contrast to the difficult, if not insurmountable, task ahead, lightness filled her like a balloon. Who needed a hovercraft? Mouse was sure she could fly.

Snatches of amiable conversation drifted back to her as she entered the main cabin. Mouse ran her fingers through her hair, trying to smooth out the tangles that constantly infested it. *This is hopeless*, she thought with frustration. *Was it always this knotty before I cut it off the first time at the Summit?* She could not remember. Mouse sighed, jamming her hands in her pockets instead. The hovercraft guttered, snapping Mouse's thoughts to the present. Its high, constant drone slid in pitch to a sluggish hum. The voices up front quieted.

Mouse turned, shooting a concerned look at Fraeda. "Did you feel that?"

"So I wasn't imagining it," Fraeda replied, frowning.

"Uh..." Toma's worried voice came from the cockpit. "Why does it sound like that?"

With Fraeda behind, Mouse crossed the cabin in a flash and hopped down into the crowded pit. The interior lights dimmed to red as they arrived.

"Welcome back to the land of the living," Toma muttered under his breath as Mouse charged in. "We missed you."

She gave him an appreciative smile, but it was fleeting. Her eyes wandered to the hovercraft's flickering control board.

"What's up, Rhavin?"

"I do not know." Nonplussed, he shook his head as he manipulated buttons and switches. "Nothing here has changed, but still, we lose speed."

Mouse ran her fingers over the glassy surface of the navigation panel, bringing up the pre-flight checklist of all fluid and power levels. She scoured the data, searching for any indication of the problem. A blinking gauge caught her eye. Mouse squinted at it, incredulous.

"It's the bidnythine. The crystal... it's drained."

"How's that possible?" Toma asked. "You just checked the gauges like a week ago. It was almost at full power. Aren't they supposed to last for years?"

"Yes, it was fine," Mouse said, giving the others an anxious look. "But it's not anymore. All the energy is just... gone. We'll be out of power within the half hour."

Linnea slammed her fist down on the dashboard with a curse. "Mother must have done this. She prepared a backup, in case her first work of sabotage failed. Why did I not think it would be so?"

"That would be some crafty sabotage." Mouse scratched her head, unsure of how such a thing was even possible. "Well, how close are we to free Elmnas? We should see the barrier by now, right?"

"We should be close enough to see it," Rhavin said, his brow furrowing. "But there is nothing."

Anxiety blossomed in Mouse's gut as she and the others looked blankly at each other in the fraught silence. *What in the world are we going to do without the hovercraft?*

She peered out the windshield, hoping the view might distract her from their transport's impending demise. A dismal landscape rushed by, treeless and gray. Snow swirled past, and even from within the comfort of the craft, Mouse could tell it was bitter cold.

"You're sure we're close?" she asked.

"As sure as we could be," Toma chimed in. "And we were making good time before... this problem."

"No Coats?"

"It does not seem so," Linnea answered this time. "It appears we found the only path between their forces. Nothing for miles. Of course, you can see why. It is a wasteland."

Mouse sighed softly as the hovercraft guttered once again. "Great. Plenty of problems to worry about, but at least the Coalition isn't the worst one this time."

"What do we do?" Rhavin asked. "Should we stop?"

"Yeah, do you think you can fix it like last time?" Toma asked hopefully.

Mouse shook her head. "Not unless there's a spare crystal on board."

Everyone looked eagerly at Linnea, who also shook her head.

"I took inventory of everything when it went down the first time," she replied. "If there was one, it is gone now."

"Alright." Mouse sucked in the air sharply. "Well, I guess we can make the power last as long as possible, at least until we get that border in sight. Rhavin, maybe if you shift down? Going slower should give us more time, although I don't think we can go much slower than this without falling to the ground."

Rhavin nodded, carefully decelerating until it reached the point Mouse had indicated. Mouse felt the difference immediately; they coasted into a glide and lost clearance as they slowed. She leaned forward to gaze out the windshield, hoping this place had a lot fewer rocks than the Elmnas she had traversed so far. It did, but that did not make the landscape any more inviting.

They flew over slabs of gray rock, interrupted only by patches of yellow grass. The ground rolled, as the rest of Elmnas did, but no mountains appeared in any direction through the robes of white fog along the horizon. Mouse recoiled at the sight.

Great, she thought hopelessly. *What's waiting for us in there?*

She craned her neck to peer into it, but of course, she could see nothing. It was a thin mist, not rushing toward them like a wall, but rather trickling into their midst and swirling over the bare patches of earth and accumulating piles of snow. That cheered Mouse's heart, if only a little. At least, despite the flurries and gloomy weather, she could see far enough in all directions to know that they traveled utterly alone. No man, nor craft, nor beast intruded upon the barren vale, and even the landscape itself spoke of its complete emptiness. Perhaps that was why, in the distance, Mouse noticed the peculiar organization of tall stones crowning the coming undulation of earth. She stared hard at them, unable to decide if the formation was natural or not.

"You know, it doesn't make any sense to me," Toma said, rousing everyone from their brooding silence. "Our craft is barely moving and still covering the space here without a problem. Why aren't there any Coalition patrols just... scouting the border? I've never given your typical Coats much credit where brains are concerned, but even a half-wit has to figure we're trying to get *away* from them and into free Elmnas. I mean, they managed to find us before. We should have seen something, anything, by now."

"Yes, I too have found that... unsettling," Rhavin said, looking over at Linnea.

Linnea rolled her eyes. "Why should I know about the movements of Grandfather's army? All I can say is that there are no outposts in this direction. Besides, they may not be even looking for a hovercraft any longer, remember? I destroyed the tracker, so perhaps they believe the craft destroyed as well. They may even think I am dead. As far as we know, the Coalition believes that you are still walking through Elmnas. You would not get far if you tried to go on foot through here, hm?"

"Well, it's very convenient," Toma muttered.

"Not that convenient," Mouse replied, once again looking down at the bidnythine gauge. "We're losing power faster than I thought. Should make it just past those weird stones up there."

Mouse pointed ahead. "By the way, what are those? Fraeda, you have any idea?"

Fraeda, who had been busily staring out the westward facing window, finally noticed where Mouse and the others were looking.

Mouse turned toward her to ask again, but the words never came. She watched in confusion as Fraeda stared fixedly at the stones, her skin growing paler with each moment.

"Oh, no, no, no..." Fraeda wrapped trembling hands over her face as she shook her head. "No, not there, not there."

"Fraeda?" Confusion shifted to heart-pounding fear as Mouse gazed at her friend. Fraeda covered her eyes, her head shaking so vigorously that all of her shuddered. She staggered back, slammed against the cockpit wall and crumpled. A gasping sob escaped her lips. Bewildered, Mouse looked to the others for help, but all of them had grown as pale and terrifyingly helpless as their eyes locked on Fraeda.

Mouse dropped to her knees, taking hold of Fraeda's shoulders as tears streamed through her fingers.

"Fraeda! Look at me! What is it? What's wrong? Fraeda!"

Fraeda refused to respond. Mouse jostled her, gently at first, but with increasing desperation as Fraeda continued to weep. She called her name, over and over, Mouse's voice growing shrill and horrified. Finally, Fraeda's eyes snapped open. Her hands slid off her cheeks weakly, her breathing fast and shallow.

"Look at me," Mouse repeated, trying with all her might not to scream or cry herself. "Breathe, okay? Just breathe. Good, good, keep looking at me. Alright? What is it, Fraeda? What's wrong?"

Fraeda drew a shuddering breath, but kept her eyes trained on Mouse.

"I thought... I thought it was a dream," she whispered. "I thought it didn't happen, I thought... Unseen help me, I told myself it wasn't real!"

Mouse's stomach dropped into her shoes. Every terrible vision she saw cycled through her mind. Images of horrors lurking in the mist and charging down upon her replayed with crystal clarity.

"What are you talking about?" Linnea spoke from behind them, her own voice shaking.

"I'm sorry," Fraeda breathed. "I should have realized it... I've... I've been here before."

"What do you mean? Where?" Mouse asked urgently.

Fraeda stared past Mouse, her breath shallow as she tried to speak. "The Valley of Ghosts."

25

Mouse frowned in confusion, turning her gaze to Toma. He shrugged. Linnea offered nothing either, as she tapped her toe quietly on the floor. Rhavin kept his hands on the steering, but raised his eyebrows as he looked over at Fraeda. For a moment, Mouse had no idea what to say. She let the silence hang in the air as Fraeda bit her fingernails and stared out at the odd stones, which Mouse could now identify as man-made monoliths. Fraeda's breathing had calmed, but the wild terror never left her eyes as she watched the hillock where the sinister guardians drew steadily nearer.

Ghosts? Mouses thought incredulously. *Really?*

The idea did not strike Mouse as totally foreign or even ridiculous. Ghost stories had been a common feature at the Summit for as long as she had been there, and no doubt Mouse had experienced plenty of mystical things when she had escaped. But seeing visions and dreaming dreams seemed an entirely different thing than this brand of supernatural. To be frank, Mouse never believed in ghosts. She had encountered and feared plenty of flesh and blood evils; why add invisible entities to the mix when she had never been bothered by them before?

Still, she had no reason to doubt her friend, and to ignore Fraeda's genuine fear of terrible danger would be both cruel and foolish. Mouse sighed, gathering herself as she placed a reassuring hand on Fraeda's shoulder. Fraeda's gaze snapped back to Mouse.

"I'm trying to understand," Mouse said slowly. "What is the Valley of Ghosts, and why are you so frightened by it?"

"An old battlefield... *the* old battlefield, where the greatest army of Elmnas fought the Coalition in the Last War. It was a massacre. Thousands upon thousands died. Many say this is where the war was truly lost." Fraeda nodded toward the standing stones. "The stones mark its boundary. To go beyond them is... it is madness."

"She's afraid of a hundred-year-old graveyard?" Linnea scoffed openly.

Even though Fraeda could not hear the ridicule, Mouse shot Linnea a dirty look on her behalf. Still, as much as Mouse hated to admit it, Linnea had a point.

"I still don't understand," Mouse tried again. "It's unpleasant to think about, and I'm sure it'll be creepy to go through, but... all the ugliness and real dangers are long gone."

"You're wrong." Fraeda wiped her nose, and, even with her blotchy face and reddened eyes, she managed to glare at the group fiercely. "It's more dangerous than you realize. It's cursed. I should know."

Toma kneeled down beside Mouse, meeting Fraeda's gaze. When he spoke, his words came softly.

"But we don't. Fraeda, what happened?"

Fraeda took a deep breath, expelling it shakily as she gathered her thoughts. She stared out the window again, her hands trembling as they continued to approach the fallow battleground. With one more cleansing breath, she began to speak.

"When I was still very little, my family, my clan – I think they must have known the Coats would take me away once they figured out I was deaf. They tried to save me, all of us, by getting away. I don't remember much, but I guess we tried to escape to the free north by way of the Valley of Ghosts. Even then, before all this, there were not many ways, and for a family as poor as mine, I cannot see that there would have been any other way. It's still there now, the memory... sneaking along Coalition blockades all along the border... soldiers and rifles always in the distance. I didn't speak then, couldn't speak then, but I still remember my father with his fingers to his lips, or his hand over my mouth..."

Fraeda shook her head, a tear squeezing from her tightly shut eyes. Still, she went on.

"We had some pack animals, I think, because I remember getting to the stones and... they couldn't bear it. The animals just went berserk, and we lost most of them. But we went on, into the field, and... oh, how can I explain it? It was like a dream. It got dark. I could barely see anything. My parents were holding my hands, my siblings with them, people in front of us and people behind. We should have been fine, but we weren't... we weren't alone. Something, some *things*, everywhere in the dark. I could see them, these... living nightmares, and what was worse, I could *hear* them too. All inside my head. If that was what hearing was like, I never wanted to hear again.

"I don't know what happened after. So much confusion. All around me, people fighting, running, tugging me this way and that... in the end, we didn't make it through. Somehow, my family got me out. But not everyone did. We lost them, people I wish I could remember now, forever. But I forgot... I forgot because I could never be sure it was real. It was so much like a bad dream. And the Coalition, when they finally did take me, that was nightmare enough."

Fraeda opened her eyes, terror-stricken. "I'm sorry. I can't go that way. I just can't."

"It's okay." Mouse patted Fraeda on the back as Fraeda leaned into Mouse's shoulder. Mouse looked at Toma as Fraeda cried again. He stared at the floor, lips pursed in serious introspection.

"Hey, what do we do?" Mouse whispered, nudging him.

Toma looked up, shaking his head hopelessly. "What can we do?"

"I will tell you what we cannot do," Rhavin said loudly. "We cannot fly any further. Perhaps it is time to brace for landing."

Mouse jerked her head toward the gauge, which was so low it did not register any fuel at all. It blinked rapidly at her as it emitted a high, angry beep.

"Of all the unlucky people in the world..." Linnea muttered, anger dripping from her words.

She followed them up with a colorful curse. Still, Mouse could hear the fear behind the facade. Mouse roused Fraeda with a quick shake.

"We're touching down. Grab a seat!"

Fraeda sniffed, but she nodded her understanding. Without speaking, she got up and moved to the couch where Linnea was already buckling in. Toma helped Mouse up and barred her way out of the cockpit.

"Stay here," he prodded, and before Mouse could object, he held up a hand. "I'll be fine. There's another seat back here somewhere."

He hopped out of the cockpit. Mouse spun, aware now of just how feebly their craft teetered through the air. Rhavin tried everything he could to slow it further, but the craft did not respond. Unheeding momentum carried the craft onward now. He gave up, turning all his attention to steering into a gliding landing. Ever so slightly, the craft angled downward. It would be a softer descent, but not soft enough. Mouse plopped into the copilot's chair and quickly threw straps over her chest and lap. Her fingers fumbled with the buckles when the soft hum of the engine sputtered and quit. Mouse looked up and gasped. The ground was rising to meet them. She threw her hands over her eyes.

The hovercraft hit the rocks with a colossal crack and screeched obscenely as it slid over the ground. Mouse's body flew forward against the straps painfully, the impact stealing her breath. Still, the buckles held. She bounced back into the seat, her head snapping into the mercifully cushioned headrest. Eyes still closed, she could feel the craft twisting and skipping over the stony hillside. She gripped the armrest, gritting her teeth as she waited for the craft to overturn. But though it sounded as if it were being torn to pieces, the ship never rolled. With one last, horrific screech, it scraped to a stop.

Mouse opened her eyes. Emergency lighting bathed everything in a dull, red glow. Before her, the panels continued to blink warnings of power failure. She raised her gaze to the windshield, squinting into the strange brightness of day outside the dim interior. Only paces away, the standing stones reared up in front of them. She could see now that the cluster before them was only one of many. Tall, rounded obelisks formed a loose perimeter across the rolling hill. The largest gaps, it seemed, used to contain stones, but whether torn down by the elements or by the work of human hands, the silent guardians no longer remained in those places. Beyond the gap, the rocky slope eventually tumbled into a grassy plain.

This stretched on and on, empty and flat for many steps into the plain. Beyond that, for as far as the eye could see, staggered mounds rose across the great expanse. A light mist crept along the flat passages between them. Mounds disappeared into the gray in the distance, and Mouse could not see what lay beyond even them. Mist, she supposed, but not the thick, completely opaque mist that heralded the approach of the Mistwolf. No, this was something else. In that lonely and desolate place, a shadow fell, one that Mouse felt as well as saw. It had no source. With no trees, no mountains nearby, no change of light that filtered through the gloam of the red-clouded sky, the shadow had no reason to exist. It just... was. Mouse shivered.

A soft noise inside the cockpit shook her from her thoughts. Mouse turned, remembering now that Rhavin sat beside her. He gripped the steering, a look of shock frozen onto his normally cool features. Other than the rustle of his slight movement, the craft remained deathly quiet. Mouse tried to clear her throat, and this time, Rhavin actually moved. He shook his head and blinked at her as she spoke.

"Is... is everyone alright?" Mouse croaked.

There was some creaking and shuffling before she got an answer.

"Yeah, you?" Toma replied.

Mouse turned again to Rhavin, who simply nodded, wide-eyed.

"Yeah, we're okay."

"I wonder," Linnea said loudly, her annoyed voiced echoing around the interior. "Why we did not bring the hovercraft to the ground *before* we were forced to make a crash landing?"

No one answered, but Mouse was sure everyone felt as stupid as she did for not thinking of it sooner. She sighed, winced as she pulled the seatbelt away from her sore chest and shoulders, and stood.

"Come on," Mouse said, gesturing to Rhavin. "We mangled this thing. Better get out before it collapses."

Again, Rhavin nodded, and with trembling fingers, unhooked himself from his seat and followed her quietly out of the cockpit. Mouse stepped into the cabin. Toma and Linnea were already on their feet, trying to gather their things that had been tossed all around by the crash. Fraeda remained on the couch, staring past Mouse and into the cockpit. From there, Mouse knew she could just glimpse the world outside the windshield, and she knew what Fraeda was staring at. She stepped in front of Fraeda's frozen line of sight as she approached. As if breaking from a trance, Fraeda slowly gazed up at Mouse.

"Oh, we have landed, haven't we?" she said softly. "Everyone is well, I hope?"

Mouse nodded. Fraeda took a deep breath and again glanced past her. Having surveyed the Valley of Ghosts, Mouse felt she could hardly blame Fraeda's fit of terror now. She bent toward Fraeda, wishing she could suppress the creeping sensation at the nape of her own neck. Mouse ignored it instead, placing her hands on Fraeda's shuddering shoulders.

Well, she can't look past me now, Mouse thought, holding Fraeda's anxious gaze.

"Are you okay?" Mouse asked. "Can you walk?"

Fraeda nodded numbly and began to unbuckle from the seat. Mouse smiled encouragingly, or at least tried to; Fraeda's behavior and the threatening creaking of the craft had begun to unnerve her. Once Fraeda was moving around, Mouse quickly busied herself with gathering her own things. She walked gingerly, wincing at every tottering squeal of the cabin beneath her feet as the others also worked in tense silence. Danger, whether from the hovercraft itself or from something beyond its shut doors, seemed a palpable presence among them. Mouse nearly jumped out of her skin when someone finally spoke.

"Will the door open now that the power's dead?" Toma looked nervously at the bay door, his low voice still too loud for Mouse's comfort.

"There is an emergency release," Linnea answered, her quieted voice also too much for Mouse's liking.

With a hesitant step forward, Linnea reached for the release. The door protested, groaning as it flew open. Mouse shielded her eyes to the bright landscape outside. An icy wind whipped across the opening and against the back of the hovercraft. It shifted beneath Mouse's feet precariously. Linnea peered tentatively out the door and shivered before looking back at the others.

"How I would rather not go out there," she said.

"Well, we're not getting anywhere fast in here," Mouse sighed.

Linnea nodded, her teeth already chattering. She pointed to the couch. "There is a compartment beneath there with seasonal clothing. I could have never believed how cold it becomes up here, but Constan always did think of everything. I suppose we shall need them now."

Fraeda opened up the compartment, withdrawing five heavy black cloaks. They bore no Coalition insignia, but their quality make betrayed their Gormlaean origin.

"Boy, can't imagine we'll make good impressions on the free Elmlings with these." Toma frowned.

"There isn't anything to do about it," Fraeda said, handing Toma a cloak from the top of the pile. "As Linnea has noted, winters in Elmnas are certainly not known for their mildness. I'm sorry to say our choices are risk being mistaken for a Coalition soldier or freezing to death. It is now just a matter of what we believe would be worse."

"Hard to say. Depends on if your northern Elmlings are the 'shoot first, ask questions later' types," Toma muttered.

Still, with an air of resignation, he shook out his cloak as Fraeda distributed the rest. Mouse slid her hands over the top of the heavy fabric, hiding her now-cold fingertips in the warm folds. The biting wind outside had already begun to chill the hovercraft cabin. Mouse hated to think of what it would do to them on the open plain. She threw the cloak over her shoulders and thrust her hands through the slightly too large arm holes. Fastening the brass clasps upon the cloak's front and pulling the hood up, Mouse immediately felt the difference. She stroked the arms and front of the cloak as she nodded her approval. Maybe they risked confusion, capture, and hostility after entering free Elmnas; at least she knew she would hardly ever feel the cold once they got there.

"And we shall want to take the rest of the rations, too," Linnea said.

"What about the holomap?" Rhavin asked. "Can it be repaired?"

Linnea held up her bag and shook it. "I doubt it, and even if we do, I cannot say what help it will offer farther north, but... it is in here. Along with Fraeda's."

"It's the best we can do," Mouse said.

Grabbing her pack, she stuffed it with all the extra food and supplies she could carry. The others did so as well, and soon she was following them out the hovercraft door.

Mouse hopped the foot or so down, her feet slapping against hard, cold stone. The wind gusted icily across her face and stirred small drifts of snow along the rocky ground. Sad patches of spiky grass grew in the small clefts between the half-buried stone slabs. To the left and to the right, Mouse found the same barren view; and she was sure if she stepped around the downed hovercraft, she would find more of that nothingness behind them. Ahead, the guardian stones of the ancient battleground rose up, marking the descent into the Valley of Ghosts. Outside the hovercraft, Mouse found it more difficult to see beyond. She squinted down at it. All that she saw in it only moments before was oddly obscured.

"Is it just me, or is it... darker?" Toma asked.

Rhavin shivered beside him, gazing upward. "Something is darker, but it is not the sky. Perhaps Fraeda spoke more sense than we understood."

Linnea huffed and threw her hands in the air. "Not one of you has any sense, is what I think. Look at my ship! Do you know how long it shall take us to get *anywhere* without a hovercraft? It could be months! And that is assuming we do not freeze, or starve, or get captured, or murdered by bandits, or eaten alive by wild beasts, or—"

"Oh, just stuff it, would you?" Mouse said sharply. "Yes, we are in trouble. With all that we've been through so far, are you surprised?"

Linnea opened her mouth, but chose not to voice her stinging retort. She crossed her arms over her chest and stared stubbornly in the other direction instead.

Mouse sighed, looking back at the hovercraft. Yet again, Linnea had a point. One glance told Mouse it had been mangled beyond her capability for repair, and even if she could fix it, then what? They still had no power, and obviously no other way to get the craft airborne again. She snorted in frustration, crossing her own arms as she surveyed the landscape. Miles and miles of flat wasteland went on from east to west.

She's right. With nothing out here in either direction, who knows how long we'll last? Mouse thought.

She glanced at Fraeda, who stood with her back to the rest of the group, eyes still fixed on the Valley of Ghosts. Mouse shuffled over and tapped her on the shoulder. Fraeda jumped.

"Oh! Mouse," she said with a sharp breath. "What is it?"

"I'm sorry," Mouse grimaced, feeling terrible for startling Fraeda, and just as bad about what she needed to ask next. "Look, we don't have many options right now. You know better than any of us what we're up against out here. How big is this battlefield? Can we honestly go around it? It seems to me we can't go in any direction without running into Coats."

"Well..." Fraeda cast an uncertain glance over the valley and to either horizon. "I think we might be able to walk a few miles that way before we're in trouble."

Fraeda pointed west, and Mouse tried, and failed, to stifle a groan.

Will we ever make it to Titans' Rest? Or have we already wasted too much precious time for it to matter?

Mouse's shoulders slumped at the thought. Fraeda wrung her hands anxiously.

"I know it's out of the way, but..." Fraeda cast a terrified look at the standing stones. "You don't know the danger. You can't know. And once we find a safe place to cross, I'm sure we'll find good help for the rest of the journey. The free Elmlings will know what to do."

Frustration bubbled up inside Mouse, but it was no use getting angry. For Fraeda's sake, she pushed it down. Turning away, she called for the others.

"Come on, everyone!" Mouse clapped her hands together with faux cheeriness, but she was sure the barely suppressed sigh of annoyance betrayed her true feelings. "Let's not waste any more time. Fraeda thinks we have a good shot this way, so we should try that."

Rhavin and Toma, engaged in low conversation, looked over at her. Toma frowned.

"But there's nothing down there. We can all see that. What if we—"

Mouse dropped all pretenses of optimism and shook her head with an aggravated snort. "Listen, just... let's see if there is another way that doesn't involve Fraeda going catatonic on us, okay?"

Toma exchanged a look with Rhavin, raising an eyebrow, but said nothing else. They picked up their packs as Mouse shouldered hers. Turning on her heel, she strode away from them before anyone else decided to argue, but her quick pace didn't keep Linnea's muttering from reaching her ears.

Rolling her eyes, Mouse clambered up and out of the small cleft that their craft had tipped into. Mouse finally stood up at full height on the small edge some yards from the hovercraft. She glanced back at it one last time, her gaze lingering upon the wreckage, twisting like tin in the gusts of wind that tore across the plain. It was a sad sight. Mouse knew she should hate even the idea of the hovercraft. It was an emblem of her oppression and her people's near extermination. Still, she could not quell the excitement, the joy, the child-like curiosity that came over her when she thought about its ingenuity. The realization that she could never tinker with this particular craft again grieved Mouse in a way she hadn't grieved before.

Goodbye, she thought sadly. *Thanks for saving my life.*

Mouse pulled her cloak more tightly around her face as the wintry air blasted her, no longer impeded by the shallow gully or the little protection of the hovercraft's bulk. She tucked her hands in her sleeves and began to walk, keeping the standing stones at her right. Much closer now, the stones loomed above Mouse's head at maybe fifteen feet high. She could make out the details now, too – stones of an alabaster hue, unlike the slabs of dark gray they trod upon. Yellow and brown lichen inched up the stones from the base and obscured some of the weathered, ancient carvings that covered them. Whether runic words or images, Mouse could not tell, but they seemed to belong to an Elmnas far older than the one she was only beginning to remember. Silent as the valley below, the stone guardians gave no further clues to their mysterious meaning. They did, however, grow more ominous the longer Mouse looked at them. A chill ran down her spine. With her next step, she put more distance between herself and the markers.

It was not long before Fraeda fell in stride beside Mouse, her fidgeting hands wringing the sleeves of her cloak. Mouse tried not to sigh again as Fraeda glanced across her at the valley. She tried to imagine what Fraeda was feeling instead. Guilt at her frustration nagged at Mouse's mind. She caught Fraeda's worried gaze the next time it flitted to the valley.

"Hey, I'm sorry how much this bothers you."

"It's fine," Fraeda said with a dismissive wave, but her strained voice said otherwise.

"Well, it's creeping me out, anyway," Mouse said. "I guess we won't be sorry to cross into free Elmnas somewhere else."

Fraeda let out a shaky laugh. "Yes, for sure. I do think we can find a way over if we just..."

She halted and stopped speaking. Mouse had walked two strides before she realized Fraeda was standing still. She turned, shocked to see all the color had gone from Fraeda's face.

"What is it?" Mouse whispered.

"Don't you... feel that?"

"What?"

Fraeda did not answer. She turned, scanning the horizon. Her eyes grew wide.

"There."

Mouse wheeled around, shielding her face against the wind as she squinted off into the east. A black speck hurtled toward them, growing in size as it careened toward them. Its slick surface reflected back the rust-colored haze of the sky. It was unmistakable. A hovercraft.

"What are you..." Toma started, freezing in place as Fraeda and Mouse looked past him in horror. He tried to scoff, but the alarm was all too clear in his voice. "I don't want to look, do I?"

"They have found us!" Linnea cried. "Run!"

Mouse looked at Linnea, opening her mouth to confirm her fears. But Linnea pointed in a different direction. Mouse searched the surrounding wastes, her eyes finding a second black speck roaring up from the south. Her breath caught in her throat: yet another shadow, this one flying from the western horizon, approached steadily in the far distance.

Mouse turned back in horror. The first hovercraft was coming on far faster than she realized. The speck grew larger and larger, taking shape as the smooth, expanded hull of a transport craft. Canons mounted on the sides spoke of the vehicle's intentions. The other two crafts appeared much the same. There was no doubt about it now. The Coalition was coming, and they had them cornered.

26

Icy fear gripped Mouse's heart, constricting it until her blood froze solid. It was all she could do to turn and gaze at the horror-filled faces of her friends. They stared back at her, mouths open, unable to speak. The sound of whirring drifted faintly toward her, and the ground rumbled beneath her feet. She looked down at them, shell-shocked, as pebbles danced along the gray stone.

Someone grabbed her arm tight. Mouse looked to her side, barely comprehending the person clutching her, tugging her arm. Someone yelled her name.

"Mouse, Mouse!"

Mouse's legs unfroze and turned to putty instead. Her knees buckled, but still, she moved. Around her, Fraeda, Toma, Rhavin, and Linnea clustered and held tight to one another. They were inching backward. Her back bumped against a weathered stone. She flinched and jumped away from it, realizing at once what it was. A hand tugged her back against it.

"Stay here," Fraeda said, shaking her head. "It's all we can do."

Mouse tried to speak, but her tongue stuck to the roof of her mouth. Numbly, Mouse reached for her holster, withdrawing her weapon. Feeling began to come back into Mouse's limbs, clarity in her mind where panic had blinded her. She looked around.

Fraeda stood at her left, still holding tightly to Mouse's free arm. Toma pressed against her at her right, with Linnea and Rhavin standing close at his side. Each had weapons drawn as well, pointing outward from where they stood. Mouse turned her attention forward, and once again, her stomach somersaulted.

The three hovercrafts had converged and were now facing the five. Though the sight was enough to melt any of the courage Mouse had begun to gather again, several odd things struck her all at once. First, the hovercrafts remained far off, well behind where their poor craft met its fate. Given their speed and trajectory, they should have been only paces away. What was more, they had grounded. When had the Coalition ever parked in the midst of an attack? Curiosity overwhelming her fear, Mouse squinted at the crafts.

"They're completely powered down," she said, frowning. "That's... insane. Why would they do that?"

"Beats me," Toma replied, his voice shaking. "They should've blown us to pieces by now."

"There is, at least, one reason." Linnea gulped and turned to the others. "They want us alive."

Mouse swallowed. The others exchanged bleak glances as the hovercraft hatches hissed open.

Out of the right and left crafts came a dozen Coats each. Armored and grim-faced, they lined up across the wasteland and faced them. Mouse frowned as she noticed not energy rifles, but sabers and crossbows in their hands. Out of the central craft, however, only came one. The lithe, muscular form of a woman stood in shadow just inside the open hovercraft door. Her rich cloak and long, black hair billowed out beside her, catching in the sudden gust of harsh winter wind.

"My, my," she called, a mockery of cheer ringing in her voice. "What do we have here?"

Linnea drew a sharp, horrified breath. Within moments, Mouse could guess why.

The woman hopped down with athletic ease, her charcoal armor gleaming splendidly despite the dull expanse around her. She pierced them with malevolent eyes as her ruby-red lips grinned murderously. Even at that distance, Mouse could see the family resemblance.

"Oh yes, I see now," the woman continued, shading her eyes and squinting. "Linny, darling, you have made some friends, have you? Be a dear and introduce them to Mother. I am most pleased to meet them."

Linnea's breath came hard and fast as she backed against the standing stone. Mouse did not have to see her face to know the terror that must be written there. She could feel it. Her own heart galloped around her chest as she stared into the face of Prime Ambassador Tyranna Vipsanius.

"Have courage," Rhavin whispered solemnly. His knives flashed between his fingers. "We shall not let her lay a finger upon you."

Mouse and Toma murmured in assent. Linnea said nothing, but as Mouse glanced at the Coalition traitor, Linnea nodded slightly. She stood straighter and raised her pistol in shaking hands.

"No?" Tyranna took a few steps forward. "Well, never fear. I have done my research."

The Prime Ambassador swept the group with a wicked sneer.

"The Ameliorite Sister, I believe, an Elmling. I did not catch your name, but I can only presume it is you. The Priory would send their regards, but I am afraid they are... indisposed."

Mouse felt the pinch of Fraeda's panicked grip even through her cloak.

"The Dell boy. Berr-Toma, is it? Have you checked in on Breythorn Farm recently, hmm? Naughty boy, you really *should* listen to your parents from time to time."

Toma growled and raised his pistol. Tyranna smirked before moving on to Rhavin. She frowned.

"A Heibeiathan. Odd. And I notice *not* your betrothed, Linny. I hope you know this has made some trouble for Mother."

She clucked her tongue as she turned to Mouse. Mouse gulped.

"And of course, there is the ringleader of this little venture. Prisoner 146. Color me impressed. I had to do a little more digging on you, but I believe I've found you out. Of course, you might not remember me, thanks to your stay at Misty Summit. But I shall tell you what they called me when I wore this."

The Prime Ambassador pulled something from her cloak and placed it upon her head. Her silver helmet, tinted red by the sky, sat low over her forehead, where a nosepiece stretched down and nearly met the two sharp sides covering her cheeks. Mouse stared open-mouthed at the black horns on either side of the helmet's temples, polished and sharpened to perfection. The Prime Ambassador curled her red lips into a vicious smile.

"The Slayer of Samras."

Pain, terror, and anger ballooned inside Mouse as a locked door opened in her mind. Like flashes of lightning, images streaked in, playing in unrelenting succession. That night... the night she lost everyone, everything. The flames, the bodies, the screams – there was something else. Something else that Mouse had forgotten. Right before Papa left her. In the center of Shomroh, in the rage of the fire, a figure stood. A woman. Her cloak and dark hair streaming behind her, hellfire shining upon her silver helmet and its curving, black horns, a hateful sneer on her perfect, red lips.

Mouse squeezed her eyes shut, willing the images rattling in her brain to go away.

"You," she choked, tears rushing down her hot cheeks. "You were there."

"Probably," Tyranna answered flippantly. "I burned a number of Samrasine villages that week, and to be quite honest, I do not remember all of them. Strange, I distinctly remember being thorough. Then again, your kind are like weeds. You can uproot a whole colony and raze the soil, and still, somehow, you keep popping up."

With a howl of rage, Mouse leveled her pistol at Tyranna.

"Mouse! No!" Toma cried.

It was too late. Mouse squeezed the trigger.

She blinked, waiting for the searing blast to rip from the barrel. It never came. Mouse pressed again and again. Nothing happened. Tyranna laughed.

"Oh, my, I forgot to tell you, your weapons will not work here. Were you not curious as to why your craft gave up the ghost? Indeed, that is the peculiar thing about the border, and what a shame. I do believe you might have struck me otherwise."

Mouse gritted her teeth, embarrassment at her stupidity and anger at her failure, leaving her speechless. But Rhavin shouted out instead.

"We have other means of fighting!" He flashed his knives dangerously. "You will not touch us."

"Cute," Tyranna said, but the amusement was gone from her voice. "But foolish. Do you not know when you are bested? Linnea, I taught you sense, did I not? You cannot fight us. I see you know death waits for any who enter the Valley of Ghosts, or else you would have taken refuge there already. You know you cannot escape. There need not be bloodshed. Come quietly. Come home. Do you not want to see Father again? He misses you so. Make him happy."

"I do not think so, Mother," Linnea said shakily. "It would not please him if I went with you."

Tyranna's mouth twisted in disgust. "Is that so? Do you always do what pleases Father, or will you ever have more use in your miserable life than that?"

Linnea said nothing. Tyranna sneered.

"I see. Then what must be done will be done."

The Ambassador held up her arm and twisted something on her wrist. As she did so, she signaled to her hovercraft. Elite soldiers bearing an insignia of a single lion jumped to the ground. Mouse shrank at their size and weaponry, but the sight that followed could have brought her to her knees. A final, enormous figure stepped toward the hovercraft door. He barely fit in its frame. A shock of red hair exited the door as he bent beneath it. The soldier hefted a battle axe as he stared right at Mouse with brilliantly green eyes. She knew those eyes, eyes once kind and worthy of her deepest trust. They looked back with predatory detachment. Nothing was left of the soul once behind them.

"Red," Mouse whispered hoarsely.

27

"Give me Linnea and Prisoner 146!" Tyranna shouted. "Kill the others!"

Crossbow bolts soared toward them as the five dived behind the standing stone. They clattered on the hard ground and shattered pieces of the ancient rock. Without looking, Mouse could feel the surge of soldiers coming toward them. Footsteps from Tyranna's elite force pounded toward them as well as the two other crafts. Behind them, Red roared, the sound entirely unhuman. Mouse's blood froze.

"I'm so sorry, we have no choice," Fraeda whispered, tears falling down her cheeks. "Hold on."

She closed her eyes, reaching for Mouse's hand and squeezing it painfully tight as she jerked her the other way. Suddenly, Mouse understood. She looked beside her, and Toma's gaze met hers. She reached out her other hand. Fraeda pulled, and Mouse came tumbling behind. Toma followed after, Linnea and Rhavin fumbling to link as they ran. The clanking of soldiers' boots and rattling of bolts grew louder in Mouse's ears. She ran.

The ground shook as she pounded over the shale. She did not dare to look back. Shivers crawled over her despite the sweat and heat beneath the heavy cloak. Still, urgency afforded Mouse no moment further of hesitation. Fraeda continued to pull. With a gasp as if she were plunging into icy water, Mouse slipped down the slope.

Hand in hand, they stumbled into the valley. Stones rolled underfoot as Mouse scrambled along the increasing decline. It was steeper than she realized, dropping from the butte above some dozens of feet into the valley rising to meet her. Toma pulled away from her, working hard to keep his momentum from carrying into Mouse and bowling her over. He found her hand again as the grass softened her footfalls. She slipped on it, nearly falling to the ground. Toma yanked her upright, and Mouse found her feet beneath her just as the slope leveled. Fraeda pulled even harder, breaking once again into an all-out run.

Mouse breathed hard as she followed, taking in the valley as it streamed past. Thin mists swirled across the ground, ebbing and flowing like an ocean tide. The shapes of the mounds rose ahead, very close now, but cast in such shadow that Mouse could not rightly see them. A pervasive, strange twilight had fallen over everything. Mouse shot a glance upward. A low-hanging ceiling of fog obscured even more of the ever-clouded sky, and no longer did the midday light stream down to them.

No light at all, Mouse thought, her scalp crawling. *How is that possible? What is this place?*

Mouse tried to shake off her growing sense of the sinister and focused on what lay ahead instead. But there, the gloam only thickened. What she had once seen by the light of day above, she could not make out now. For all she knew, the Valley of Ghosts would never end. The farthest of the mounds disappeared into the shadow that had no business being there in the first place. Still, they ran on, never stopping, never giving the Coalition an opportunity to cut them down.

"Wait!" Linnea shouted from behind Mouse.

The sound fell dead in the air, and Mouse realized just how quiet everything was around. She had been aware of the sounds of running, their breathing and the swish of feet through the grass, but there was nothing else. Nothing at all.

Mouse tugged hard on Fraeda's hand and dug her heels into the ground. Fraeda stopped abruptly, wheeling around to face Mouse and the others. Her face was wild and flushed, and her eyes wide and white. Fraeda heaved with the exertion of the run, holding her ribs with her free hand. Still, she squeezed Mouse's fingers in hers and shifted her feet anxiously, ready to flee again at a moment's notice.

"We need to keep going," Fraeda said breathlessly. "We can't rest here, even for a moment."

She turned, but Mouse tugged again. Anger broke through the exhaustion and the fear.

"What?" Fraeda said, her voice sharp.

"The soldiers. What happened to them? They're not... there. I cannot hear them anymore," Linnea said haltingly, stepping closer. "They were right behind us. Where could they have possibly gone?"

Fraeda squinted to read her lips in the gathering dark, her face softening as she did so. She nodded, empathy returning to her features, her fear clearing for a moment.

"Yes, I understand now. You are right. I don't know what to tell you. Nothing I say can explain it. It's because... we are here."

"But they were right behind us!" Toma added, gesturing back to the slope.

Mouse glanced back, shocked that she could only see a thin line of sky above the ridge behind them. It was far. Farther away than it should have been. All light fled unnaturally below. Nothing moved in the valley. No one came over the plain behind them.

"I don't think they just turned around!" Toma exclaimed, shaking his head. "It doesn't make any sense!"

"This isn't the sort of place where anything makes sense," Fraeda said, shuddering. "You don't understand now, but you will. Now please, listen to me. Don't let go of each other, not even for a moment. You're going to... see things. Hear things. Things that may or may not be real. I'm beginning to remember it more now... what happened the first time I came."

"And what did happen?" Mouse asked tentatively.

"There are no words for it," Fraeda said numbly. "I wish I could explain. But then... you'll see, won't you?"

"But *why* is this happening?"

Linnea huffed. Mouse thought she would have thrown her hands up in frustration had Toma and Rhavin not been holding them. Even so, Linnea could not hide the mounting fear plain on her face. She drew a long breath as Rhavin answered.

"It is hard for your people to understand," Rhavin said quietly. "You do not believe in the thin places, the haunted places. But they have always been there. This is doubtless one of them. We do best to heed Fraeda's warnings of the evils we shall find."

Mouse's gaze shifted uncomfortably from Rhavin, to a somber Linnea, a puzzled Toma, and finally, to Fraeda, who pursed her lips and nodded slowly in agreement. Mouse did not know what to think. Surviving evils that existed in a cold reality wrought by cruel people was one thing; how exactly were they to manage evils that belonged to some otherworldly realm?

Far off, miles away, a tortured cry rent the air.

Mouse froze. She stared into the paling faces of her friends as moans and screams answered the first in the valley all around.

"It's starting," Fraeda breathed. "We need to go."

Cries followed them as they bolted, each of them running as hard as they could. Soon, the mounds reared up out of the shadows before them. Fraeda swerved, dragging her train of followers behind. As they passed, one by one, Mouse began to understand what they were: graves, hundreds of them, filled with who knew how many bodies of the fallen in that great, ancient war.

The blood-chilling screams faded and died. The silence behind Mouse stretched on, and she got the distinct and horrible feeling that those voices would never be heard again. Still, they ran, hotly pursued by shadows that never relented.

LION

A stitch formed on Mouse's side as Fraeda finally slowed to a jog, and then to a brisk walk. But Mouse suspected Fraeda hadn't slowed because she was winded; rather, the darkness had grown so thick that they could no longer see feet in any direction. Mouse chanced a desperate glance behind her once more, seeking comfort in the thin line of reddish sky. It had gone.

Mouse's gaze snapped to Toma and the others behind her as she tried to make out their faces. She no longer could. The heaving breaths, the shuffling footfalls, and the heat of sweaty palms against hers remained the only signs that she was not utterly, completely alone in this night.

But she was not alone.

She could feel it now. Something passed near enough for her to feel a breath of icy air against her cheek. Mouse shivered, biting her lip to keep from yelping in fear. She squeezed Toma and Fraeda's hands harder, but she did not need to. Their death-like grips crushed her fingers against each other as a shape moved beside them.

Mouse forced herself to look, to face her foe, whatever it might be. She knew without seeing it was no Coalition soldier. A morbid, despairing corner of her heart almost hoped it was a Mistwolf. At least then she would know what they came up against. But no lupine shape emerged. No low growls or keening howls met her ears, nor could she smell the pungent mix of rot and sulfur that preceded them.

Whatever this was had no shape, and yet, more surely than the ground that was beneath her feet, she knew it was there. She felt it more than saw it, an undulating blackness darker even than the gloom surrounding them. It crept beside them, keeping pace as its form swelled and shrank like the deep breaths of a heavy sleeper. Mouse wanted to speak, wanted to warn her friends, but nothing came out. It drifted closer.

She gasped as Fraeda's shaking voice broke the tense silence.

"Don't... don't let go. Please. Keep walking. Even when it reaches inside you."

253

"What is it?" Linnea asked in a shuddering whisper. "What is that thing?"

"Things," came Toma's hoarse voice, and Mouse realized he was almost pressed against her. "They're all around us."

Mouse twisted wildly, her heart leaping into her throat as she saw that Toma spoke the truth. Shadows glided beside them on her left and on her right. An amorphous darkness pursued them from behind. Another icy breath of air touched her face and penetrated to the bone. Mouse whipped to look to her right, from where it had come. The black shape had come nearer. If she had wanted, she could reach out her hand and touch it. The thought alone made every hair stand on end. Still, she could not look away. Transfixed, she stared at the consuming darkness.

Its shape changed.

Mouse froze, watching in horror as it morphed. Finally, the lupine head and enormous, powerful limbs she had grown to dread more than anything grew out of the darkness. Its jaws opened and shut, a guttural growl in its throat. The smell hit her all at once, and she gagged.

No, no, please, not that.

The wolf head turned toward her, as if thinking. Glowing red eyes blinked. As it considered her, arresting gasps and moans of terror escaped from her friends.

"No, not you, anyone but you!" Fraeda cried in Elmling.

She sounded as weak and as pitiful as a child. Her grasp weakened in Mouse's hand. Mouse squeezed tighter, and Fraeda breathed in sharply.

"Don't let him touch me, don't let him near me!" she squealed.

A terrible scream from behind jerked Mouse from Fraeda.

Linnea, Mouse realized.

"Mother, no... Mother please! Please don't hurt him, please!"

Linnea's hysterical screams rose all the louder. Mouse wanted to cover her ears, but she couldn't. She dared not let go. Below Linnea's screams and Fraeda's weeping, she heard Rhavin, rapidly speaking in

Heibeiathan, each utterance growing into a frenzied shout. Behind Toma, she felt him tugging, fighting, trying to escape. She squeezed Toma's hand, but he had fallen silent and nearly limp. Only two words came from his lips as he crumpled to the ground.

"I'm... sorry."

The wolf head watched with curiosity as Mouse tried to pull him to his feet. Toma would not budge. She wanted to cry, she wanted to scream, but she could muster nothing but desperation. Fraeda thrashed against her, pulling as hard as she could to escape Mouse's tenuous grasp. Overwhelmed, Mouse glanced again at the shadow Mistwolf. Her friends' words, their uttered, anguished, groaning and writhing, terrified Mouse more than the sight before her.

I know this now.

The words slithered out of the shadow wolf's mouth, rasping like a serpent's scales as they reached her. Mouse stared in renewed horror as the wolf shape again began to change.

It is time, 146.

The shape stretched, the lupine legs and shaggy head retracting. It congealed into a man, and by its changed voice she knew it: the Supervisor, the one who took Red from her forever.

"Leave me," she whispered shakily. "You aren't real."

But it's time to play.

The voice and the shape changed again. The man shortened and became thin, arrogant, predatory. Mouse shuddered as Slim's yellowed teeth leered back at her.

Won't Mousey come and play? I got some new tricks for you. I do. And look how you've grown. Oh, the things I'm gonna do to you.

"You're dead!" Mouse shrieked. "I saw it! I heard you die!"

Oh Mousey, Slim laughed. *Do you really believe that any of your nightmares can die here?*

The odor of rancid breath filled Mouse's nostrils as Slim continued to laugh. His black fingers reached toward her and stopped inches from her throat.

So many fears, the rasping, slithering voice said again. *What to choose?*

Again, the shape changed, morphing into the green, dead eyes of Red, the sneering face of the bounty hunter, shifting easily into the Prime Ambassador. Smoke filled Mouse's lungs, and she coughed as she breathed in the smell of burning corpses. Tears stung her eyes as the shape remained feminine. But this time, it was loved, familiar. Two dark eyebrows knitted together in sorrow and concern as her mother's face resolved out of the shadow.

Hiiri, don't leave me here! Don't leave me to die!

Mouse wept openly now, unable to look away from her mother's face. Her expression had twisted into one of excruciating pain. Flames licked at her torso and consumed the skin on her arms and neck.

Hiiri! Hiiri! Why? Why would you do this to me?

"Mama," Mouse choked. "I didn't... I..."

Her mother pointed a burning finger in her face. Mouse nearly puked at the smell of charred flesh beneath her nose.

It's your fault. They came for you, they came for the Harbinger! You did this, Hiiri! You killed us all!

Mouse slumped, wracked with grief and guilt. Vaguely, she was aware of the two hands in hers. She had forgotten why they were there, and who the hands belonged to.

What does it matter, anyway? Mouse thought in tortured despair. *Nothing matters any longer. I deserve this.*

The black shape that was Mama slithered toward Mouse. It grabbed hold of her, entangling her in its endless tendrils, pulling her inside the black thing's fatal embrace. Mama was wailing now, wailing in the throes of an agonizing death that would never end. It had her now. Mouse would be consumed. But even as she succumbed, she felt it recoil and hiss as one tendril touched her hip. In the midst of the screaming and burning, a thought occurred to her.

Why?

Like light piercing the darkness, the thought of her Cardanthium dagger still in its sheath burst into her mind. It roused her, if only a little, and Mouse turned her head from the black shape already against her cheek.

"Toma!" Mouse called weakly. "Toma! Can you hear me?"

She remembered now what was in her hands: the lives of her friends. She squeezed her fingers, grappling to keep hold of Fraeda who had no strength left to squeeze back. The darkness wailed louder, angrily, and it filled her ears, slipped inside, and began choking her like poison. But Mouse could feel the dagger now, too, burning against her side, bright and hot. She tried to look at where she knew it would be. In the black curtain, a sliver of light shone from her holster. Dull as it was, it was something. It was hope.

"Toma!"

"Mouse..."

Toma's voice cracked with anguish. Mouse's heart ached at his pain. It pulled her out of her own misery, if only for a moment, giving her the strength for what she must do next. She pulled Toma's hand to her side, pushing back her cloak as she pressed his fingers against her belt loops.

"Hang on!"

"No..." he moaned.

Tears brimmed in Mouse's eyes. She could not breathe. The darkness had fully covered her now, and she felt Fraeda slipping out of her grasp. Mouse moved as if through mud. She slipped her hand out of Toma's weakening grip, slapping his hand against her side. Whether he caught on or not, she could not tell. She stretched for her dagger, an unbearable heaviness pressing down on her chest and suspending her hand in an invisible morass. Her knees buckled as her feeble fingertips grazed the hilt. All the comfort of human touch disappeared. Toma and Fraeda had dissolved, and she could no longer sense them. Despair crushed her as the screams of her dying mother overwhelmed every sense. Mouse felt her own life ebb with every anguished wail. This was it. She was alone, finally, utterly alone.

No.

A voice, not her own, but not the darkness, either, reached inside her. Gently, it pulled at her, tugging her from the miry depths she had sunk to. Light flashed across the black sky. Mouse blinked at it, the shape still imprinted in her mind after it had gone.

Phoenix.

It was only a moment, but it was all Mouse needed. New strength flooded her as she withdrew the dagger. The light that came so dimly before blazed mightily in her fist. Mouse slashed, and the dagger struck. She could not know what it struck, but Mouse felt the resistance of the dagger, heard a bestial shriek of pain, and gasped for air as the heavy presence suddenly withdrew. Her mother's wailing stopped. The dagger flared all the brighter, pushing the screeching darkness away.

Mouse waved the dagger overhead. A new fear filled her as she searched for her friends. Ahead, Fraeda lay on the ground, hardly moving. Mouse lunged forward, grabbing her ankle as she swung the dagger wildly through the air. Something let out a high, terrible whine as it took flight. Mouse pulled, and Fraeda stirred feebly. Mouse tried to stand to reach her, but felt something pull against her side. She turned, brandishing the dagger, only to find Toma's wild, wide-eyed faced looking up at her. His fingers were still hooked on her belt loop.

"Help me!" Mouse said desperately.

He glanced back.

"The others," he said hoarsely.

Mouse stumbled over him, holding the dagger in front of her. She could see two inert shapes just outside the blade's glow. She jumped to her feet and slashed above them.

By its light, she saw one of their hunters in its true, profane form. Thin, red eyes stared back, malevolent and greedy as it stretched black, spindly claws toward an unconscious Rhavin. It opened a circular, saw-like mouth. Rows upon rows of teeth lined the cavernous emptiness. It sucked in a rasping, rattling breath.

Mouse plunged the blade, its point finding purchase between the hungry eyes. The thing screamed, louder than any of the others, and by its scream Mouse knew it had been mortally wounded or sent out of Reidara for good. Like escaping air, it hissed away until it was gone.

Her dagger blazed triumphantly and flooded her with a strength she never knew. With the shout of a warrior, she jumped to her feet and pursued the lingering dark shapes. How many there truly were, she could not guess, for each fled before the holy, sharp light of the Cardanthium and shrieked at the scourging touch of its razor edges. Into the shadows they disappeared, and with them went the suffocating night that had fallen upon the valley.

A thin, gray light filtered through the fog above. Like the rise of the dawn, it increased moment by moment. Mouse stretched out her hands before her, the unexpected rush of relief at their welcome sight bringing new tears to her eyes. She turned, those tears falling freely down her cheeks as she found the upright, breathing, living forms of her friends huddled together on the grassy ground. Mouse rushed toward them as Fraeda looked up at her, still gasping, arms thrown around a shuddering Linnea. Still, Fraeda's eyes shone wet with joy and hope.

"You did it," she whispered.

Mouse laughed, wiping her damp cheeks with the back of her hand. She gazed down at the blade still clenched in her fist.

"No, I'm not so sure that I did."

28

Mouse replaced her dagger and stepped closer. The others, still gaining their bearings, roused to look up at her.

Linnea, still beneath Fraeda's comforting wing, lifted a shaking hand to the hem of Mouse's cloak. She stared up with bloodshot, but grateful, eyes. Mouse placed her hand against Linnea's and squeezed. It was clammy and cold, but alive.

Rhavin muttered something in Heibeiathan, bowing deeply and steepling his fingers in something like a blessing toward her. Mouse smiled as best she could. She turned last to Toma. He managed his own fragile, thin smile before reaching out and slipping his fingers through hers. Mouse's stomach fluttered. She flopped down beside him, and before she could stop herself, rested her head against his shoulder. He let out a contented sigh.

"All the same," Fraeda said, swallowing. "We are alive, thank the Unseen, though we shouldn't be."

Mouse wanted to say something, but her ragged, exhausted lips could not form the words. She studied the faces of her friends again. With their pale and wild countenances, they looked as she felt – puzzling out their dual desire both to understand and to never speak of what had happened to them there in the Valley of Ghosts. Mouse cast a glance over her shoulder, back from where they had just come. An unnatural semi-darkness that deepened into twilight shadow fell behind them. She could only think of the intense gathering of angry clouds before a particularly violent thunderstorm. It veiled from sight whatever waited in the valley as well as the danger they had narrowly escaped at its edge. She could no longer be sure that southern Elmnas even existed beyond the battleground's borders. The longer she stared into the darkness, the harder it was to discern the reality from the dream.

At this revulsion welled up inside Mouse. Try as she might, she could not dispel the image of that thing that became every one of her worst nightmares, forcing itself into the deepest recesses of her mind. The slimy contamination of its evil touch made her skin crawl all over again. But worse still was the truth behind the nightmares. Her thoughts drifted back to the moments before their escape. Each new revelation hit her like a blow to the chest. The loss of her home, her family, her past... all that had been at the hands of the Slayer of Samras, the Prime Ambassador.

Linnea's mother, Mouse thought in disbelief.

It shook her to her core. But even as she looked again at Linnea, expecting a new wave of hatred to fill her, it never came. For the first time since she met her, Mouse saw Linnea for what she was: a victim, a survivor, a lost girl searching for a way to make things right. Just like her.

Mouse nestled a little closer to Toma, wishing the other awful truth she had learned would end in some peace like the last. But as her thoughts turned to the red-haired soldier roaring after her, she could not imagine how.

Was it really Red?

The soulless eyes flashed back into her mind. Though she tried, she could make no sense of it. The Red she saw today was younger, stronger, changed in a way that seemed entirely out of the realm of possibility. But as Mouse dwelled upon those eyes, she could not come to any other conclusion. They were empty and terrible, as devoid of humanity as the rest of the Taken at Misty Summit, but without a doubt, they were his. Mouse shivered.

Toma placed his arm around her, and whether he meant to do so or not, drew Mouse closer. Sinking into the warmth radiating from him, she closed her eyes and imagined a world without the fate of her loved ones already sealed or hanging in the balance. Mouse imagined the end of the war, a bear hug from a restored and whole Red, and growing old, no prison walls or wilderness wanderings, but a warm hearth and a quiet, peaceful home. She imagined falling asleep... just like this. For the first time, she imagined things she never dared to dream before, and despite everything, dared to hope it could be.

"Hey."

Toma spoke softly in Mouse's ear, stirring her from her fantasy. She sat up, shaking off her weariness as she remembered where they still remained.

"What's wrong?" Mouse replied.

"Nothing," Toma assured her. "I was just wondering... if any *good* things we see here in this place are real."

"I'm not sure," Mouse frowned. "Why?"

Toma pointed. "Well, how about that? Do you think that is real?"

Mouse gazed ahead. In stark contrast to the valley behind, the light had grown, almost reaching the daytime brightness she had come to long for. It touched the last of the burial mounds ahead and grew steadier and more real as it washed up a ridge and over the last of the tall, somber standing stones that watched along the valley's far boundary. At the top of the ridge, where Toma pointed, Mouse made out puffs of smoke and crackling, cheery flames.

"A campfire?" Linnea shook her head in disbelief. "Could it really be just... a campfire?"

The five weary travelers all stared hopefully at the fire. Mouse squinted in concentration as something moved behind it. The bald head of an elderly Elmling bobbed into view. Though still a long way off, Mouse could make out the diminutive aged form stooping over the fire and pulling off a steaming kettle.

"I hope so," Rhavin replied, rubbing his arms. "It is a welcome sight."

"That man... Why do I get the feeling I know him?" Fraeda murmured.

The old man turned his face toward them, a knowing smile on his lips. With one gnarled hand, he stroked his long, white beard, and with the other, beckoned to them. Mouse's mouth hung open as another set of familiar green eyes met hers. An image formed in her mind as a voice echoed in her ears.

Without thinking, she clutched at the master key, the one that had spelled Rhavin's freedom from Needar's Circus and salvation for them, thrown by those same old, knobby hands. She cleared her throat.

"I... I think I do."

29

71st of Sun's Wane
High Security Detention Facility
Location Undisclosed

Dervish slouched drowsily against the wall of his cell, his legs stretched in front of him and his head resting against the cool cement as if he were already sleeping. To anyone watching, Dervish knew that's what they'd think. He breathed in and out in the slow, even rhythm of deep sleep, his crossed arms moving with the rising and falling of his paunch. But with his cap low on his forehead and his body still, they could not see his scrupulous gaze roving everywhere. No one could comprehend just how many whispered words made it to his ever-listening ears.

Mouth shut. Eyes and ears always open. Myergo had plenty of sneaks and snitches, but not one of them could measure up to Dervish. He was downright professional. Maybe that was why Myergo had kept him around all these years, trusted him, and had even seemed to like him. Well, as much as Myergo could like anybody. And maybe that was why he got to share a cell with him –

only him – in the depths of this high security Coalition prison facility.

Dervish's eyes darted to the corner where Myergo waited. He had been provided a small table, a stool, a loaf of bread and wooden goblet of wine. Surprising luxury, as far holding cells went in Coalition prisons. But Myergo had not accepted the hospitality. The bread and wine lay untouched. His massive hands remained patiently folded upon the rough table's surface. He had taken to the stool, however, and his enormous frame was perched and curled atop it like a resting dragon. The dim light of the cell obscured most of his face in shadow. From where he sat, all Dervish could see were his two black eyes, shining with calculating malevolence.

"You have been silent long enough," Myergo said, his gravelly voice just loud enough for Dervish to hear. "What have you gathered so far, my crafty friend?"

Dervish did not move as he answered. "Not much. The rest of our lot are being held on another level. Guards don't seem to know what to do, though. Waitin' on orders from higher up, it seems."

Myergo let out a rumbling, wicked chuckle. "As expected. We shall know soon."

Dervish cocked his head at this remark and eyed Myergo suspiciously. "What're you on about?"

"You shall see," he answered.

Myergo's face split in an evil grin, which showed all of his pointed yellow teeth. Despite himself, Dervish recoiled. Pleased as he was with the work and the pay the crime lord offered him, Dervish trusted Myergo about as far as he could throw him. That terrible smile usually spelled doom for someone; sometimes enemies far off, sometimes once-trusted associates close beside. And he had occupied Myergo's inner circle long enough to know that no one was safe from it.

Myergo did not speak again. Dervish returned his attention to their prison, taking note of every detail. He had occupied space in plenty of prisons, but none quite like this. Their cell, though rather bare, was in pristine condition. It even had a latrine in the back corner, an isolation barrier erected just high enough to afford a bit of human dignity. Outside of its black metal bars, the level they were taken to had appeared much the same. Sterile, slate gray walls stretched along the cell corridor, and though not exactly inviting, had looked far cleaner than any place Dervish actually chose to frequent. He had known at once that the Coalition only kept their most influential, powerful criminals here. Myergo certainly qualified. It contrasted markedly with the level below them, which Dervish and Myergo had passed on their way up. Dervish had expected one of those cells for himself; crowded with violent lowlifes, dingy, damp, and cold, smelling of sweat and excrement. This was new. But to his experienced gut, it did not feel remotely safer. A different sort of danger presented here, and it was making Dervish jittery. *What in blazes are those filthy Coats up to?*

Down the hall, a security lock beeped, whirred, and hissed open. Dervish could hear the door unsealing and swinging aside. He pulled his cap lower, ears and eyes straining as low voices echoed along the corridor. Heavy boots stomped in first.

Coalition Sentinels? Dervish wondered. *No, something higher even than that.*

Lighter boots followed, tapping against the floor with a hollow but melodic echo. Even without seeing, Dervish could distinguish the boots' superior quality. Expensive. Rare. He had only known of the wealthiest of the Coalition elite to have access to such things. Dervish's chest tightened. Behind them, one other set of feet followed. The door swung closed and beeped as it locked. The footsteps proceeded toward them.

Dervish sat up, no longer interested in offering a pretense of being asleep. He looked askance at Myergo, searching for recognition, anger, even concern. Nothing. Myergo remained coolly seated as before, the sinister grin fixed in place.

The two Coalition personnel arrived at the cell door first. Dervish looked them up and down, trying to hide his surprise. Red and black cloaks hung over their right shoulders, revealing an impressive array of gleaming, charcoal-gray body armor. Sleek helmets covered their faces, a darkened shield protecting and hiding their eyes. Dervish had no doubt they were attentively watching, however. Their gauntleted hands rested threateningly on the latest energy pistol models, and the butt of a powerful rifle peeked over their left shoulders. Curiously, no insignia marked out their rank or order. One of them reached for the cell door, unlocking it with an encoded card. The door whirred and slid open. The two men stepped inside and took station on either side of the cell door.

Mr. Expensive Boots was still taking his time, pausing every few cell doors along the corridor. Dervish listened as he whispered to the person stalking behind him, but it was so low and secretive that even he could not make it out. He would have leaned forward to get a better view, but he felt the burning gaze of the secret Coalition guards upon him, even through their tinted visors. Dervish did not dare move, but watched the floor in silence as the footsteps drew ever nearer. Both curiosity and dread competed inside Dervish. *What Assembly member would show his face here?*

The mysterious visitor strode into view, and what color had ever been in Dervish's pallid face drained completely. With arms crossed behind his back, the man entered the cell. Dervish stared at his immaculate, dark uniform and sweeping black cloak, both accented with specialized crimson embroidery. Dervish's eyes darted to the white insignia emblazoned above his right pectoral – a chevron and three bars above the Coalition twin lions. He quickly hopped to his now shaking legs and wiped sweating hands on his filth-encrusted trousers. The man glanced at Dervish down the end of a strong, aquiline nose, his inscrutable eyes studying him. With terror, Dervish averted his gaze, remembering himself and the appropriate gesture of respect. It had been a long time since he had shown any such respect to any Coat, but with this one, Dervish would grovel at his feet if he thought it might appease him. The man turned his attention to Myergo.

Myergo's grin broadened.

"Supreme Chancellor," he crowed with amusement, dipping his head. "What an unexpected delight."

Supreme Chancellor Vipsanius narrowed his eyes, the withering look melting any remaining courage Dervish might have felt.

"Watch your forked tongue, Myergo. You have already drawn my displeasure. Do not irritate me further."

Myergo's grin twisted into an ugly grimace. "Your troops ambush me and my people in the midst of legitimate business, and *you* have something against me? I recall a contract between us—"

"Which you have broken, you ignorant fool," the Supreme Chancellor hissed. "Fling mud in your own pigsty as you wish, but you have transgressed more than I can stomach. You have interfered with Coalition movements, overstepped agreed boundaries, and have brought an army into view of the public. I should have you and every single one of your pathetic cronies beheaded in Pardaetha's streets tomorrow. Little else would bring me more satisfaction."

Judging by Myergo's changed expression, he comprehended and believed the force of the Supreme Chancellor's threat. Dervish remembered well the contract forged between Myergo and a Coalition page. He himself was there as a witness. It was what empowered Myergo to act as he pleased, as long as he stayed within the contract's bounds. Even then, the page had warned of swift and merciless retribution. Myergo had never experienced such retribution before, but Dervish knew of many of his company who had. Run-of-the-mill criminals who preyed on the wrong people or got in the Coalition's way unfailingly met grisly ends.

Myergo paused, considering his next words. To Dervish's surprise, no malice dripped from them, echoing something like respect instead.

"There was a reason. A reason that concerns you, Honored One."

The Supreme Chancellor's unreadable eyes bored into Myergo. "Then speak, and save your miserable hide."

Dervish wanted to look away from Myergo's face, but couldn't.

Never before had he seen the crime lord in such a position. He was cornered like the Mistwolf he had caged not too many days before, and Dervish wondered if he would lash out in a blind rage or cow to the Supreme Chancellor's undeniable power over him. Myergo remained placid, but the emptiness of his black eyes spoke of the animosity seething below the surface. Like that same Mistwolf, he would strike if given the chance. But Myergo was no unmastered beast. He spread his hands plaintively.

"I was merely trying to take care of a problem for you," he said. "Do you recall a certain Elmling, what those people call a Guardian? I had him, the one known as Blade, before I was betrayed by *your* bounty hunter."

The Supreme Chancellor laughed, a cold, hollow laugh that made Dervish's blood freeze.

"And you lost both of them in the Aruacas Rainforest. I know this, Myergo, and I also know about your abject humiliation at the hands of that ridiculous Jackal Syndicate. Your utter failure is hardly a defense."

Myergo glowered. "Why, then, have you come?"

"To renegotiate terms," the Supreme Chancellor replied. "I can have use for you yet, provided you do not fail me again."

"And if I refuse, you kill me, yes?" Myergo said icily.

The corner of the Supreme Chancellor's mustached lip quirked up. "Not exactly, Myergo. Such a waste, such a pity to put that behemoth, predatorial body of yours into the ground."

Supreme Chancellor Vipsanius stepped aside and looked behind him outside the cell door. He motioned for the remaining person to enter. Dervish watched as an oldish, balding man with black spectacles and a long, white coat strode in behind him. His eyes, perceptive and penetrating behind the glasses, swept over Myergo and then to Dervish, lingering. Dervish did not like that look, not one bit. He focused on Myergo instead, who was still trying to work out what the Supreme Chancellor could possibly mean. *And what does he mean?* Dervish wondered with trepidation. He glanced again at the scientist, who studied the two inmates like he might study the dissected entrails of a particularly interesting specimen.

"You see, Dr. Endiatus here has made some incredible breakthroughs in his field. Progress, Myergo, progress that pushes the limit of what humanity has ever imagined possible. What would you say if I told you we have engineered a way to bend the will of any living creature? Yes, even a Mistwolf, Myergo. An entire pack of Mistwolves, at your command and disposal. And not just mere beasts. Men. Men transformed into perfect soldiers. What would you say to that?"

At this, Myergo bared another fanged grin. "I would say that you are a madman. But I would like to see you try."

"Very well," the Supreme Chancellor answered, and that impenetrable gaze turned to Dervish. For his part, Dervish met it, compelled by the overwhelming sense that cowardice would mean his immediate doom. But Dervish was not courageous. He never had to be. His place was in the shadows; he was meant to be unassuming. Dervish was disposable.

"Yes, very well," the Supreme Chancellor mused. "This one will do, Doctor."

The two guards pounced. Dervish staggered beneath their sudden onslaught, kicking and screaming as his cap flew from his greasy hair.

"Gerroff! No!"

Dervish struggled in their iron grips. His arms pinned and useless, he kicked once more. An armored boot slammed into the back of his legs. He howled as his kneecaps smashed against the floor. Tears of agony blurred his vision, but he could see Myergo's hulking form rear up from behind the table.

"What is this?" Myergo demanded.

Supreme Chancellor Vipsanius shook his head and clucked his tongue. "Patience, Myergo. You wanted to see, did you not? Watch."

Myergo growled, but paused, his chest heaving and fists clenched as he glared at the Supreme Chancellor. The crime lord could easily kill the Supreme Chancellor and the doctor, Dervish believed. He might even stand a chance against the elite Coalition guards. But Myergo waited.

He ain't doing a thing, Dervish thought with despair. His stomach plummeted. Sweat dripped down the back of his collar. His terrified eyes roved between Myergo and the Supreme Chancellor, a stuttering, mumbled plea forming on his lips. It never came. His throat went dry as he caught sight of Dr. Endiatus removing a small leather case from his jacket and rolling it out upon the table. He attached a gleaming needle to a syringe of blood-red liquid.

"What's that?" Dervish asked hoarsely. "What're yeh doing?"

Dr. Endiatus flicked the tiny glass bottle. He pushed his spectacles up the bridge of his nose and gave the Supreme Chancellor a curt nod.

The Supreme Chancellor lifted his wrist and pulled up his sleeve. The strange device clasped around it shimmered as he adjusted it. "Proceed."

Dr. Endiatus approached. A gauntleted hand grabbed a fistful of Dervish's hair and yanked it, forcing his head upon his shoulder. Dervish fought again, but the vice-like grasp was stronger. He could not move. He could only watch as Dr. Endiatus examined his exposed throat. The needle hovered above his carotid artery.

"Myergo," Dervish whispered. "Do something."

The needle plunged into his neck. Dervish squealed in pain, but only for a moment. The slow dribble of blood and another strange sensation spread from the pierced place. It ebbed through Dervish with the galloping beat of his heart, rushing into his brain. His vision clouded. Time slowed. Every thought and worry fled. Dervish's world went black.

But something new entered the darkness. Dervish gasped for breath, opening his eyes. A pinprick of red-hued light filtered in through each pupil, then spread. Dervish could see. He could see as he had never done before. All the world rushed toward him. The room around resolved into utter clarity. Every inch of it was his. He felt it, all of it, and it belonged to him, all that he could see and reach. And nothing would escape his rapid, roving eyes.

Dervish let out a wild laugh. He tried to dart forward, but bonds restrained him. Anger suddenly coursed through him, and he gnashed his teeth at the visored helmets that kept him from rising to full power. He could feel that power now as he never had before. All his senses tingled. But gone now was all that ever held him back. Gone was every inhibition, every self-preserving notion, every cowardice, love, hope, and fear. Even the pain had disappeared. With every heartbeat, it ebbed away from every wound, old and new. He felt only his strength, his wrath, his ecstasy, his hunger.

Dervish lashed out, throwing off the metal grip of the armored guards who held him. He surged from the ground, springing to his feet with a physical prowess the old Dervish could never have dreamed of possessing. With a savage kick, he knocked one guard off balance, and then grabbed the other by his helmet and slammed him into the cell bars. He heard them gasp in surprise, moaning in pain as they scrambled out of his reach. Dervish flexed his pulsing muscles. He roared with raging exhilaration.

"Ah, now you see it taking full effect. When the Praepotentia Serum enters the body, it first empties the man of his humanity. He becomes a feral shell."

Dervish cocked his head. He recognized that these were words being spoken around him. Human language. Language he once cared for, but had no real use for now. He scanned the room, baring teeth at the other fleshy, weak forms of life. The weakest one scurried out of the bars, followed by another and the two armored things. He hated them. He hungered for them. He wanted their sinews between his teeth.

The fleshy speaker continued as the cell door clinked shut. He raised his wrist and placed his fingers on a black dial. "But with this device, I fill the shell. And it does my will."

Attack. A silky voice cooed in Dervish's head. *Kill. Be filled.*

Dervish gazed hungrily at the one human left before him. He snarled toward it.

"Dervish, my friend," the human said, holding up its massive hands. "Stop."

Kill. Take what you want.

Dervish wanted to crush those great hands. He wanted to rip the thing's head from its shoulders and lap up a river of blood. It was big, but hunger and hate filled Dervish; so overwhelming it was that he pounced forward.

Dervish upended the table into its chest. It splintered against the human and the wall. Force. Such almighty force. He roared with satisfaction. The human staggered backward. Streaks of shiny, new blood blossomed on its front. Dervish leaped forward. He reached for the neck. One great hand swatted him away. Dervish landed in a heap of table debris. Its splinters cut him, but he felt no pain. Only rage, only thirst, only lust for blood. Dervish ripped a splintered piece of wood away from the frame and sprang back at the human, growling. With one hand, he plunged the makeshift stake into the human's bicep. With the other, dug fingernails wherever they would find purchase. The human shouted, cried out. Still Dervish raked the skin away with feverish ferocity. He smelled blood. Almost tasted it. The human pushed Dervish away, but his jaw opened wide. He clamped down on the arm that would hold him at bay.

Dervish heard his scream and bit down harder, tearing away flesh, but a rough kick sent him sprawling across the cell. His head cracked against the opposite wall. Blood ran down over his ear and neck, but Dervish did not stop to even wipe it away. He would never stop. Never, until his rage was exhausted and his hunger satisfied. And he could rip this man to shreds and swallow him piece by piece and still need to be filled.

Dervish lurched toward him. *Kill. Attack. Be filled.*

"Enough!" the human roared, his bleeding chest heaving. He ripped the splintered wood out of his arm and chucked it on the floor. "Stop him. You have made your point."

Wait.

A wave of new sensation rushed over Dervish, and he paused.

Rest. Your time will come. Yes, rest.

Dervish's eyelids grew heavy. He curled up on the cell floor, grinning as drowsiness overtook him. Voices with little meaning floated around him.

"What have you done to him?"

"What I shall do with every man, woman, and child who dares to be a thorn in my side. He is wholly mine. Imagine it, Myergo, every rotting prisoner, treasonous dissident, asylum inmate, and worthless fool turned to a new purpose. These, the disposable, plucked from the trash heap and put to true use. I shall make them a force unlike anything the world can even begin to fathom. Behold! A visceral terror that neither man, nor beast, nor nature herself can halt unless I command it so. Do you see now?"

There was resignation in the other voice. "What do you demand of me?"

"This army I am creating still requires an intelligent human touch. Lead these to Elmnas, subdue it as you will, and consider your offense against me forgiven. I shall even release you back to your dominion, if you so desire. But if you refuse, or even think of revolting against me with the power I offer, your fate will be worse than that of your friend."

Dervish closed his eyes completely now, resting his head against his torn and bruised forearms. A few drops of his own blood made it to his lips, and he licked at it with pleasure, tasting the commingled blood of the human still upon him. Dervish had never felt better in his entire, miserable life.

"We have an agreement," the voice replied, hoarse with surrender. "It shall be done as you say."

About the Author

Kaylena Radcliff is the author of several books and a number of short stories, articles, and poems. Aside from writing, she serves as a magazine editor, church planter's wife, and a homeschooling mom of two. She drinks a lot of coffee.

When not working, Kaylena drags her loved ones on long hikes through Pennsylvania's beautiful forests, joyfully plays keyboard piano with little talent, and indulges in all things nerdy. You can find her on Instagram, Twitter, and Facebook @kaylenaradcliff.

Made in the USA
Middletown, DE
22 May 2023